The Heat of the Moment . . .

At a full sprint, Enid picked up the sword and put herself between the young squire and the bigger, older bully. She met his sword with her own in a parry so powerful that his weapon broke in two. Crying out, he dropped the hilt, clutching his wrist and staggering back to gape at her.

She froze, the sword at her side, hearing the stunned silence all around her. Every gaze was focused on her, and she saw herself as from a distance, a woman too tall, too strong, clothed in a gown, but carrying a sword. Sir Blakemore watched her with cold, calculating eyes.

The skill was hers, Enid thought, but the abnormal strength was not. And she'd used it in front of all of her husband's fellow knights. She'd made a grave error.

Geraint would hear of this. So would the others. How would she explain herself? She moved away from the crowd, hearing the low buzz of conversation swelling behind her.

She heard Geraint's name mentioned, and Enid stiffened, worry and dread knotting her stomach.

"But he is one of the high king's favorites," a stranger said. "Maybe Arthur does not wish Sir Geraint to do battle. He is obviously being groomed as the king's counselor."

"He will not be a favorite if his wife is discovered to be a sorceress," Blakemore said coldly.

Their voices faded, and soon Enid was alone.

Don't miss the first
Knights of the Round Table novel . . .
Lancelot

Or the next in the series . . .
Gawain

Knights
of the
Round Table

• • •

GERAINT

GwenRowley

J
JOVE BOOKS, NEW YORK

THE BERKLEY PUBLISHING GROUP
Published by the Penguin Group
Penguin Group (USA) Inc.
375 Hudson Street, New York, New York 10014, USA
Penguin Group (Canada), 90 Eglinton Avenue East, Suite 700, Toronto, Ontario M4P 2Y3, Canada
(a division of Pearson Penguin Canada Inc.)
Penguin Books Ltd., 80 Strand, London WC2R 0RL, England
Penguin Group Ireland, 25 St. Stephen's Green, Dublin 2, Ireland (a division of Penguin Books Ltd.)
Penguin Group (Australia), 250 Camberwell Road, Camberwell, Victoria 3124, Australia
(a division of Pearson Australia Group Pty. Ltd.)
Penguin Books India Pvt. Ltd., 11 Community Centre, Panchsheel Park, New Delhi—110 017, India
Penguin Group (NZ), 67 Apollo Drive, Mairangi Bay, Auckland 1311, New Zealand
(a division of Pearson New Zealand Ltd.)
Penguin Books (South Africa) (Pty.) Ltd., 24 Sturdee Avenue, Rosebank, Johannesburg 2196, South Africa

Penguin Books Ltd., Registered Offices: 80 Strand, London WC2R 0RL, England

KNIGHTS OF THE ROUND TABLE: GERAINT

A Jove Book / published by arrangement with the author

PRINTING HISTORY
Jove mass-market edition / March 2007

Copyright © 2007 by The Berkley Publishing Group.
Cover illustration by Aleta Rafton.
Cover lettering by Ron Zinn.
Cover design by George Long.
Text design by Stacy Irwin.

ISBN: 978-0-515-14263-1

JOVE®
Jove Books are published by The Berkley Publishing Group,
a division of Penguin Group (USA) Inc.,
375 Hudson Street, New York, New York 10014.
JOVE is a registered trademark of Penguin Group (USA) Inc.
The "J" design is a trademark belonging to Penguin Group (USA) Inc.

PRINTED IN THE UNITED STATES OF AMERICA

10   9   8   7   6   5   4   3   2   1

Knights of the Round Table

· · ·

GERAINT

Prologue

. . .

THE Ceremony of Revelation had been sched-
uled for the night of a full moon. Enid had spent
two months training, studying, and anticipating this moment. Not everyone who requested the tutelage of the
Lady of the Lake had her wish granted. But Enid had
been chosen to represent the Donella tribe, and their
looming fate must have persuaded the Lady.

Alone, Enid stood beside the lake, which reflected
the moon like a second white eye in the night. She saw
the Lady in the distance, walking slowly toward her,
wearing the same white tunic as Enid, though the
Lady's shone with an unearthly light. Her face was fair,
but unlined, betraying no age. Mist rose on the lake in
her wake, creeping to shore, wrapping about her ankles,
moving ever onward toward Enid.

Enid's heart was pounding so loudly that she was

surprised she couldn't hear an answering echo. Her mouth was too dry to swallow. What if she had been deemed unworthy? What if all her effort here was for naught? How could she return to her tribe, to her father, the chieftain, and tell him that her plan to strengthen the defense of their tribe had not worked? He had heard rumors of one of the lesser kings of Britain growing impatient with his own boundaries. The Donella tribe feared to be gobbled up by a stronger, larger foe. And although the high king, Arthur, was not in question, there were many kings beneath him who would try to widen their boundaries at the expense of a small tribe.

Enid could not let that happen. She, a warrior woman by training, had been chosen to learn the secret fighting techniques of the mounted knights and bring the knowledge home. She would make her tribe strong, so that no one dared to attack them. But to do that, she needed protection in the unfamiliar world of men and armor. The Lady of the Lake had deigned to consider helping.

The Ceremony of Revelation would be her answer.

As the Lady approached, the mist crept outward to meet Enid. It was cool and moist against her feet, but prickled with a power that was not of nature. The Lady's grace made her seem to float there in front of Enid, and the effect was awe-inspiring.

"Enid of the Donella," the Lady said.

Though she spoke softly, her voice boomed with a new echo, and Enid flinched.

"Aye, my lady," Enid responded.

"I have spent these many months in the knowing of you, in understanding your place as a warrior woman, and your innate ability to give a young man courage by just your touch. I have watched you work; I have listened to your desperation to help your tribe. I have deliberated on how I might aid you and have decided on these gifts of magic."

Enid could not control her gasp of relief and excitement. She had been deemed worthy!

"You will be among strangers, out in the world. My first gift is the enhancement of beauty, so that all find you pleasing and unthreatening."

Enid tried not to frown. She hadn't thought herself *un*pleasing.

"My second gift is the strength of ten men to aid you in battle. In the coming months I will teach you the use—and not the abuse—of it. Third, you will be able to sense the presence of magic, aiding you in the defense against it. Use this wisely, for it will not grant you powers to *fight* magic, an important distinction."

Enid nodded as if she understood, although she wasn't all that certain. But that was what the next few months were for: learning how to use her magical gifts.

"Last, I will teach you the ability to disappear within the shadows, to cloak yourself from your enemy. This is not a tool to be used in battle, but when stealth is required. Remember now that the use of this magic is not endless. You are granted these gifts for a short period only, and they must be replenished beneath the moon every third night. I will teach you the ritual over time, but tonight I will perform it with you. Give me your hand."

Enid obeyed, and to her shock, the Lady produced a curved dagger. Giving Enid no time to react, she made a small slice across Enid's thumb, and blood began to drip.

"Hold it above the water," the Lady commanded.

Enid turned to the moonlit lake, but was hard-pressed to see where the edge of the lake lay, with the mist that hovered at her feet. She took several steps forward until her toes brushed moisture, then held her bleeding hand in front of her. As the blood disappeared within the mist, the Lady began to chant words that Enid could not quite hear. A wind seemed to come from nowhere, swirling around her, making her sway.

"Step into the water."

Again, she obeyed, then gasped at the power that rose upward within her, crackling through her suddenly upraised arms, arcing in a bolt of lightning that reached between her and the shining moon. The light faded, but it still seemed to exist inside her, its secret power humming through her body, changing her. Her skin felt alive with it, her senses heightened, her muscles more alert than she'd ever felt them. She thought she could swim the entire lake or climb high mountains.

The last of the wind faded away, the mist receded, and the glow of the Lady's garments dulled. Then it was simply Enid and her teacher.

The Lady rubbed her hands together. "You have much to learn before I can allow you into the world with these great gifts. Shall we begin?"

Chapter 1

* * *

THE woman's sword arced high in the air, flashing sunlight as it swooped to parry away her opponent's weapon. Sir Geraint, prince of Cornwall, watched the fight from the back of his horse, concealed by trees, unwilling to distract the combatants. The woman stood taller than any he'd ever seen, long limbs firm with sleek muscles. She wore a sleeveless leather jerkin that only covered her down to mid-thigh. Her blond hair was pulled back from her face, leaving naked the intent focus of her eyes. Geraint could not take his gaze from her, so absorbed was he by the grace of her movements, the power of her stroke, the skill evident in every turn of her body.

The man she fought was obviously a ruffian, panicking, flailing his sword, as she drove him across the sunlit clearing toward the edge of the woods. When she could have killed him, she merely raised welts with the flat of her sword and drove him away into the forest.

She stood still, her breathing normal even though she'd exerted herself. Blood ran down her upper arm, a remnant of the ruffian's desperation. She looked at it impassively and then shrugged.

But to Geraint, that was her life's blood, and he feared for her. Before he could move to aid her, he heard the crash of underbrush, saw another horse leap a fallen log and land in the clearing, barely an arm's span from the woman. A villain raised his sword to her, this time from above her in the saddle, as if fighting a woman wasn't already dishonorable.

Tapping his heels into his horse's flank, Geraint sprang from the cover of the trees and saw the woman back up, as if to take them both on. Her expression was fierce, challenging—she believed she could win. She made him believe it, too, and his admiration only surged higher.

But he wheeled his horse about and charged at her enemy. The man wore no armor, no padded brigandine like Geraint had to protect his chest. But he fought bravely, meeting Geraint's sword again and again. With just the pressure of his knees and heels, Geraint guided his horse in a dance about his opponent, leaving his hands free to absorb blows with his shield and wield his powerful sword.

His opponent toppled off the back of his horse to avoid a particularly well-aimed thrust. Without stopping, he somersaulted back to his feet and took off running into the forest. The horse, after rearing and screaming, galloped off in a different direction.

Geraint twisted in the saddle, but to his relief the woman was still there. She wore an approving grin that made his heart sing. By God, he was turning into a poet at just the sight of her.

He dismounted, sheathed his sword, and came to stand before her. Most women barely reached his shoulders, but this blond goddess came up to his eyes. He thrilled at the size of her, imagined covering that long body with his—

And then regretted his unchivalrous thoughts. She was a lady in need of protection, although it was obvious she'd been forced to learn to protect herself. Was she alone in the world? What had happened to her that she'd had to learn a man's art of war?

When she smiled at him, with white, healthy teeth between full pink lips, it was as if the sun burned brighter.

"A good afternoon, kind sir," she said. "You have my thanks for your aid."

He reached for her hand, and although she stiffened with obvious suspicion, she let him lift it to his lips. "Sweet lady, helping you is the highlight of my life."

"Then you must have had a deprived life," she said gently, her melodious voice full of good humor. "I will admit, I thought you a third enemy."

"And were ready to slay the two of us, though we be mounted and you on the ground."

"I am still ready, should you prove false." She pointed her sword tip into the ground and leaned upon the hilt.

He put a hand to his heart. "Ah, to battle you with swords between us would grieve me deeply. There are other ways for a man and woman to battle."

She arched a blond brow. "Must it be a battle be-tween us, then? Can we not declare a truce?"

"A truce, aye," he murmured, gently taking the wrist of her injured arm and turning the wound into the dappled sunlight. "You have injuries I should tend."

Her smile faded, and she tugged back, though he didn't release her. "You need not—"

"The blood continues to flow, my lady. How could I, in good conscience, leave you to take ill?"

The smile once again appeared on her lips, and he experienced a profound relief. He did not want to be parted from her, not yet. He had never before felt this drawn to, this enthralled by, the mere presence of a woman, a stranger unlike any he'd ever met before. A lifetime was not enough to uncover the secrets of such a woman. And now he could not stare into the depths of her blue eyes long enough, with their pale color as unusual as she was. He was surprised that he could even form a coherent thought.

Enid felt her breathing catch at just the interest in the stranger's eyes. Men had never looked at her in such a way before. She was a warrior woman, meant to train young men. She'd always been one of them, talking of battle strategy and how to keep one's sword polished and sharp. With women, except her sisters and mother, she was usually awkward with speech. But this man, this warrior knight, made her speechless in a different way. The concern in his eyes was almost embarrassing. When he studied her minor wound, she wanted to blush. Even her skin felt hot, though the day was cool. And his smile . . . She could not keep her gaze from him, from his handsome face with the slightly crooked nose, down the lean cheekbones to his broad, blunt jaw. There was the shadow of a dimple in his chin.

But it was his skill with the blade that could have made her swoon, were she the type. His horsemanship amazed and captured her. His ability to fight while riding was just what she wanted to bring back to her people. Had fate led her to the perfect answer to her problems? If only seeing into the hearts of men was one of the Lady's gifts.

Still holding her wrist, he led her to a rock in the shade. She laughed when he brushed it off before allowing her to sit.

"Is there a stream nearby?" he asked.

She nodded. "It is just behind that copse of trees."

He looked where she pointed. "I'll return in a moment."

"But I can walk there."

"You might grow faint from lack of blood."

"I have had far worse, Sir—Sir—?" She tilted her head as she watched him.

"Sir Geraint," he answered, still frowning at her wound.

"I am Enid."

He grinned, and the effect so close to her was blinding.

He repeated her name in a low, smooth voice. "My lady Enid, excuse me for but a moment."

He went back to his horse, which grazed contently in the meadow grass. He took something from a bag attached to his saddle, followed her directions to the stream, and then returned with a damp cloth and something that resembled wet mud in his other hand. When she tried to take the cloth from him, he gave her a disapproving look.

"It is on the far side of your arm—you won't be able to see it."

She didn't protest again. She let herself enjoy the rarity of a man taking care of her, gently cleansing the blood from her arm, and then applying the wet, cool mud.

"Should I ask what is in that concoction?"

"An old Cornish remedy for insuring a healthy recovery."

"You are of Cornwall?" she asked with interest.

The land shared a border with her tribe, but their people were very different, and hers kept themselves secluded.

"Aye, although I also serve King Arthur."

"The high king at Camelot?"

He gave her a wry grin. "You sound like there might be another."

"Oh, nay, I have heard of the wonders of it, of course, but I have never been there."

"I am bound for Camelot myself. I could escort you there—or anywhere else." He sat back on his heels, letting go of her arm. "Unless you are merely separated from your party."

"Nay, I travel alone."

He arched a black eyebrow. "A woman alone?"

She grinned. "Think you I cannot defend myself?"

"Nay, but I am worried you must defend yourself often."

"I have been journeying for several days, and that was the first attempt at robbery."

"Probably because you look so fierce."

She showed her teeth in a grin. "I am."

He grinned back, and for a moment it was as if they

shared a communication not of words. His spirit was like hers, full of adventure. The fact that he recognized the same in her and still thought her a woman worth flirting with was an aphrodisiac such as she'd never experienced.

His smile faded. "You truly are alone?"

"For right now."

"Could I—"

They heard the neigh of another horse, the sound of undergrowth parting. Enid's sword was in her hand, and she was halfway to her feet.

Sir Geraint touched her arm. "He is with me."

Even as the second man brought his horse to a halt and dismounted, she told herself that she was now alone with two well-armed knights. But she had always been a good judge of character, and she could not look on Sir Geraint and think he meant her harm.

Or was she being naïve? Perhaps such a man was even more dangerous to her.

The second knight was of middling years, with a full gray mustache that twitched with amusement as he looked between them. "Sir Geraint, I did not know that our meeting had turned into a romantic outing."

Enid felt herself blushing, another rarity in her life. Men had always joked about such things, and she had responded in kind. Imagining she and Sir Geraint as lovers made her think thoughts that were dark and hot and seductive.

Sir Geraint rose to his feet. "The young lady is alone."

"Ah, and you were rescuing her. I thought I saw a man or two scurrying away from here."

"She did not need my rescue," he said, glancing at her in amusement.

Not many men would have so easily given up the
credit for helping her. He was comfortable with himself.
More and more he looked like a man who could help
her—though he could not know it. No attraction was
worth breaking her oath to her father about the secrecy
of her mission.

The second knight dismounted from the saddle
stiffly and gave a great sigh. "These old bones are not
what they used to be. I appreciate you meeting me
halfway, Sir Geraint."

"I am honored." Geraint turned to her. "Sir Albern,
may I introduce the lady Enid."

Enid rose to her feet, and Sir Albern had to look up
at her. But to his credit, he only grinned and shook his
head.

"Count on you to meet the unusual ones, Sir Geraint."
He pulled a rolled parchment from the pouch at his
waist. "What you've come for, lad. Send the high king
my regards, along with this missive." He glanced at Enid.
"I'll be on my way."

"I was just going to make camp, Albern," Sir Geraint
said. "No need to rush off in haste. Do you not want a
warm meal and a night's rest before you journey back?"

When the older knight glanced at her again, Enid
lifted a hand. "Do not think I mean to interfere. I, too,
need my sleep."

Sir Albern exchanged a look with Sir Geraint, who
shrugged and said, "I am certain that the lady Enid
would not wish to share a fire alone with me."

She gave him a cocky grin. "In exchange for your
company, gentlemen, I will provide dinner."

Both knights looked alarmed.

"Lady Enid," Sir Albern said, "please, it is not seemly that you should serve us in so common a fashion. I would feel the basest of men should I allow—"

But with a wave, she entered the forest, leaving the men to discuss their private business while she was gone. To her surprise, Sir Geraint caught up with her before she could take another step.

"Lady Enid, you have been wounded. Allow me to—"

"If you insist on helping me, Sir Geraint," she interrupted, "let us make it a contest to enliven our evening. We will see who can bring back supper first."

He took a step closer to her. The trees surrounded them; the sun was hidden from them. It was an intimate moment that made her realize she didn't know what to expect of him—and she wanted to find out.

"And the prize?" he murmured.

He was not even looking at her eyes, but at her mouth, as if he wanted to kiss it. She had kissed men before, but always in the way of instruction. She had never felt passion from it. She thought that might not be true with Sir Geraint.

She smiled and backed away from him. "The prize is the right to sleep closest to the fire. What other prize would be so suitable?"

He reached for her, but she eluded him with a laugh and disappeared into the forest.

• • •

ENID had won their little contest—her rabbit had been skinned and on a spit before Geraint had even returned to their camp. He could not keep his eyes from her. She sat at Albern's feet, listening enraptured to the tales of his days as a knight under Uther Pendragon. When she glanced at Geraint, she gave him a cocky grin and nodded toward the fire. He bowed low and held his rabbit forward.

"A meager offering," he said.

"And one that is too late," she answered sweetly.

Albern laughed. "The girl told me of your wager. It would seem she has got the best of you."

"So it would seem," Geraint said. He did not truly mind losing to Enid, not when she looked so adorable and proud of herself. For the first time, he wondered at what kind of place had raised such a woman.

When both rabbits had finished cooking, Geraint took over the duty of cutting apart the carcasses and handing over portions. He bade Enid drink the ale from his horn, and she pronounced it finely brewed. He felt as proud as if he'd made it himself, rather than the brewer at Camelot.

At last the sun set, and they were all sitting on blankets before the fire. Geraint picked at the grass beside his blanket and stole looks at Enid, who, bathed in firelight, looked as remote as a queen. He could recognize no emotion on her face as she stared into the fire. He told himself that he should inquire into her life, into her family, but a deeper understanding told him that she would only tell what she wanted him to know.

Would such knowledge spoil how drawn he was to her? Did he want her to be of the real world—or like this: mysterious and different, full of strength and shadows?

When Enid looked at him, his awareness of her boiled higher.

"Sir Geraint, you say you serve King Arthur."

Albern lifted a hand. "He is not a mere knight serving the high king, my lady."

"Albern," Geraint said in a warning voice. Did he want her to know who he really was? Would his identity change everything, drive her away—or bring her falsely close?

Enid looked at the old knight with interest.

"My lady, young Geraint here is a future king himself. His father is the king of all Cornwall, and Geraint his only son. Now can that not recommend him in your eyes?"

Enid's gaze slid back to Geraint, and he felt it assess him.

"A prince among other knights," she murmured, her voice carrying neither approval nor condemnation. "Yet you serve the high king."

"Do not we all?" Geraint responded.

She did not answer, and he found that disturbing. But perhaps she only meant servitude in the military sense.

"He does not just serve the king," Albern went on heedlessly. "He has become a trusted councillor, a man whom King Arthur consults on matters of diplomacy."

Geraint barely kept himself from grimacing. He did not want Enid to form opinions about him because of what he did, but rather who he was. He felt that way about her—it didn't matter her background or her family. All that mattered was this shimmering interest, this . . . desire.

He admitted to himself that he wanted her. She did not deserve his lust, but she inspired it. It was a raw, sinful, needy emotion that made him forget everything he was, in the need to be part of her. He was grateful that Albern was encamped with them, for he feared his own reaction should he be alone with Enid through the dark night.

Chapter 2

• • •

THOUGH Enid listened to Sir Albern's bragging about Sir Geraint's accomplishments, she surreptitiously watched Sir Geraint.

He was very uncomfortable being praised, another mark in his favor. He looked only at the fire, except for an occasional grimace when Sir Albern's boasting irritated him. She found herself smiling at his every wince, hiding it behind her hand when Sir Geraint glanced at her in desperation and tried to guide the conversation down another path.

She decided to help him. To change the subject, she said to Sir Albern, "Are all of King Arthur's diplomats trained as knights?"

"Nay, Sir Geraint is an unusual man," Sir Albern said jovially, giving the poor younger knight a broad wink.

"Are the knights trained at Camelot or at their own estates?"

Sir Geraint's gaze focused on her so quickly, she wondered if she had betrayed too much interest. But he let Sir Albern keep talking.

"Training must continue at all times," the older knight said. "Camelot's tiltyard is full of Britain's finest warriors, preparing in case the Saxon threat becomes an invasion."

She nodded as if only in politeness, when instead her mind was racing. Camelot would be the ideal place for her to study and learn the knights' skills. Had the Lady given her gifts she didn't know of, perhaps the ability to find luck in her favor? For surely her meeting with Sir Geraint could not be mere coincidence.

Yet this awareness between them would make things difficult. For the first time she was attracted to a man, and he to her. How could she reconcile her mission for her people with her interest in this prince of Cornwall? She told herself she could not give in to it, could not be distracted. But he might be the key to her tribe's very survival.

She glanced at him again, only to find him watching her with eyes the same green of the forest. She held his gaze and told herself that she would be the one to control this attraction they shared.

But he looked down her body boldly, and she felt herself shiver. This might be a dangerous game to play.

"And where do you call home, Lady Enid?" Sir Albern suddenly boomed.

She collected herself enough to remember her rehearsed answer for such a question. "I am from a small woodland tribe far south of here. We are hunters and farmers."

"And the women are warriors?" Sir Geraint asked softly.

"Nay." She lowered her eyes, wondering how she was going to get out of saying more.

"Then you were forced into something not meant for women?"

She mutely lifted her eyes to his, only to find him suddenly angry. He broke a stick in half and tossed it into the fire. She wanted to know what he was thinking, but she could not ask, not without risking even more questions. It suddenly seemed important not to have to lie to this man.

He didn't seem angry with *her*, for he served her another portion of rabbit with the gentlest of hands. He even blew on the hot meat before handing it to her. In his face she saw sadness now. Did he regret his display of anger? She was relieved.

Sir Albern looked between them, and seemed to have finally run out of things to say. He bid them both a good night and rolled into his blanket near the fire.

Enid and Sir Geraint stared into the fire in silence for several minutes. She listened to the call of the owls far overhead and the buzz of crickets. It was a peaceful, intimate moment, worth savoring.

Sir Geraint cleared his throat. "Where do you travel on the morrow?"

She sighed. "I have nowhere to be."

Seeing his jaw clench, she held her breath.

"Then allow me to escort you to Camelot. You shall have all the time you need to decide what to do next."

She gave him a tremulous smile and felt ill having to do it. "I accept your offer. My thanks."

He grinned back with a relief that amazed her.

"Then sleep now, my lady Enid. And trust that I will protect you."

And she did.

Geraint heard her breathing even out, knew the moment her consciousness left her and she slept. He was humbled that she trusted him, when it was obvious she had had little reason to trust the men in her life. When he had cleansed her wound, he had seen other scars on her arms, some faint, some more recent. Her family must have neglected her, and the thought still made him so angry. He wondered if she had been forced to learn to defend herself because her family wouldn't. Or was she truly alone in the world, though she claimed herself a member of a distant tribe? She needed protection—*his* protection. He wanted to offer his sword arm to her. The fact that she was strong in her own right made him feel even more certain that she needed him. He would take her to Camelot and show her what the civilized world had to offer. Perhaps she would stay. Perhaps . . .

He fell asleep imagining the possibilities.

• • •

IN the morning, Albern left them, and Geraint watched Enid wish him a farewell with the respect she'd obviously been taught for her elders. Someone had molded compassion and kindness into a woman with the body of a warrior, making her intriguing.

More than intriguing—her very differentness jolted

him once again. As he filled his water skins in the stream, she began to disrobe a little way down the bank. Her beautiful face was serene, unperturbed that he watched. Was she giving herself to him? Did she think his offer of escort came with a price? From his knees, he gaped up at her, but he couldn't speak, couldn't protest—and felt like the very worst sort of man because of it. Just like the men who'd abused her.

She pulled the jerkin over her head, leaving only a thin shirt without sleeves. It hung low to her thighs, rippled in smooth folds across her hips. And then she pulled it off, and she wore braies about her hips, a man's low-slung undergarment. And above it—

He dropped the horn he'd been filling into the shallows.

Her breasts were full and rounded, glowing in the early morning sunlight. When she lifted her arms to release her hair, he barely held back a groan. The fall of yellow curls swept along her shoulders and obscured her breasts from his hungry view.

She waded into the water, splashing herself and shivering. He realized she was taking a morning bath, and he didn't like himself for the disappointment that swept through him. But his cock certainly didn't care, for it pulsed with a hard, continuous ache.

But how could he remain disappointed when he had such a glorious sight to behold? And in what tribe was it permitted for men and women to bathe so openly?

When the water reached her thighs, she bent over to reach below the surface. He choked trying to swallow. She came up with a handful of sand and began to rub it into her skin, shivering all the while. He watched while she cleaned her body, felt his mouth fall open when she submerged herself to clean more intimate places.

At last she turned toward the shallows, her wet hair streaming down her shoulders. Geraint looked away, fumbling for the horn he'd forgotten just as it had begun to float away. Out of the corner of his eye, he watched her don a clean shirt over her wet skin. It clung to her. He turned away, trying to control a shudder as he used every bit of willpower not to take what seemed offered to him.

But she was not of his people; she didn't know what she did to him.

Or did she?

"Sir Geraint?"

He glanced over his shoulder at her; she had not donned her leather jerkin yet. She was tying back her hair, arms upraised, her shirt riding just high enough that he could see the edge of her wet braies peeking out.

"You seem . . . shocked by my bathing," she said hesitantly, letting her arms fall to her sides. "Do your people bathe infrequently?"

He gave a shaky laugh. "Nay, it is not that. In my kingdom, men and women do not usually bathe so freely before each other."

Her lips parted in dismay. "I have . . . embarrassed myself before you?" She reached for her jerkin and couldn't seem to find the opening in her haste.

Geraint rose to his feet and went to her, taking her hands to still them. She looked up at him in distress, drops of water falling from her hairline to merge with her wet shirt.

"You could never embarrass yourself before me," he murmured, reaching to cup her face.

He knew he shouldn't have touched her, but once he did, he was lost. Her skin was soft as the finest silk. He let his thumb brush her lips; they were moist and full and trembling. Her eyelids fluttered, and she swayed. He wanted to gather her into his arms, to hold her close, to protect and keep her safe.

Instead he bent down and kissed her lightly on the lips. Her eyes went wide, and they stared at each other, mouths separated by but a breath.

"Stop me, Enid," he whispered. "I should not—"

But she put her hand behind his head and pulled him to her. She did not kiss like a shy maiden; her mouth was open to him, and her tongue darted between his lips with a boldness that shocked and aroused him. With her body she caressed him, fitting herself against him until he desperately wished he were without garments. They kissed and licked and clung to each other. It took every inch of his control not to thrust himself against her for relief.

He broke the kiss, gasping. "Ah, Enid, you are wondrous. You should marry me."

She laughed at him, and he gave a shaky laugh in return as they parted. But what had him so confused was that in that moment, he meant it. He wanted to spend his life learning everything about her, because she would be the adventure of a lifetime.

• • •

SIDE by side, Geraint and Enid rode their horses down a dirt road on the way to Camelot. Enid could not remember enjoying a day more. Geraint had a quick mind and a ready laugh. Though he knew much about the world that she was ignorant of, he never made her feel unintelligent. He freely shared his knowledge, and it was obvious he had an adventurer's love of the unusual.

Which was probably why he'd kissed her.

Often throughout the day, her mind wandered to that kiss. It had aroused in her a hunger she'd never experienced before. She knew of the ways of the flesh from experience, but only in the application thereof. Not the immersion, not the sensual experience of giving her heart and soul to a man.

For the first time, she wanted to share more than her body. The thought held no fright for her; she was not forbidden by custom from enjoying the pleasures of the flesh.

But she sensed that this sudden, intense relationship with Geraint of Cornwall could hold hidden dangers. Already he had mentioned marriage to her. Though spoken in jest, it seemed a strange thing to mention to a woman one had known for a day.

So she steered their conversations away from anything about her personal feelings for him. This wasn't difficult, since she wanted to hear all about what it was like to be a trained knight. She had so many questions, and he answered them all freely. In return, he questioned her about her own training, but never asked *why* she'd learned it. She was grateful and curious at the same time.

That night, they found a few trees to camp beneath in the middle of an endless field of grass. As fox roasted on a spit over the fire, they sat side by side in awkward silence. Once the sun had set, the same intimacy rose up all around them, and she found she could think of little else but his kiss. She tried to concentrate on the moon, felt its pull, knew she had another night before she had to renew her gifts of magic.

But always there was Geraint, watching her. When she reached to add another log to the fire, he took her hand in his and looked into her face.

"Such beauty, you have," he whispered.

A blush seared its way across her cheeks. "But I am not like your women, Geraint."

"You will be at ease with them, Enid, I know you will. You will be the envy of many. Your eyes are like stars, winking in the night at me."

In confusion, she found herself blinking at him, which made her feel foolish. She tried to turn away, but he caught her arms, slid his rough palms down until he held her hands.

"Your skin seems bathed in the moisture of dawn, so soft."

She caught her lip between her teeth and no longer fought him. He seemed so sincere that she found her heart caught in his words. Was this love? Could she already be losing herself to him?

He rubbed her hands between his, then turned her palms up.

"My hands are rough as leather?" she finished for him.

He whispered her name, then bent his head and pressed his mouth to her palm.

Her insides seared with an ache that this gentle man treated her so tenderly.

"I would take away all your pain if I could," he murmured against her skin.

For the first time, she wished she had no urgent mission, nothing to stop her from reveling in her enjoyment of Geraint. And then she realized that as long as she learned of his people's training methods over the next few weeks, what was to stop her from enjoying him as well?

She lifted his hand and brought it to her face, kissing the palm as he'd done to her. With her eyes closed, she smoothed his hand down her face and neck, then even lower, over her breast. All of her garments separated them, but she didn't care. She held his hand to her, then opened her eyes to find him staring at her in shock. Were the women so shy where he came from? For a moment, she regretted her boldness, but then she reminded herself that it was *her* he was drawn to.

He suddenly pulled her to him, and she found herself seated on his lap, straddling him. His thighs were hard beneath her; she could feel the warmth of his stomach at the juncture of her thighs.

They stared at each other, both breathing raggedly.

"You have bewitched me," he whispered. His hands trembled at her waist, but went no farther.

Helplessly, she answered, "I did not mean to." But had she? Was this part of the Lady's gifts? No, the enhancement of her beauty only made her pleasing; surely it could not change the feelings that existed between her and Geraint.

"Your innocence is part of your power, part of your allure."

Innocence? She felt a pang of regret that she could not offer him that, when it seemed purity was something his people worshiped.

Geraint licked his lips. "I have never enjoyed myself more than I have with you. I don't want this to end."

She touched his face, savored the rough feel of a day's growth of beard. "Geraint, every day has an ending. You cannot change that. But we can make tonight last." She slid against him, used her woman's body to pillow the hardness of his erection. Though he inhaled sharply, she hurried on. "We can—"

"We can make all of this last," he said earnestly. He held himself so still, trembling against her. "My words of this morn seemed foolish at first," he rushed on, "but they've grown on me all day. Be my wife, Enid."

In the dark of the night, laughter did not even occur to her. She knew he was serious. She was flattered and intrigued and touched.

"Geraint, our worlds are so very different."

"Then let us make a new world together. That is what a marriage is, is it not?"

After loosening the laces at her neck, she pulled her jerkin off over her head. "Let us explore this world, Geraint. I don't want you to feel that you have to offer marriage to me. I freely offer to share myself with you." She brought his hands to her breasts, now with only thin linen separating them.

He stared at what he held, unmoving, then with a groan he touched her, letting his thumbs brush her nipples. With a cry she arched back, pressing their hips even harder together. She pulled at the leather skirts of his jerkin, lifting up until she could settle against him even deeper. Only their undergarments separated them now. He was hot and hard against her. With his hands he brought her closer, lowered his head, and pressed his open mouth to her breast. When his tongue touched her, she shuddered even harder against him.

This was desire; this was passion. No wonder she could only teach the basics of lovemaking, not this riotous emotion. How could one explain this? How could one even counter this?

"Marry me," he murmured against her breast.

With her last reasoning, she told herself that she could not imagine how their worlds would fit together. And how she could hold back secrets from a man she called husband.

"I cannot!" Then she cried out his name, pressed and rocked herself against him.

But he pushed her hips away from his until she was perched on his knees. "I cannot in good conscience continue," he whispered raggedly. "It would be a dishonor to you and my feelings for you. I have fallen in love with you, Enid."

She gaped at him. "How can you love me?"

He leaned back on his hands, eyes closed. "Ask me how I know the sun will rise? That might be easier to explain. But it is a truth I know deep within me, Enid. I will not use you as a concubine."

"Does what I want not matter?"

"We want the same thing—each other."

She crawled off his lap and knelt before the fire, hugging herself in the sudden cold. When he tried to put his arms around her from behind, she stiffened, but he didn't relent, just held her to the warmth of his chest.

"Is there someone else, Enid?" he whispered against her hair, close to her ear.

"Nay, no one. I have never had such feelings for a man."

"Then perhaps you love me, too."

She said nothing—what could she say? *Did* she love him?

He lay a blanket on the ground, then drew her back against him to lie behind her. He covered them both with another blanket, using his body to warm her.

Was this love?

Chapter 3

· · ·

IN the morning, Geraint came awake with Enid in his arms. At first he remembered nothing of the previous evening; it was only the rightness of her with him, and how he would be content to awaken like this for the rest of his life.

But she didn't want to marry him. She could not trust that something that had sprung up so quickly between them could be real.

He understood her mistrust. She was obviously used to being alone. Perhaps she was running from the cruel family who'd misused her. He would make her see that she belonged with him, that what they shared was a rare, precious gift to be savored, not thrown away.

She stiffened, and he knew that she was awake. He would not pressure her. She rolled onto her back and looked up at him tentatively, blinking the sleep from her eyes.

He smiled at her. "A good morning to you."

Her look was wary. "And to you."

"Today is the day you shall see the wonders of Camelot. I promise you won't be disappointed."

She slowly sat up, never taking her eyes from him.

He grinned and shook his head. "Nay, I have not forgotten what happened between us last night."

"What almost happened," she said in a low voice. "You did not wish to continue."

He glanced down her body, and with just a look he was ready for her. "Believe me, I wished to continue. But I love you, and I want more than that for us. I vow that I'll convince you of that."

A little tension seemed to go out of her shoulders, and a half smile hovered on her lips. "You are very certain of yourself, Sir Geraint, prince of Cornwall."

He lifted an eyebrow. "You could be a princess."

With a laugh, she said, "And such a responsibility is supposed to tempt me?"

"It would tempt most women."

She rose to her feet and stood above him, hands on hips, letting the breeze flutter her shirt against her body. "I am not most women."

"I am counting on that."

• • •

DURING their morning ride, they were joined by more and more travelers on their way to King Arthur's court. Geraint saw the many wide-eyed looks Enid received, and she handled it all with an equanimity that he was proud of. She was a strong woman; he would do well to rule with her at his side someday.

But he wanted her to know the joys of being a part of a community of people, something she must know little about. Just before they were to take a turn in the road that would reveal the majesty of Camelot, he drew her aside, away from the other travelers.

"Enid, I have a request of you."

She smiled at him, and he saw her excitement, the way her eyes followed the people passing them on their journey, especially a troop of knights in armor.

"Anything, Geraint," she said.

He told himself it was natural she be so distracted on this great adventure. But he wanted her attention.

"Enid, please."

Her smile faded as she looked him in the eyes. "I am listening."

"These people at court will not understand about your skill in battle."

She stiffened. "I will not lie."

"I am not asking you to. It is obvious by your garments alone that you have been raised differently than most. I am only asking if you would withhold from training while you're here. I want all—especially the women—to be at ease with you, to get to know you."

"And the fact that I have the ability of a warrior will stop them?" she asked coolly.

This was going badly. He reached for her hand, glad she let him take it. "I want you to have the chance to make friends, to see what kind of life I can offer you."

Her expression softened, and she gripped his hand

harder. "I will not fault you should your people reject me, Geraint. We cannot control others. I appreciate the fact that you care enough to try to protect me."

"I love you."

She didn't flinch; her smile only deepened and grew more intimate. "Thank you. I give you my word that I will not train while I'm at Camelot."

He grinned and kissed her hand before letting her go. "You have my gratitude, Enid—and my heart."

As they rode beneath two gatehouses and into the inner ward of Camelot, Geraint watched the awe on Enid's expressive face. Surely she had never been among so many people, from lowborn peasants and dairymaids to foreign princesses and ladies-in-waiting to Queen Guinevere. He tried to ignore the looks of shock and open curiosity that Enid constantly received. It was only natural.

But when she made her entrance into the great hall of Camelot itself, it became silent as a tomb at the mere sight of her. Little children pointed, ladies gaped open-mouthed, and men stared with hostile curiosity.

He had wanted Enid to marvel at the wonders of the stained glass window cut high into the wall, or at the rich tapestries that chronicled the high king's reign. But instead he saw her face redden as she stared around her. She drew herself up, calm amid the frozen speculation. And he was never more proud of anyone in his life. He held his arm out to her, and she set her hand on his forearm. He led her forward as if she were a princess in truth, instead of the one he wanted to create by joining with her before God.

"Sir Geraint?"

The crowd parted at the sound of King Arthur's

voice as he walked forward, away from his raised dais. The high king was a man at ease in the position of power he'd held since boyhood. He wore a simple tunic, not the royal robes of the kingdom. But his bearing marked him as a king.

Enid sank to her knees before him, and King Arthur gave her an interested glance before smiling at Geraint.

"Sir Geraint, I did not know that when I sent you on a simple mission, you would find a way to complicate it."

Geraint bowed to the king and handed over the roll of parchment from Sir Albern. "Sire, the missive you requested. And may I introduce the lady Enid, a traveler in need of your protection."

"I assume you have done a decent job of protecting her so far," the king said dryly.

Laughter circled the room, and Geraint made himself relax. He'd barely protected Enid from his baser self the past night, but King Arthur didn't need to know the details.

"Lady Enid, be welcome at Camelot," the king said solemnly, but with a hint of amusement in his eyes. Enid rose to her feet, and King Arthur studied her. "I think you've probably done well protecting yourself before you met Sir Geraint."

"I did, sire," she said in a clear voice. "But it was not nearly so enjoyable."

As the crowd roared with laughter, Geraint felt his face redden as if he were a youth. Enid looked about her in confusion.

King Arthur raised a hand. "Go in peace, Sir Geraint. There is nothing more you need to hear from me. I think you have things well in hand."

• • •

WHEN Enid descended to the great hall before supper, not many people noticed her except Geraint, and that was how it should be. It was amazing how a change of clothing rendered one just another person in a crowd. Geraint was speaking to a man she did not recognize, yet when he caught sight of her, his face lit with a grin that warmed her clear to her heart. She wanted to see that grin every day of her life.

She *must* be in love. She could think of little else but him while they were parted.

But what was she to do about it?

Geraint met her at the bottom of the stairs, and took her hand to kiss it. "Enid, you look stunning."

She fingered the skirt of the blue gown she wore and blushed. "The queen's ladies said it was far too short. It will take time to make garments to fit me."

"I love seeing your ankles." He put her hand on his arm and drew her through the crowds to a remote corner with a cushioned bench.

She laughed as she sat down. "You would not care if I were naked."

"Oh, I'd care, believe me. I would have to fight every man here for the privilege of kneeling at your feet." He smiled at her and leaned close. "So how did it go today?"

"The ladies were very kind, but they did not know what to make of me. I am so much taller. And though I am skilled on a field of battle, I kept tripping over their spinning wheels." She smiled. "Do you think there is hope for me?"

His amusement faded, and he looked at her with sincerity. "If you are willing to try."

"I am," she breathed, watching his lips, wanting his kiss.

He squeezed her hands gently.

She was very willing to try anything just to be with him. While she'd been with the ladies, she had considered their plight. Just like her, each would eventually marry and live in her husband's household. She had always assumed the same thing for herself—why should marrying Geraint be any different? And Cornwall was so close to Donella that she'd be able to see her family regularly.

As for her magic, it would be gone soon, and she would be like other women. Well, other women with military skills. But if Geraint loved her knowing that she was a warrior, all would be well. Her mission would be over soon. He was a soldier; he would understand.

Geraint was watching her now, and by her very silence she knew that she encouraged his hopes.

"Enid?" he whispered her name. "Have you considered my request? Will you marry me?"

Her whole life was balanced precariously on this decision. But how could she leave him? How could she go back to a world he wasn't in?

"Geraint." She said his name softly, simply. "Know that I love you."

He smiled. "Your heart already told me that, my sweet. But what is your answer?"

She closed her eyes on a sigh of pleasure at his endearment, but she could not put off the inevitable. "Geraint, you must understand that there are things I cannot tell you right now concerning my family and my tribe. In a few months, I will want to return home to visit them. Can you accept that?"

His face darkened. "No one deserves all you've done for them, the heavy burden you bear alone."

"Regardless, I have sworn an oath. Can you accept these mysteries that are a part of me, and trust that I will tell you when I can?"

"Enid, I watched you fight a man with a sword as if you were born with the skill. Do you not think that the very mystery of you is pleasing to me? I want to spend each day discovering a new thing about you. Know that the things that have hurt you in the past will hurt you no longer. I will be your protector now."

She stared at him in shock, fighting her growing hope. He had agreed to her conditions.

He slipped from the bench to fall to one knee. "Will you marry me, Enid?"

There was nothing left to think about. "Aye, my love. I will."

He hugged her so hard that he lifted her clear off the bench. Setting her on her feet, he said, "I knew that you would marry me. I told the priest so."

"The priest?" she said, laughing. "I thought you were dealing with your soldiers this afternoon."

He waved that aside. "They can make do without me. But I was hoping for a wedding, so a priest—and King Arthur—were whom I needed to talk to."

"You told the high king about us?" she said with a gasp.

"I did. And he said if you agreed to be my bride, he agreed to allow us to marry. He trusts my judgment. Would tomorrow be too soon?"

She felt her excitement giving way to trepidation. "Tomorrow?"

"Enid, trust in me. I can wait no longer to make you my wife. The world is full of dangers—why deny ourselves happiness?"

She could think of no rebuttal—didn't want to think any more about refusing him. She wanted to be his. A part of her knew that things between them were moving much too fast, but she kept telling herself that everything would work out, that their love could conquer anything.

• • •

THAT night, with the moon calling to her fiercely, Enid gave in to one of the secrets she could not tell her betrothed. With water from a basin, she summoned the Lady's power. With her arms, she pulled in shadows to cloak herself from prying eyes. In a castle housing hundreds of people, guarded by the best soldiers and knights of the realm, she could not risk being seen.

She avoided the patrolling guards, and the great hall itself, where so many servants made pallets before the immense hearths. She escaped through a small door which led from the women's apartments to the lady's garden, and from there she sprinted across the open wards.

She heard the soldiers calling to each other from inside their barracks and the sound of dogs barking as she passed the kennel. Of course the poor animals could smell her, but the houndsman, after a look around, only hushed them and went back to his bed of hay.

After borrowing a rope from a storage shed, she ascended the winding staircase in a corner tower and went out onto the battlements. The cold wind made her shiver as she tied off her rope and let it slither to the ground outside the castle. She froze when a pair of guards passed her, but she was not discovered. The moon's shadows were at her bidding.

After pulling the back of her skirt up between her legs and tucking it into her belt, she climbed down the rope, using her feet against the curtain wall. She knew that just a year before she would not have had the strength for such dangerous work. But the Lady of the Lake had agreed with her mission, had trusted her with the power of unearthly strength. And Enid used it gladly.

By moonlight she found the pond she'd seen from the road. No human sound disturbed the magic of the night. When she was naked, she accepted the buzz of her skin as she stood at the water's edge. With a small dagger, she made a tiny slice in her finger and held it over the still water, letting several drops fall. Then she raised her arms and beseeched the night sky in her own tongue for the power it had so recently begun to grant her. The trees began to sway with a wind she could not feel at first. The whisper of their branches was another language to her ears, and she swayed with them. She placed one foot in the water, then the other.

The sudden energy that shot between her and the moon, replenishing her powers, was invigorating, restoring her sense of purpose, her knowledge that she was doing the right thing, though it be a secret from her future husband.

When finally the light faded, and she was simply Enid, standing in a pool of water, she waded back to the embankment and donned her garments again.

• • •

GERAINT was drunk. Several of the knights had begun plying him with ale hours before in the great hall,
as they tried to persuade him to reconsider marriage.

Geraint held up his tankard. "To my future wife!"

There was a chorus of groans and boos. Sir Rowan
and Sir Maxwell slumped on their benches across the
table from him, shaking their heads.

"You are far too young to marry," Rowan insisted,
wiping his mouth on his sleeve.

"Or maybe he needs a woman too badly," Maxwell
said with a guffaw, "and she will not give in without a
priest's blessing!"

"Go ahead and laugh," Geraint said. "I will be a
happy man tomorrow, and the rest of you will only have
your envy to console you."

Rowan looked like he was about to protest, but suddenly he stiffened, his face mottled white and red.

Maxwell peered at him. "You look ill, my friend."

Rowan suddenly bolted to his feet and began to run
for the double doors that led outside.

Geraint stood up.

Maxwell dropped his head to the table. "He doesn't
need us to witness his folly."

"Mayhap he needs us to make sure his folly does not
become worse."

Maxwell didn't move. "There's a good man,
Geraint."

Geraint was quite proud that he didn't stagger as he
crossed the hall. Two sentries gave him amused looks,
but they didn't try to stop him as he pushed through the

doors and went outside. The air was cool and fresh, and he was so busy enjoying it that he almost forgot the stairs leading to the ground, though they were lit with torches. He staggered down them without falling and found Rowan on his knees clutching a water trough.

"Tell me you did not foul the horses' drink," Geraint said, laughing.

"Nay, but I thought I might need to dunk my aching head."

As Geraint stood over his friend, smiling, something strange came over him. The wind suddenly picked up, and it must have chilled his skin, because he felt goose-flesh rise. And then he saw a flash of lightning in a cloudless sky.

He blinked stupidly. "Did you see that?"

Rowan hiccuped. "I only see water."

"I just saw lightning, but heard no thunder." He waited, but it didn't repeat. "It seemed so close."

A feeling of foreboding swept through him. Was the solitary lightning bolt a sign from the heavens? He told himself it was the ale making him feel so morbid. He was about to be married to the most wonderful woman in the world—who refused to tell him her secrets. Was God trying to tell him something?

Sir Rowan grabbed his leg. "Your assistance, please."

Geraint helped him to his feet, but he couldn't stop looking at the moon, as if waiting for confirmation that a storm was approaching. But the wind died away, and he was left feeling . . . unsettled.

"Let me help you back inside," Geraint said.

Sir Rowan clutched his shoulder and swayed. "Are we in a hurry?"

"I just need to see to my betrothed."

"Tonight?"

"Aye, tonight."

"But do not ladies need a night to reflect on the purity they're about to lose?" Rowan laughed softly to himself.

Not Enid. She kept offering to give herself to Geraint without vows of any kind. He reminded himself that her tribe did things differently than the Britains—like bathing no matter who was watching.

He shook off these strange thoughts. Everything would be fine once he talked to Enid.

He escorted Rowan back inside, propped him up next to Maxwell, and then went looking for Enid's bedchamber. He knocked softly, but there was no answer. She was probably asleep. He turned to leave . . . and hesitated. He just needed to make sure she was safe. Something just felt . . . wrong tonight.

"Geraint?"

He whirled around and saw Enid standing in the corridor, looking uncertain. She still wore her gown, though she had retired hours before.

He kissed her cheek. "I am sorry to disturb you, my sweet."

She smiled. "I can tell you've been enjoying your evening."

"The odor of ale, eh?"

She only shook her head indulgently.

"I saw lightning on a clear night, and for some reason I had to come check on you."

She stiffened, and he knew he'd offended her.

"Forgive me—the drink is playing with my senses," he said. "You were probably using the garderobe."

"Surely 'tis better than hiding behind a bush for my private needs, as we did on our journey."

She glanced at her chamber door.

"You must be tired," he said. "You could not sleep on your last night as a maiden?"

With a shrug, she said, "My mind was awhirl. Too much excitement, mayhap."

He stepped aside and let her open the latch on her door. As she moved past him, he happened to notice a stain on the front of her skirt, and loose thread at the bottom, as if the hem had ripped.

"Enid, what happened to your gown?"

She glanced where he pointed, then blushed. "You will think me foolish, but I am not used to wearing skirts. I stepped on the hem going upstairs and fell."

He touched her arm in concern. "Are you bruised or bleeding? Should I send for a healer?"

"Nay, Geraint, but—" She turned to face him, lifting her chin with a resolute expression. "I am not sure what kind of marriage we can have if you question me whenever I'm not exactly where you think I should be."

He blinked at her. " 'Tis the drink, Enid."

"Is it? Are you changing your mind about me?"

He opened his mouth to protest, but she cut him off.

"Because I would understand. You could come to my chamber now, and I would give you everything you might want of me, without any vows, if that's all you need from marriage."

"You know 'tis not, Enid," he whispered. "I love you."

"And I love you."

He kissed her good night, then waited until she'd

closed the door. He stood looking at it foolishly. He didn't only want her body; he had vowed to trust her. Surely it must be the ale making him so suspicious. He needed to sleep.

Enid kept her back to the door, holding her breath until her lungs ached. But Geraint didn't knock. She let out air with a heavy sigh of relief.

What was she doing? Geraint wanted her regardless of her secrets. But the moment she did anything unusual, he seemed suspicious. And this marriage would be filled with the unusual, as she studied a knight's training.

He had promised to trust her—but she couldn't trust him. What kind of relationship was that?

Should she leave Camelot? Find another place to learn military skills? But where else would she be able to have this kind of ready access?

By the gods, was she only using Geraint to fulfill her mission?

But she loved him! She wanted a life with him, and it would only be a few months more, and then there would be no secrets between them. She wasn't using him; she could refuse to marry him right now and still be allowed to remain at Camelot, secretly learning from them.

She just couldn't bear to live her life without him.

Chapter 4

• • •

FOR Geraint, the wedding and the midday celebration passed in a blur of frivolity that seemed to be happening outside himself. Within, he was full of clarity and purpose and certainty. Enid was his destiny—seeing her smile and her happiness were all that mattered. And when they were finally left alone in his bedchamber, never more to be separated, his contentment was complete.

She was his. He would show her his commitment and love, and eventually she would trust him with the secrets that haunted her.

But for now, she trusted him with her body, and it was enough. He peeled her beautiful gown down, kissing each scar revealed. He ached for what had been done to her, what she'd been forced to bear, putting aside the rage that festered inside him. He was gentle as he caressed her skin, pleasured her breasts. By her cries he knew when she was ready and entered her with great care so as to cause her as little harm as possible.

But there was no maidenhead to sunder. She was not a virgin. For a frozen moment they stared into each other's eyes. This was one of her painful secrets. But how could he blame her, after the way she'd been raised? A woman forced to learn skills to defend herself against the world. She might even have been raped.

So he put aside the sorrow he bore for her, hushed her protests, and made love to her as she deserved, many times over through the night. She brought eagerness and power to their bed, even if she did not bring purity. She made him so happy, and he vowed he would never give her cause to regret their union.

• • •

AMID the summer splendor of the lady's garden at Camelot, Enid laughed as her new husband lay her back in his arms so he could feed her grapes one at a time. They reclined on a bench, partially hidden by climbing roses.

She chewed and swallowed, then smiled up at him. "We are displaying our happiness before the entire court. Surely we are making someone uncomfortable."

"Think of the inspiration we provide," he murmured into her ear. "Mayhap there will be more love matches at Camelot, because everyone will envy us."

She told herself this, over and over, but regardless of what Geraint said, a feeling of unease had not left her since the consummation of their marriage last night.

Now he knew she'd had another man before him. She still remembered the shock in his eyes, so close to

hers. She'd been ready for anger, but instead a sweet
sadness had altered his expression, as if he would accept anything she was. He had wanted no explanations.
How could she not love a man like that and want to remain with him always?

"I think it was a mistake to leave our room," he said,
his hands combing through her hair.

She closed her eyes on a sigh at the rush of pleasure.
"You know you have your duties, Geraint."

"And I also have a new wife to care for. No one will
miss us."

She found herself hesitating, her mind clearing, as she
caught sight of knights returning from practice at the tiltyard. Their leather garments were covered in sweat and
spatters of blood, and they laughed and traded stories and
exchanged coins wagered on personal contests. It was
that world she knew, that world that her husband belonged to as well. She was so grateful to find a man who
understood her. After all, he'd seen her in battle, knew
that she had not been raised as the women of Britain.

"But, Geraint," she said, "what will King Arthur say
if you neglect your duties?"

"He has a wife, though she be a queen, my sweet.
And he gives her the devotion she deserves." His hand
slid around her waist, his thumb brushing beneath her
breast. "Let me offer you mine."

She gasped and tried to remember what she'd been
saying. Geraint was so distracting. With but a touch, but
a word, her mind strayed to their bedchamber and the
secrets they shared within. If she was not careful, she
would lose all that she was, in service of this need to be
joined heart and soul and body with him. Her training in

the practice of lovemaking had not prepared her for the sensations that his love inspired in her. For of course, she'd never allowed another man to give her pleasure, regardless of what her student experienced while she taught him.

Reluctantly, she sat up and tied back her hair, chasing away his questing fingers. "You promised to show me the wonders of Camelot. We have barely left our bedchamber since yesterday."

He laughed, but he seemed eager to display for her the impressive accomplishments of his high king. Arm in arm, he led her proudly through the inner ward.

Guilt began a slow simmer inside her as she realized that Geraint unwittingly helped her mission by guiding her around Camelot. She promised herself she was only going to learn how they trained even the lowliest of knights, something that surely was not a secret among his people. The Donella did not wish for war; they only wanted to protect themselves, and Enid was honor bound to help them.

She studied everything her husband showed her. She knew she displayed too much interest in the blacksmith's art, but armor was something her people did not know how to create and must learn in order to survive. She admired the barracks housing soldiers on the second floor of every outbuilding in the inner ward. There were stables and carpenter shops and sheds and kennels. Geraint tried to spend extra time showing her the kitchen gardens, but plants were her sister Olwen's love, useful with the healing arts Olwen learned from their mother. Enid found herself impatient for what she really wanted to see.

She heard the sound of metal on metal before they were even through the gate separating the inner and outer ward. The tiltyard, the second home of every warrior, spread out below them down a hillside, framed within massive stone walls. Enid pulled up short and merely stared. Knights practiced their jousting at the quintain, a dummy that spun and knocked them from the saddle when they hit it incorrectly. Pairs of men fought each other with sword and dagger and axe. At the far end, archers aimed at targets braced by bundled hay.

She stared in silent awe. The skill evident in King Arthur's knights brought home how inadequate her own father's soldiers really were. Enid's people were of the forest, fighters of skirmishes on foot; the skill of their sword arms usually ended combat. For they had none of the protective armor of King Arthur's men. The mounted cavalry who could fight from horseback would slaughter her people. Her resolve to help them only strengthened. Her husband would understand.

The sounds of the castle faded from Geraint's hearing as he stared at his wife. He never tired of studying her, as if she were a rare tapestry come to life. She looked out over the tiltyard, her pink lips parted with excitement, her shoulders thrown back, her body tense, as if at any moment she would attempt to draw a sword that was no longer at her side.

He knew she had battle training to rival his own, but as her devoted husband, he would protect her now. Never again would she know the fear of being alone against her enemies. He could not imagine a family, a home, that would so little protect its women.

But he could not fault what training for battle had

wrought in her body. She was tall and long-limbed, lean of muscle, stronger than any woman he'd ever known, and he had selfishly taken pleasure in that.

He called her name softly, but she didn't seem to hear him, so eagerly did she watch the knights and squires training.

He touched her arm, trying not to feel annoyed. "Enid?"

As if she came out of a stupor, she turned slowly to look at him. "Geraint, let us go down among the men. The training fascinates me."

"Enid—" he began heavily.

She turned to face him, taking both his hands in hers. "I know I am dressed inappropriately," she said. "I will not interfere or try to display my skills, but Geraint, 'tis what I know how to do."

Her voice was laced with sincerity; her blue eyes, pale as mountain ice, beseeched him. He did not want to refuse her anything, but he had to try to make her understand.

He kissed the backs of her hands. "But you have *me* now, my sweet, and the protection of my arm."

She smiled at him, but he sensed a disturbance in her emotions as she looked back at the tiltyard once more. He would have to be more patient, he told himself, even as he gave in to her entreaty. He smiled, entwined her arm with his, and led her down the slope to where the knights trained. She grinned her excitement, and then had eyes for only the soldiers. If he didn't trust in her love, he might easily be jealous.

But she had the queen's ladies now to train her in the ways of women. Soon, she would understand that she was not alone in the world, that she had a husband now who loved her.

Geraint desired her trust more than anything else, for what was a marriage without it?

The sounds of combat grew ever louder as they approached, men cursing, grunting, shouting challenges, and the ever-present clash of metal on metal. Clouds of dirt raised by booted feet shimmered in the air.

Sir Blakemore, one of his sparring partners, broad and bearded, came over to the edge of the yard, and after a brief nod to Enid, looked Geraint over.

"You are not dressed to train," the knight said.

Geraint grinned. "How observant of you. Can you not see I am with my lady wife?"

Blakemore shrugged and said in a low voice, "You have been gone too long. Are you not to lead a troop to scout the eastern border of King Arthur's lands in a sennight?"

For a moment, Geraint felt like a youth again beneath the critical eye of his father, but all he did was nod. "I shall be well prepared."

"If you call lounging between a woman's thighs a preparation," Blakemore said darkly.

Geraint stiffened and rested his hand on his sword. "You say such things in front of my wife?"

Blakemore reddened and glanced away, wiping his sweaty face on his arm. "My apologies, my lady."

Enid smiled. "I freely came to the tiltyard, Sir Blakemore. I knew what to expect. And perhaps I shall forgive you if you demonstrate again how you found the weakness in your opponent's armor with your sword."

Blakemore straightened up and looked at her with

interest, even as Geraint withheld a sigh. He could hardly blame Enid, since he was the one who'd agreed to bring her. He found his irritation simmering just beneath the surface. He despised this new feeling of jealousy. He had won her to wife; why was that not enough for him?

Blakemore walked like a strutting cock back into the center of the yard. The knight called out instructions as he broke apart the thrust for her, move by move. Enid leaned on the rail and watched avidly, as if she were committing it to memory. Surely no other woman had ever taken such an interest in a knight's accomplishments. He almost found himself wanting to remind Enid of his own skills.

But that would only encourage her. Instead he fell to his favorite new pastime, watching Enid, from the excitement that widened her mouth and lit her eyes to the way she gripped the rail and leaned over it. And then he caught her twitching, and he realized she was imitating Blakemore's movements.

Sighing, he shook his head and put his arm around her shoulders. For one moment he felt a startled tension surge through her body, as if he were an enemy. Almost immediately she relaxed, and her soft laughter was full of chagrin.

"Forgive me, my husband. I forgot I was not on the tiltyard myself."

He smiled as he kissed her. "I will give you other things to think about."

◆ ◆ ◆

THAT night, long after Geraint had fallen asleep, Enid lay awake, the bed curtains closed around them.

Geraint's breathing was slow and methodic, with only the occasional growl of a snore that she found endearing. She knew she had to be in love if she found a man's snoring so captivating.

Her body tingled with energy, and she felt suddenly smothered in the darkness. Very slowly she pulled the bed curtains back, her body alive with the night sky. It was as if her power didn't want to leave her body and needed her to come be one with the stars and moon, woods and water. It was still so new to her that she didn't know what to expect.

Her body was not her own tonight. She pushed back the coverlet, slid from the bed, and walked to the window. The shutters were already thrown back, and at the touch of the moon, she felt something stir inside her, an energy that seemed to crackle with heat. She closed her eyes to will herself to accept its very alienness, but in the end she stepped away from the window.

If only she could tell Geraint everything, ask for his help. But she could not forget his dismay with her need to visit the tiltyard, and the way he wanted her to be one with his people. There was no magic here, no destinies like hers. What if he outright forbade her to finish her mission? What if he was disgusted with the powers she was imbued with? But the magic would be gone when her mission was complete.

He had other things to worry about now, like the troop he was to lead, according to Sir Blakemore. She sensed a wariness in the other man in regard to Geraint. According to Sir Albern, Geraint had been working with King Arthur as an advisor. It was obvious he had not trained for some time. She would just have to make sure he spent part of the day tomorrow with his soldiers.

But to her dismay, he spent the morning introducing her to more women, finding more gowns and smocks for her to wear, and admiring her attempts at embroidery while he distracted her by laying with his head in her lap. She was alternately worried and pleased and exasperated.

In the great hall, just before the midday meal, she saw Sir Blakemore brooding when he noticed Geraint, then turning and talking to several other knights, who glared at her husband.

"Geraint?" she murmured.

But he was distracted by a maidservant handing him a leather wallet bulging with food. He glanced up at Enid, wearing an excited smile. "Aye?"

"Do you not see Sir Blakemore? He is upset with you."

Geraint turned his head toward his comrade, but only shrugged. "He has never been married, and does not want to understand a husband's need to be alone with his bride the first few days of his marriage."

"But we needn't be separated while you train. I could come watch you, maybe even practice—"

Geraint's smile fled, and he spoke softly. "They will not understand that you were raised differently, Enid. You gave me your word, now I ask you to trust me in this."

He searched her gaze with his, and she wondered if he saw that she did not trust him completely, not yet. Her stomach burned with the guilt, but not enough to betray her mission or her people. Silently she watched him sling two drinking horns over his shoulder.

"Where are we going?" she asked.

Kissing her quickly, he took her hand to lead her through the crowds milling about the trestle tables. She watched him ignore Sir Blakemore, who turned away in obvious disgust.

"There's a beautiful wood nearby," Geraint told her over his shoulder. "It is the most romantic place, with a stream that leads to a small pond."

She could not explain that she'd already been there.

• • •

THEIR private meal was glorious. Geraint made her forget everything but him. It was only when he escorted her back to the great hall, flushed with his kisses, her hair tumbling down around her shoulders, and her gown grass-stained, did reality intrude. He went off to a council of King Arthur's closest advisors, and Enid found herself alone. She strode purposefully outside to the tilt-yard. She might not be able to disobey Geraint and train, but she could watch and absorb the lessons, in hopes that she could later find time to practice.

She boldly walked up to the same rail and leaned upon it to watch the men train. She devoted an hour's attention to jousting, knowing that her people needed to become more comfortable fighting on horseback. But then she went back to watching the sword fighting, her favorite discipline.

At first the knights regarded her warily, but in the way of men, soon they were trying to impress her. The ones who suffered for it were the squires, with years of training left before they had the ability to become knights. One particular young man's plight called to her the most. He couldn't have sixteen years yet, and his body was still gangly and thin with youth. He was no match for the men who trained around him, but still he continued to try. He reminded her very much of her brother, Dermot, who at fourteen was just beginning his training with the warrior women. Dermot was too proud to accept tutelage from his sister, of course, much as she ached to help him.

This young squire, his brown hair wet with sweat, made her feel the same maternal ache. He had no confidence in himself, she saw, as she unconsciously moved closer to him. He was fighting a bigger, older squire. Though they used blunted swords, her chosen squire kept falling back, repeatedly failing to parry in time to miss a stinging blow to his arms. She almost called out instructions, but caught herself in time.

She held her breath when he was knocked to his knees, his sword sliding across the packed earth near her feet. The other boy came at him from behind, his broad face full of triumph, his sword raised high.

At a full sprint, Enid picked up the sword and put herself between the young squire and the bully. The older boy couldn't stop his motion, though she saw the shock register in his face a moment before she met his sword with her own in a parry so powerful that his weapon broke in two. Crying out, he dropped the hilt, clutching his wrist and staggering back to gape at her.

She froze, the sword at her side, hearing the stunned silence all around her. Even the horses blew out their breaths and waited. Every gaze was focused on her, and she saw herself as if from a distance, a woman too tall, too strong, clothed in a gown, but carrying a sword. Sir Blakemore watched her with cold, calculating eyes.

Gathering her wits, she turned to the instructor and said, "I could not allow him to strike such a cowardly blow. Forgive my intervention."

"Did you not see what she did to me with strange magic?" the bully cried, holding his hand against his chest. "I was not going to hurt him!"

The skill was hers, Enid thought, but the abnormal strength was not. And she'd used it in front of all of her husband's fellow knights. She'd made a grave error.

She knelt down in front of the young squire. He had fallen onto his backside, braced on his hands, staring up at her in shock. After setting his sword beside him, she put a hand on his shoulder. The power of a warrior woman surged within her like a rising tide, and though it was daylight, she could see the faintest glow where their bodies met. The boy's wide eyes saw it, too, but he didn't tremble, didn't flee. She watched his face, saw the relief and amazement and thrill capture his expression. Looking at her with wonder and gratitude, he took her hand and kissed the back of it reverently. It was in moments like these where she most appreciated her calling as a warrior woman, a teacher to young men. This was no magic granted from the Lady; this was her destiny, her one gift as a member of the Donella. Every young man needed confidence, and by her touch she could grant it for a lifetime.

Embarrassed, Enid rose to her feet and almost stumbled, forgetting how drained she always felt. No one moved to help her except the squire himself, who jumped to his feet.

"Allow me to assist you, my lady," he said, taking her arm.

With a smile, she pulled away. "I am fine. You return to the field. Believe in yourself."

He grinned. "Aye, I will."

Heavily, she walked away from the tiltyard, hearing the low buzz of conversation swelling behind her. When she reached a wooden bench in the shadow of a storage shed, she sat down and closed her eyes.

Geraint would hear of this, she knew. So would others. How would she explain herself without giving everything away? Her thoughts muddled, she let her consciousness drift. She had no idea how long she sat there, gathering her strength, but she came back to herself at the sound of male voices. The shed was between her and the knights.

And they were knights, because she recognized the voice of Sir Blakemore.

"The king will understand," he was saying to an unknown number of men. "Geraint is not prepared to lead us. He follows the witch's skirts more than he trains with us."

Enid stiffened, worry and dread knotting her stomach.

"But he is one of the high king's favorites," a stranger said. "Maybe Arthur does not wish Sir Geraint to do battle. He is obviously being groomed as the king's counselor."

"He will not be a favorite if his wife is discovered to be a sorceress," Blakemore said coldly.

Their voices faded, and soon Enid was alone. She hugged herself and rubbed her arms as if a chill had invaded her very bones. She didn't resent being labeled a sorceress. She knew how different she was from these people.

But how could she tell Geraint that his friend had betrayed him?

Perhaps the high king wouldn't believe such rumors. Would not King Arthur trust the prince of Cornwall over a mere knight? And she yet had to convince Geraint that he must return to his men.

Chapter 5

. . .

AT supper that evening, the massive great hall was lit by torches, full of the sound of pipes and harps. Tapestries celebrated the great deeds of King Arthur and his knights. Geraint had been a part of it, and was soon to be privy to more. He had a beautiful wife, a future kingship of his own, and a high king who was pleased with his performance this afternoon. Geraint's command of the language of Gaul and his knowledge of the country itself had proven valuable. He was feeling well satisfied, especially with his position at the high table.

The representative from the king of Gaul was being feted this evening, and the court of King Arthur glittered its welcome, especially with the beauty of the ladies, who with just a demure lowering of their heads

could distract any man. Maidservants anticipated their
guests' every need, from food to fill bellies to cushions
for weary feet. Goblets of wine, a gift from the foreign
king, whetted the appetites of the guests, and the bread
was set out on silver plate rather than used as trenchers
to hold the rest of the meal.

At Geraint's side, Enid glowed beneath the thousands of candles. Her excitement and awe was a palpa-
ble thing, and Geraint wondered if she'd ever seen such
a feast before. One of the queen's ladies had gifted Enid
with a wine-red gown that actually reached her ankles, a
rarity since they'd not been here long enough to have a
proper wardrobe sewn. Laced beneath her breasts, the
gown displayed her embroidered smock beneath. He
wanted to pull apart the laces with his teeth and—

He realized that Enid was watching him, wearing a
knowing smile beneath her blushing cheeks. He was
so lucky that she was not shy about the intimacies of
marriage.

He leaned into her, let his lips brush her ear, felt her
shiver. "I do not suppose that you have eaten your fill,"
he whispered.

She giggled, and the girlish sound pleased him. How
had he ever deserved her?

"And what would your king think if we left his feast
so early?" she asked.

He bit her earlobe gently, felt her twitch, and then he
moved away. "He would say that I am a lucky man, just
as he is."

"You compare me with the queen?" she said with
astonishment.

He saw her glance at Queen Guinevere, ever remote —
and beautiful in her white gown.

"Nay," he answered softly. "She is her own woman,
as you are. But you shall be my queen someday."

She stared at him wide-eyed for a moment, unsmil-
ing, and Geraint felt a moment's worry. What could she
be thinking?

Then she laughed and shook her head. "From what
you tell me, your father is yet hale and hearty. I shall be
an old woman before I am queen."

"Without matters of state, I will have more time to sit
at your side, an old man daydreaming about his old wife."

She pushed at his shoulder playfully.

A young squire, brown-haired and lean, approached
them carrying a platter with morsels of beef and lamb
laid out to resemble flowers.

As the youth presented the tray, bowing, he looked at
Enid and said, "My lady, I made sure to find the best for
you. Each selection has been chosen for its tenderness,
so that it will please you. I am Lovell of Exminster, and
I am your humble servant."

"Lovell, it is good to know your name," she said softly,
glancing at Geraint with what could only be uncertainty.

Before Geraint could ask a question, the squire
turned to face him, his expression full of grave concern.

"My prince, no matter what anyone says, or how
they try to slur her, I greatly appreciated your ladyship's
help this afternoon."

Geraint glanced in astonishment at his wife, who
winced and shrugged, but again, the squire spoke before
she could.

"She was brave beyond any measure of courage,

especially for a woman. Her courage is only equaled by her beauty and kindness."

Enid's face blushed red. "Lovell, please, you do not need to—"

But at that moment, there was a great cheer as buxom serving maids paraded into the hall, dancing between the tables and benches, bearing over their heads trays of cooked, stuffed swans so realistic that they still seemed to swim. Geraint expected his wife to enjoy the pageantry, but she continued to look worried, which made him uneasy. How could helping a squire at Camelot require feats of bravery in a time of peace?

Lovell continued to dote on Enid, but soon everyone had been served, and he was forced to retire, still bowing as he backed away from her. The voices died down as the guests concentrated on the meal, and although the minstrels still played, Geraint was able to speak to Enid.

"So what did you do to so impress a squire?" he asked lightly.

Her smile was strained. "I spent the afternoon watching the knights train."

He frowned, but said nothing.

"Another squire was taking unfair advantage of Lovell, and after knocking the boy's sword away, he was about to strike a blow to his back—"

"With a blunted sword?"

She sighed. "Aye, I know no grave injury would have resulted. But he was using all the force he could, and before I knew it, I had picked up his sword and blocked the blow."

He tensed, wondering who in the great hall already knew that his wife had demonstrated her warrior training.

For the first time, he thought of what his father, King Erbin, would say—that once again Geraint had made a rash decision marrying so quickly.

Enid was watching him with resignation. He took her hand, and her shoulders sagged with relief. It wasn't her fault that she was not of his people. But he'd asked for discretion, and she hadn't been able to give it today. It was one thing for him to accept that there were secrets about her past that she would reveal in time; it was another thing to be disregarded as if his wishes didn't matter.

He sighed. "Is there anything more I should know?"

"The boy's sword broke at the hilt when I countered. It caused . . . quite a stir."

"You are a strong woman, Enid."

She shrugged and looked away. "I overheard Sir Blakemore call me a sorceress."

Geraint stiffened, and he searched the hall with his gaze until he found the man—standing at King Arthur's side and whispering. At that moment, both the high king and the knight looked right at Geraint. He knew damn well what they were discussing.

He had thought he'd known Blakemore well, but for the man to go to the king instead of talking to Geraint directly . . . it could only mean he'd been searching for a way to discredit Geraint and had finally found one. He was a coward, to use Enid in such a way.

She was watching Blakemore, too, and she turned back to Geraint with worry darkening her fair eyes. "Forgive me, my husband. I am so used to protecting the new warriors amongst my people that I never even hesitated to interfere."

God's Teeth, did she have to protect *boys* in her tribe? "Are the men so useless?" he finally asked with disgust.

"You misunderstand me, Geraint." She hesitated, as if weighing what she could reveal. "That is my position in my tribe. I am a warrior woman. Like my ancestors before me, I am of the elite women who initiate young men into the arts of battle. When their training is through, they join the men who guard our borders. We give them confidence and the courage to succeed. I could not stand there this afternoon and watch such mistreatment amongst fellow soldiers."

"You train the men," he said slowly, trying to comprehend such a place. "You were not . . . forced to learn to protect yourself, because the men did not provide it?"

She looked puzzled. "Of course not. Most of the women of my tribe do what you would expect of women. Although I admit," she said, looking around at the various people near them, "our women are expected to contribute more to the society of our tribe, and are given equal consideration when decisions are made. Here, unless they are servants, the women are required to do nothing except sew and be beautiful."

Geraint rubbed his hand down his face. "Ah, Enid, a high king's court is not the same as a castle in the countryside. When men are gone long, women are left to run great households. Most do not sit and wait for a man to worship them."

She looked relieved. "That is good. I fear I would not be able to accept adoration."

Some of the tension between them eased. "You do not want me groveling at your feet?"

"Well, that is different, of course. Where else should a husband be?"

"A little higher up, mayhap."

Once again, an exquisite blush swept her cheeks. He studied her and imagined her on a tiltyard, training soldiers. The force of command such a thing required seemed so very foreign to her. She was his wife, the soft place he would return to each night for the rest of his life.

But although he kept telling himself that it didn't matter, some dark part of him wondered at the man who'd reached her first. He doubted now that it had been rape, not if she lived and worked with men.

And would she understand that she could not continue training men when they returned to his father's castle in Cornwall? "Enid, you have to—"

But he was interrupted by Lovell again.

"Sir Geraint," the squire said with excitement, "the high king spoke to me—me!—and asked me to relay the message that he wishes to meet with you and your bride in his private solar when the feast is through."

"Inform the king that I will do as he commands."

Lovell seemed to think this a great honor, but Geraint knew what Blakemore had told King Arthur. Enid met his gaze, worry evident in hers.

"Everything will be fine," he said.

Or was he reassuring himself?

• • •

FOR once, Enid was glad to be clothed as the other women of Camelot. She walked down the torchlit corridors of the castle, her hand on Geraint's raised forearm.

She wanted to be a part of these people, to not call any more attention to herself than she already had.

She could still see the shock on Geraint's face when she had told him about her warrior woman status among her tribe. He'd obviously thought that she'd learned to fight because she had no one else to defend her. She was almost affronted for her father—but she was beginning to understand the world her husband resided in. Dread seeped into her at the thought of everything else she had yet to reveal. But if she was lucky, her mission would be long finished before she had to explain it.

But right now, nothing was more important than this meeting with the high king.

Two armed soldiers guarded the entrance to the solar, but let Enid and Geraint pass without questioning their identities. Obviously her husband's reputation as the future ruler of Cornwall did him in good stead.

They stepped through the double doors into a large room, where tapestries covered every wall to keep out drafts. There was a throne on a dais at one end of the room, but King Arthur was not in it. He sat at a table, dictating to his clerk. Gone were the crown and robes of state. He was but a man in a fine doublet and hose, surrounded by men who waited to serve him.

He looked up and saw Geraint and Enid. Though there were circles of fatigue beneath his eyes, his gaze was calm, full of a rare intelligence and perception that made Enid feel laid bare. Her nervousness began to skirt outright fear. She wasn't used to feeling afraid, but this man held their fate in his hands.

"I am finished here," King Arthur said to the roomful of people. "Please leave us."

The clerk, several counselors, and soldiers all dutifully filed from the room. Enid felt their curious stares, but no one dared question the king.

When the room was silent, King Arthur gave them a considering look. "I was pleased that you chose to celebrate your marriage at Camelot, Sir Geraint. I hope your father approves of your bride."

Enid tried not to take that personally.

"He has yet to meet her, sire," Geraint said. "He trusts my decisions."

But she was beginning to read the subtle, hidden expressions on her husband's face, and she could not help wondering if that was true. A king was usually consulted on who would rule at his son's side.

"Then you are brave," King Arthur said mildly, "for King Erbin is a man in control of his kingdom."

"Well I know it, sire."

The king turned his penetrating eyes on her. "So where did you meet your husband, Lady Enid?"

She laced her hands before her. "In a clearing in a woods a day's journey from here, sire."

The king arched an elegant brow. "You were just . . . waiting for him?"

Enid glanced at her husband, not knowing how much of the truth she should tell.

Geraint smiled at her. "My wife is concerned that I might be embarrassed by her, but I am not. Lady Enid is a warrior among her people, sire, and she was defending herself against a ruffian when I first saw her."

She let out the breath she'd been holding.

"Then you must be quite the swordswoman to impress

Sir Geraint," the king said, sitting back and folding his arms across his chest.

"She trains the young men of her tribe," Geraint said.

"Skilled enough to instruct." The king nodded slowly. "Where is this tribe that puts such important training in the hands of women?"

She had left home prepared for this question and what would be necessary to protect her people. Her husband watched her curiously, and she promised herself that she would tell him the truth—later.

"I am from many leagues south of here, sire, where two rivers form a boundary around marshland."

"Your tribe resides in a marsh?" the king asked skeptically.

She gave him a secretive smile. "There is much hidden within."

"I see. And you do not wish to share the exact location."

"Nay, sire. I have my people to protect."

She waited for the king to refuse such secrecy, but he only nodded.

"I understand, Lady Enid. Does your land yield many women such as yourself?"

"I know not what you mean, sire."

"Women with the strength to cause a sword to break in two?"

"It was a blunt sword. Perhaps it was not well made."

"My captain of the guards assures me that it was. Yet the strength of your parry cleaved it asunder."

"I can say nothing about the sword, sire, but I can answer your question about women warriors. We are rare even among my tribe, and only train the men. We do not normally fight at their side."

The king nodded, and then said softly, "In regard to the incident today, one of my knights claims sorcery."

"The man who claims such a thing is only envious of her skill," Geraint said harshly. "Let Blakemore come to me with his complaints."

"And how did you know it was Sir Blakemore?"

"I saw the manner in which he spoke with you at supper, sire, and yesterday he uttered a slur against my wife."

"Such behavior will not be given credence, Sir Geraint, but he also claims that you have been neglecting your duties."

"I am a newly married man."

"With an important assignment yet to come."

"Did I not serve you well today?"

There was an edge to Geraint's voice that the king could certainly not miss.

King Arthur rose to his feet. "You did, Sir Geraint, and We are grateful," he said formally. "But you must not lose the trust of your men. You may retire now. A good evening to you, Lady Enid."

He nodded to her, and she nodded back.

"Rest well, sire," Geraint said.

He presented Enid with his arm, she rested her hand upon it, and they left the king's solar. Geraint said nothing as they walked through endless corridors until they reached their own bedchamber. When they were alone, she helped him remove the fine robe he'd worn to supper, and when he was in shirt and hose, he paced their room silently.

She knew that this argument was not over between Sir Blakemore and Geraint.

"You lied to the king," he said suddenly.

"Aye."

"You do not live in a marshland to the south."

"Nay."

"King Arthur is an honorable man."

"Not everyone among his court can be."

"What about me?"

There was a terrible pause, and the tension rose between them until it was almost unbearable.

"I trust you, my husband," she whispered.

"But not enough to tell me where you're from."

She felt the sting of tears that had not threatened since her childhood. She looked brokenly at Geraint. "If you insist, I will tell you. But you promised I could tell my secrets at my own pace. And I swore a vow to my father to protect our tribe."

"And you would break this vow for me?"

She closed her eyes, feeling the foolish tears trickle down her cheeks.

Suddenly, he was there, his arms around her, kissing away her tears.

"I trust you, my sweet. I will not ask you to break your vow."

"Oh Geraint," she whispered, returning his kisses until their fierce passion overwhelmed them both again.

But afterward, when he lay asleep, naked beside her, she considered the wedding vow she was breaking. She had used wine in their lovemaking, drinking much of it, splashing it against their bodies. But she had done so deliberately so that he would sleep.

She had dallied long enough, enjoying her marriage and avoiding her purpose. It was time for her to regain her own confidence. She could not allow her people to suffer. She had to finish this promise to her tribe quickly, so that she could create new vows for her life with Geraint. Tonight she would replenish her powers—and she would begin to practice the new skills she'd used today. She could train next to the pond, using the shadows to hide what she did.

She had not known how difficult it was going to be to keep separate the promises she'd made to both her father and her husband. She had tried to explain before their marriage about her secrets, but the reality of it seemed worse to Geraint now. She had to finish it all quickly, so that she could devote herself to being his wife.

Enid stood at the window naked, the shutters thrown back, feeling the pull of the moon strongly now. Her very flesh vibrated with it. She bound her hair back and dressed in her own garments—a sleeveless leather jerkin that fell to mid-thigh and tall boots that left only her knees bare. After strapping on her scabbard and sword, she gave one last glance at her husband asleep in their wedding bed, cloaked herself with shadows, and then slipped out into the corridor.

Chapter 6

• • •

SEVERAL hours before dawn, Geraint suddenly opened his eyes. He lay still, feeling in his bones that something wasn't right. Enid was not lying curled against him, as was her wont. He couldn't hear her breathing. He sat up, and by firelight he could tell that the chamber was empty. He was alone.

His head was still thick with the wine he'd consumed, and he tried to remember if she'd drunk the same amount, but he could not.

Why had she left him? And had she deliberately encouraged the wine drinking?

He wondered how soon he would regret the bargain he had made with her before their marriage. Had he been so anxious to bed her that he would have accepted any secret?

Even the night before their marriage, he had caught

her roaming the castle when she should have been asleep.

Suddenly he heard the door open and close. He could see nothing in the shadows at that end of the chamber. But Enid stepped into the firelight and looked at him as her wet hair dripped a dark line down her leather bodice.

She was dressed as he'd first seen her, like the warrior woman she was, a sword belted at her waist. Geraint suddenly felt ridiculous sitting naked before her, exposed, when she'd covered herself. He wrapped a sheet about his waist as he came to his feet and stood before her.

Her shoulders slumped as she removed her scabbard and set it in the corner.

"Where did you go?" he asked. "Or will you lie to me as you lied to our king?"

"I do not willingly lie to you, my husband. And he is *your* king," she added.

"Then where did you go?"

"I needed to train, and you would not allow me to display my skills before your knights."

"Why would you need to train, unless you planned to use your skills?"

"So by not training, do your skills disappear even as we speak?"

Stung by her words, he glared at her.

She put her face in her hands and sighed. "Geraint, I did not mean that the way it sounded. Like King Arthur, I, too, have heard the knights talk. You need to return to them, to assuage their discontent, to prove yourself their leader."

The anger he used to live with so often now crowded back into his mind. "So this has become about me, and how you think I'm a coward?" he said softly.

Her eyes went wide, and she raised her hands beseechingly to him. "I never said that, nor do I believe it!" she cried.

"Keep your voice lower, or the entire castle will know what you think of me. Or do they already know, because they have seen you sneak from my bed? Twice—that I know of—you've wandered the corridors at night."

"No one saw me, Geraint. And I did not sneak—I left to train, because you did not want to permit me what is my right."

"And who did you train with?" He heard the jealousy, knew his hurt was causing it, but he could not seem to stop himself. "Is there another man whose cowardice is not in question?"

"I do not believe you a coward!" she insisted.

When she approached, he walked away toward the fire.

"And there was no one else," she added. "I vow I went alone."

"I'm not sure what your vows mean, Enid. Maybe I never knew."

"Geraint!" Her voice was broken, sad. "You cannot believe such things of me. I love you!"

"But do you love your secrets more?"

"You said that you understood."

"I thought I could. I thought nothing mattered but our being happy together. But your behavior tonight, this afternoon on the tiltyard—even the night before our wedding!—proves my trust has been misplaced. I thought your secrecy was about how your family treated you."

She shook her head.

"I should not have accepted such a bargain."

"But you did." A tear leaked from Enid's eye as she stared at him. "So you can only love and trust me if I do what you say and behave how you think appropriate?"

"It is your loyalty that is in question—and I guess my courage, too," he added sadly.

"Geraint, do not act like this," she whispered.

"Then tell me your secrets," he implored. "I am your husband."

She bowed her head. "They are my family."

"You're leaving me no choice but to believe the worst of you, if you can behave like this at Camelot, the seat of our high king."

When she turned away, he saw her shoulders trembling. He felt bleak and alone, wondering how in one day's time, the happiness he'd thought he'd found could melt away into distrust and sadness. He was a fool, and the entire court must know it. He thought of the way he'd been lovestruck over her, how it had jeopardized his place at court and with his men.

Even after all the things he'd done to prove himself as a steady counselor to King Arthur, Geraint was still what his father always claimed him—an impulsive man. And now he was paying for it.

He had to take Enid away from Camelot, before between the two of them, they ruined any more of his reputation at the high king's court.

• • •

AFTER a couple hours of sleep, Enid awoke with a pounding head, and her face felt raw from weeping.

Slowly, stiffly, she rolled onto her back, wondering what had awoken her.

By firelight, she saw Geraint stuffing his garments into a coffer.

The love she felt for him stabbed at her heart, but so did her bitter feelings of betrayal and disappointment. He had refused to sleep at her side after their argument, and the last she had noticed, he'd been sitting before the hearth, staring at the flames. Had he spent the rest of the night in the chair?

She wasn't going to ask him, because he deserved such discomfort after his accusations.

And she, too, deserved to feel miserable, because she had disappointed him.

Did holding to her family vows make her incapable of trust? It certainly held true after their argument. She didn't trust him—couldn't trust him. And it was obvious he didn't trust her. They'd rushed into marriage without knowing each other.

She sat up slowly, drawing her smock tighter around her bent knees as she hugged them to her chest. "What are you doing?" she asked softly. Her voice sounded hoarse.

"Packing."

She flinched at his cold tone, and then panic hit and she spoke without thinking. "Are you abandoning me?"

He glared at her over his shoulder. "Do you not mean to say like the coward I am?"

She groaned. "I say what I mean, Geraint, and I never said that."

"Then why would you think I would abandon my wife?"

She remained silent, knowing that anything she said would be twisted beyond recognition.

He turned back to the coffer and resumed throwing his garments inside. "We are leaving Camelot. I suggest you pack."

"But—" She was about to ask about his assignment for the king, but realized he would interpret her concern as another accusation. "Where are we going?"

"Home. *My* home. Cornwall."

• • •

GERAINT'S meeting with King Arthur was more cordial than he'd thought it would be. The king understood his need to take his wife home. Or maybe the king just wanted to be rid of the distraction of Enid, both to Geraint and to his men. Geraint promised to return immediately unless his father had need of him.

Enid, who had little to pack, was calmly waiting for him in their bedchamber. Geraint looked at her white face and somber expression and felt a moment's softening that he cursed himself for. Then he saw her in her own leather jerkin, wearing a cloak thrown back from her broad shoulders. She didn't offer to defend herself, and he didn't bother to question her choices. She was letting him know that his opinions about her clothing no longer mattered. Maybe *none* of his opinions mattered. He felt a tightening in his gut that he told himself was anger.

Late in the morning, Geraint led Enid through the great hall, where people stared at her garments. He bid farewell to several friends, and surreptitiously watched his wife stand alone.

Together they went out to the stables and met up with his men-at-arms. Four soldiers had come with him from Cornwall and now seemed eager to return home, although they eyed Enid curiously.

Geraint performed the introductions as Ainsley buckled him into his brigandine, the short chest and back plate he wore while traveling.

"Enid, meet your traveling companions for the next week. This is Ainsley, the captain of my guard."

Ainsley, short and broad and grim, bowed his head to Enid, but continued with his task. Ainsley took everything—even this unexpected journey—with a cynical fatefulness that had saved them all more than once.

Toland and Tyler were twins whose identical calm, pleasant features masked a quick wit and a tendency to play pranks.

They bowed as one to Enid, who looked between them skeptically and asked, "Gentlemen, how do I tell you apart?"

They wore identical caps, the same plate-reinforced leather jerkin of common soldiers, and wool hose above their boots. They raised one identical blond eyebrow at each other before Toland said, "I be the prettier one."

Enid's lips twitched in a smile but she only shook her head.

The last soldier was the youngest, new to the personal guard, and far too talkative and glib for Geraint's tastes. His cap had a peacock feather sprouting from it, and the young man pulled it from his head, swept it across his body and bowed low, revealing sandy hair that curled naturally into ringlets he usually preened over.

"Enid, this is Wilton," Geraint said disapprovingly.

Enid glanced at him in surprise, but nodded to the soldier.

"Milady, this journey be far more civilized with you here," Wilton said earnestly.

"I doubt it." The moment the words were out of his mouth, Geraint regretted them.

The four men-at-arms stared at him, and Enid's eyes heated, then went cool and blank.

"Those words were poorly chosen. Forgive me."

"Only for those words?" she asked softly.

He turned away.

As the party mounted their horses, Geraint saw his men watching Enid ride like a man. Above her boots, her legs were bare until one's eye reached the skirts of her jerkin. When he'd first met her, he'd been fascinated by the inches of flesh so casually revealed. Now he wanted it hidden, but said nothing. Raising a hand, he began the procession, followed by Enid and his men. Their coffers and provisions for the journey were piled in a cart driven by Tyler, whose horse was tied behind.

They rode under the gatehouse of the inner curtain wall, the pointed portcullis suspended just overhead. Geraint guided his horse down the slope toward the tiltyard—and Sir Blakemore, who waited below.

Chapter 7

. . .

ENID guided her horse as she rode between her husband's men-at-arms. She felt weary though it was morning, despondent over the state of her marriage, but then her curiosity came to life when she saw that Geraint was heading for the tiltyard, rather than the main gatehouse. While the twins glanced at each other in confusion, Ainsley looked worried.

Only Wilton seemed cheerful as he rode up beside her. "Now, milady, you be in for a treat."

She tilted her head. "A treat? What is Sir Geraint doing?"

"His duty to the high king, o' course. Just watch."

Enid bit her lip, but pulled her mount to a stop at the same time as the soldiers. Geraint kept riding until he was abreast of the yard, where he seemed to pause until he had everyone's attention. One by one the knights and squires ceased to train and turned to watch.

She held her breath as he swung out of the saddle beside Sir Blakemore and threw his reins to a squire. The two knights stared impassively at each other before Geraint turned his back. Sir Blakemore stiffened.

In a loud voice, Geraint called, "I must leave unexpectedly today for Cornwall, and King Arthur bids me choose a replacement who will lead the troop to the northern border."

Enid knew that Sir Blakemore might have been the one chosen before, but she couldn't imagine Geraint choosing him now. Yet how to handle the situation without leaving divisive anger in their wake?

"There are two men capable of this position, but I cannot easily choose between them. I shall fight them both and then make a decision."

For a moment, only a thick silence filled the tiltyard. Then suddenly a cheer rose up, and the knights cleared the yard.

Enid looked at Wilton questioningly, but the young man only shrugged. She could not help wondering if Geraint was trying to prove to her that he was not a coward.

If their argument last night got him killed, it would be her fault.

By the gods, he could be such a fool.

"The first man I shall fight," Geraint said, sauntering away from Sir Blakemore, "is Sir Rowan."

As the cheers rose, a knight emerged from the crowd, making sure his padded jerkin was on securely.

But Enid watched Sir Blakemore, who fisted his hands on his hips and glowered.

Geraint turned in a circle, grinning as he looked at the scores of knights surrounding the yard. "As for the winner of each bout, I shall allow all of you to decide."

Shouts echoed through the yard, and dozens of men wagered coins openly. As word spread, dairymaids left their churning and kitchen maids abandoned their dirty pots to watch the entertainment.

Geraint took a shield and weapon from an eager young squire. Though the swords were blunted, two large men swinging at each other could cause great damage, and she found herself holding her breath. But she'd seen a brief display of Geraint's battle skills, and found herself reluctantly anticipating this match.

He did not disappoint her. He swung the first mighty blow, and there was an audible crack as it met the weapon of Sir Rowan. For a moment, they were suspended together, each one using all his force against the other, until Sir Rowan staggered back and the boos began.

They slashed at each other, banged shields, parried away blows, but inevitably Sir Rowan kept retreating. Enid felt a stirring within her at Geraint's strength and talent, at the intelligent way he anticipated his opponent's every move. He had obviously not been harmed by missing a few days' training.

But their argument wasn't about the training, or anything resembling cowardice, and he should have realized that. He should have trusted that she was trying to tell him the truth about his predicament with his men— and his standing with King Arthur.

She couldn't wildly cheer her husband's victory when he was named the winner by the assembled knights, but she did force a smile so as not to embarrass him. That faded when Geraint next called Sir Blakemore's name, and she watched the knight stride into the center of the tiltyard, refreshed and confident. He was a powerful man, and Geraint had just finished fighting another. Would Sir Blakemore not allow her husband to rest?

But Geraint didn't ask for a respite. He merely nodded at his chosen opponent and brought up his sword. This time the battle was more even, at least as far as skill was concerned. Within minutes, both were bloodied and bruised from the force of the blows. Enid held her breath, waiting for Geraint's strength to fail, but it never happened. It annoyed her that she felt breathless watching him, even a tad too warm. He slashed and parried, hopping away from a sure blow and sending his shield crashing into Sir Blakemore's shoulder. When the other man staggered and almost fell, the crowd roared.

But Sir Blakemore did not give up. Soon both men were breathing in gasps and lumbering awkwardly as they circled one another. Sir Blakemore slashed; Geraint stepped aside, and one-handed, whirled his sword toward the other man's neck. Sir Blakemore barely raised his shield in time, and the sword slid off it and caught him across the skull. His helmet held, though surely his ears were ringing. He went down on one knee, but instead of admitting defeat, he unexpectedly swiped Geraint's legs out from beneath him. Both men ended up on their backs on the packed earth.

Why wasn't someone calling a winner? Enid wondered, looking around in confusion. Were they going to let this go on until two of Arthur's prized knights were grievously wounded? Sometimes she didn't understand men or their bravado. Women—even women warriors—were much more practical.

Geraint rose first, and a fierce grin split his sweaty face. "Am I the winner, Blakemore?"

The other knight roared as he staggered to his feet and came at Geraint, sword raised. As Geraint parried the blow, Blakemore tottered past him.

Blakemore came around slowly, and he spoke in a haggard voice. "Tossing your bride's skirts seems to have improved your skills, Geraint."

The other knights roared with laughter at such crudity, and Geraint joined in tiredly. He slowly straightened, his sword pointing into the dirt as he leaned against it.

"After such a magnificent battle," he began grandly, then held up a hand to calm the good-natured jeers, "I declare that Sir Blakemore has earned the right to command my troop in my absence."

While money was boisterously exchanged all around, Enid watched the two knights come together and speak in low voices. Geraint's expression was stern, and he did most of the talking. Sir Blakemore nodded once and turned away, but he did not look angry. Geraint had proved masterful in handling the delicate transfer of power.

"Sir Geraint!" called a voice from the crowd.

Her husband was returning the sword and shield to its owner, but he looked up.

"Mayhap ye should challenge your wife next," said a man who didn't bother to step from the crowd. "She wears a sword like she knows how to use it."

There was laughter all around, but it was awkward and dwindled away.

Enid drew herself up, keeping her face calm and unemotional. She felt every curious stare, saw every hidden whisper.

Geraint looked at her for a moment, then put on an obvious smile. "And have her master me out of bed as well as in it?"

The guffaws were overwhelmingly loud, and she felt her face go hot, but she understood. Wilton turned his head away, his shoulders shaking, and the twins only smiled and shrugged.

Whatever else she could say about Geraint, he knew exactly what to say to men. He was gifted with speech—but didn't she already know that, from the way he'd seduced her into marriage with words even more than kisses?

• • •

THEIR first day's journey passed uneventfully beneath a rare, cloudless day. Though the circumstances were sad, Enid felt relieved to be heading toward her own home, though she didn't tell that to Geraint. Not that she could even visit the Donella tribe—not until her mission was completed.

They made camp that night in a wooded copse near a stream, and since the sky was perfectly clear, they decided not to raise pavilions. Enid ate her dried beef and cheese silently, listening to the twins and Wilton chatter. Men said *women* talked too much, she thought in bemusement. But she appreciated their conversation, glad to think about something else. Geraint never talked to her at all, unless necessary. Just a day ago there were not enough hours to say all the things they had to say to each other.

The soldiers were so busy talking—and Ainsley was trying to quiet them—that it was Geraint and Enid who first realized something was wrong. There was a sound in the woods that didn't belong there. Their gazes met across the fire, and then both were on their feet, swords in hands.

The four soldiers hastily scrambled for their weapons as Geraint said softly, "Enid, remain by the fire."

She knew that she could be at his side faster than his soldiers, but she said nothing. It was not worth another argument, especially when she knew how King Arthur's knights protected their women.

But if a battle broke out, she would be ready to join.

Before anyone could fan out into the woods, a trembling voice called, "Sir Geraint, it is I, Lovell the squire. Might I have permission to join you at the fire?"

No weapons were lowered until Geraint called his permission, and the boy came forward out of the darkness. He was leading his horse, and his face was sweaty and pale by firelight.

Geraint was the first to sheath his sword. Then he folded his arms across his chest and stared at the boy. "Do you bring me a message from the high king?"

"Nay, my lord," Lovell said, looking down at the ground.

After Enid had put away her own weapon, she left the soldiers and came to Lovell's side. "Was there trouble, because of how I helped you?"

"Nay, my lady." He hesitantly raised his gaze to hers. "But I'm too old to foster, and I have been waiting to discover who I shall be squire to. 'Tis a terrible wait, my lady." He sighed heavily and risked a glance at Geraint. "I thought I would . . . help escort you to Cornwall."

Geraint arched a dark brow. "To pass the time?"

Lovell only nodded.

"Does the king know you left his service?" Geraint demanded.

Lovell gasped. "I did not leave his service, my lord! You are in the king's service, and by helping you, I help the king, do I not?"

"You think you'll be of help, boy?"

"I can do whatever needs doing," Lovell said stubbornly. "I have been well fostered at the home of Lord Blaed."

Enid saw the twins nodding to each other as if in approval. They sat back down and were soon joined by Wilton and Ainsley, leaving Geraint and Enid to deal with the squire.

"Lord Blaed is a fine knight," Geraint said. "But if you remain with us—temporarily, I might add—will not King Arthur worry about explaining your absence to your father?"

Lovell grinned and seemed to relax. "I sent the king a message, my lord, that I would temporarily be serving you."

Geraint sighed. "Confident, aren't you?"

The boy nodded eagerly and risked a glance at Enid.

She bit her lip, wondering what Geraint would say if he knew where such confidence came from.

At last Lovell was invited by the fire, and he shared the marzipan he'd stolen from supper before he left. Besides the candy, he'd provisioned himself well, and Enid could see that Geraint was impressed. Her relief was great. She sensed she had an ally in young Lovell.

After their meal, Geraint removed his garments, then walked the five paces to the stream wearing only his braies. Enid could not help watching him after she saw the new bruises across his chest and arms. She ached to soothe him, to rub liniment against his warm skin. He denied them both such comfort, she thought bitterly.

Though her muscles were tired from the day's ride, she could not forgo her people, now that she was coming ever closer to home. She stood up and drew her sword, capturing every male gaze.

Geraint finished pulling his shirt over his head and reached for his weapon. "Is there someone else stalking us?"

"Nay, but I must train." She didn't phrase it as a question.

His dark brow lowered. What if he forbade her, as he had at Camelot? She would have to go against him, forcing his men to choose between her and him. Or she would have to summon the magic and hide herself from them, which she didn't want to have to do every night.

But Geraint turned his back, and she flinched as if from a blow. Was his disinterest a prediction of the future? Here she was about to wield a sword, when all she wanted to do was cry.

Instead she marched farther down the clearing, where the woods opened a bit to give her room. And then she went through each new move one by one, over and over again until her muscles trembled with fatigue and sweat ran into her eyes. When she stopped, she turned back toward her companions and discovered that Lovell had left the comfort of the fire to watch her.

Reverently, he said, "I have been practicing those maneuvers my entire life, Lady Enid, and never have I seen them performed so fluidly."

She gave him a tired smile and allowed him to take her sword. "You see no opponent before me, Lovell. That would make all the difference."

"Do you mind if I ask why you learned to fight, my lady?"

"Because it is my destiny among my people to teach boys to become young warriors."

His eyes widening, he looked down at her sword but remained silent.

She walked past him, past the four men-at-arms who gave her puzzled looks, past her husband, who avoided her gaze. From her saddlebag, she removed a clean shirt, then walked to the stream to remove her garments. When she was only wearing her sweat-stained shirt, she walked into the water to wash.

Chapter 8

• • •

GERAINT sat beside the fire, but did not even pretend to ignore his wife bathing—although he did offer a ferocious frown to anyone else accidentally glancing her way. By moonlight her wet, white shirt hugged her flesh like the ghostly raiment of a fairy. He could see the long line of her torso and the round firmness of her buttocks where the water lapped. He had only begun to know that body intimately, but now it seemed like he knew nothing at all. He felt helpless and sad, and so angry that Enid would not give him her loyalty, her trust.

And she thought him less of a warrior as well. Although at Camelot he'd well handled the transfer of power to Blakemore, he worried that Enid might think he was simply displaying his skill for her benefit, as an offering of proof. He didn't need to prove his courage to anyone, but she didn't know that.

Because she didn't know him.

Although he told himself he was protecting her by watching over her, he knew he simply could not take his gaze from her body as she lifted the hem of her shirt to reach beneath and wash. At least she was not totally disrobing in front of his men.

He was hot and painfully aroused, but still he watched even as she walked out of the water. He could see . . . everything . . . through the wet garment, as if she were wearing nothing at all.

She retrieved her clean shirt and stepped behind a bush to change. Her long arms pulled the wet garment over her head, and then slid the other on in its place. Her skin was damp, so she had to drag it down her body, and for a moment, Geraint remembered his hands and mouth following the same path.

His vivid memories were a taunt to everything that had happened in the last day.

But so was her body, as she walked down the bank of the stream to the rest of her discarded garments. The darkness of her nipples against the shirt seemed deliberate, and he was angry that she so displayed herself. But with another quick check over his shoulder, he saw that the men were rolled in blankets around the fire, except for Wilton and Lovell, not so far apart in age, who were talking earnestly, their backs to the drama.

After Enid was clothed, she squatted beside the stream, rinsed out her shirt, and hung it across a bush to dry. Heading back for their camp, she came up short when she noticed Geraint watching.

Did she not know the display she'd made of herself? he thought derisively. Or had she done it all to show him what he was missing?

She tilted her chin in defiance, and with a snort he turned away. But then she settled across the fire from him, wrapped herself in a blanket, and combed her fingers through her long hair to dry it in the heat. He barely withheld a groan at such torture.

"My lady?" Lovell said hesitantly.

She glanced up at the squire, but did not cease her slow combing. "Aye, Lovell?"

"You heard me mention that I have yet to be assigned to a knight."

As she nodded, Geraint found himself studying the boy with curiosity, relieved to have something else to concentrate on.

"Lady Enid," Lovell continued in a formal voice, "would you do me the honor of allowing me to serve as your squire?"

Geraint must have made a noise of disbelief, because Enid glanced at him sharply. Lovell continued to fix his worshipful gaze on Enid.

"You said you train boys," Lovell rushed on. "Could you not train me? Though you may not think so from that day on the tiltyard, I am quick to learn and easy to teach. I would work hard for you, keeping your weapons and horse in fine condition."

For a moment, Enid said nothing, and Geraint wondered what he should do. The Geraint of his youth wanted to jump to his feet and refuse, as if sharing her were not an option. But he remembered her secrets and her mistrust, and he wondered if he had any say in her life anymore.

Then she met his gaze and tilted her head. Was she asking his permission as her husband, or as the commander of their small party? What else could he do but shrug his acquiescence?

She turned back to Lovell. "Very well, young squire, you can *temporarily* belong to me. I have seen you fight, and you do need tutoring."

Instead of being embarrassed, the boy only nodded with eagerness. "Wait until my mother hears this!"

Both Enid and Geraint stared at him.

Lovell ducked his head in embarrassment. "She always says that in their own way, women are as strong as men."

Enid smiled as she tied her hair back with a leather strap. "I think I would like your mother."

"And she would surely like to meet you, my lady," Lovell said as he grinned.

"Who are your family?" Geraint asked.

"I am the heir to the barony of Exminster, my lord."

Geraint slowly nodded. "I served once with your father. A good man."

Lovell nodded distractedly, but he was watching Enid with awe and wonder.

"Find your pallet," Geraint said with a sigh. "I shall take the first watch."

• • •

ENID awoke before dawn, wrapped in a blanket dampened with dew, facing the fire. Ainsley was adding wood to build it back up, and when it flared higher, he held his gnarled hands before it.

"Have you been awake long, Ainsley?" she asked softly, sitting up to ease the stiffness in her muscles.

"Just finishin' me turn at the watch, milady."

Geraint was the next to awaken, and she covertly studied him as he sat up and stretched. Since their marriage, she'd spent mornings in his arms, awakening to kisses and the passion that always flared to life between them. Even their argument couldn't stop her feelings. He looked at her now, and she could still remember the heat she'd felt when she'd come back from her bath last night and realized he'd been watching her.

She was consumed by shivering without his arms around her. To hide her own sad need for him, she said, "Yesterday after you defeated Sir Blakemore, what did you say to him?"

He laced up the tunic at his neck. "Only that he was not to question my abilities again."

"Surely you had already proved that."

He rose to his feet and spread his blanket out near the fire. After a small hesitation, he looked at her. "I told him that a true commander and knight of Camelot would never slur a woman as he did you."

She didn't bother to hide her astonishment, but he turned away, and she knew he didn't understand her reaction. Blakemore's behavior toward her was as forgettable as an insect bite. Did Geraint not realize that he had wronged her far worse with his unfounded accusations?

She grew angry all over again.

• • •

THE days of their journey stretched out one after the other, and each evening Enid broke the monotony by training with Lovell. He was an eager, intelligent student, and she enjoyed once again doing what she did best. Often the other men-at-arms watched them and made suggestions, which helped Enid to learn their fighting techniques. Twice she had to renew her magic, but since her husband was ignoring her, she was able to cloak herself in shadows and briefly leave the campsite.

She and Geraint spoke little. He never rode beside her during the day, and at night he spread his pallet as far away from her as he could get and still enjoy the comfort of the fire. As they journeyed ever closer to Cornwall, she sensed his deepening unease, and at meals she often saw him gazing to the west with a frown. What awaited him there that he seemed to dread? If only she could ask him.

Or was he worried about introducing his new bride to his family?

As the terrain became more familiar, the high moorland interspersed with deep fertile valleys, she occasionally smelled the sea, not so many leagues away. Toland and Tyler proved themselves good fishermen, and often caught their supper in nearby streams.

Finally the morning came when the men seemed excited to awaken, and Wilton confessed that they'd be at Castle Cornwall before dark. Geraint, wearing a frown as he turned away, did not seem to share his soldiers' enthusiasm.

Halfway through the day, as they rested on Bodmin Moor before the final push to the castle, Enid took her saddlebag and excused herself to climb back down into the wooded valley they'd just left behind. When she emerged wearing the blue gown given to her by the queen's ladies, all the men stopped what they were doing to stare. She rolled her eyes at them as she plaited her hair and tied it back from her face.

"I am a woman, you know," she said crossly. For a moment she remembered feeling so feminine when Geraint had courted her. Being treated as a woman had seemed so rare and different, but now she didn't know what she preferred. Couldn't she have both, the life of a warrior—and that of a woman?

But when she met Geraint's eyes, he seemed skeptical, as if he suspected an unpleasant purpose for changing her garments. Wasn't it enough that she wanted to look her best for the king of Cornwall, his father?

As she approached her horse, she found Lovell waiting, his hand lifted to help her. Just last night she had bodily thrown him across the clearing, startling everyone. Now she was too dainty to mount her horse alone? Wearing a smile, she brushed his hand away, put one foot in the stirrup and swung her leg over. She had no sidesaddle, so she spent several minutes trying to rearrange her skirts to cover her legs. If she'd have worn her boots, that would have covered more, but instead she'd gone with useless cloth slippers. They matched the gown.

She guided her horse amidst the men, but found them all giving her frowns.

"What is it?" she finally demanded of Ainsley.

"Should ye not be ridin' with the prince?" he said pensively.

"Oh. Aye, of course."

She tapped the horse's flanks and cantered up to meet Geraint. When she was at his side, he nodded and began the last road of their journey. Just behind him rode Wilton, carrying the banner of the prince of Cornwall. Today was Lovell's turn to drive the cart.

She glanced off into the northeast and wondered when she'd be able to feel done with her mission and ready to take her skills home. Would Geraint even want her to return?

• • •

THE trumpets alerted Enid first, although Castle Cornwall was yet a league in the distance. The castle within its curtain walls sprawled across the open moor, the tallest thing maybe in all of Cornwall. The tower must have had a view clear to the sea.

As they came closer, a drawbridge was slowly lowered, and only then did she see the low marshland that circled the castle like a moat, and the mist that hung about it even in daytime, as if the castle floated on clouds.

She, who had faced the gravest peril with calm, was suddenly very nervous. She was married to Geraint for eternity—what if his family hated her? And they would, if he told them of the grudge he held against her.

Their horses clattered over the drawbridge, and it was as if they entered a village within the castle. Dozens of small thatched-roof houses were built along the curtain wall. There were open market stalls and merchants leaning out the folded-down windows of their businesses. Dogs and chickens roamed freely.

Adults and children came running, waving the banner of Cornwall and calling out greetings to their prince. Enid found herself smiling at the enthusiasm of the children, who gathered around Geraint's horse. To her surprise, he pulled pennies from his saddlebag and tossed them to the children, who shouted their glee and went chasing on their hands and knees. She assumed he'd keep moving, but he waited to make sure all the children had at least one, tossing a few extra as needed. This was the man she thought she'd fallen in love with, a kind, gentle man.

But inside him lurked suspicion and mistrust.

Their party continued up to the castle, winding through barracks and stables and other outbuildings. Ainsley and the other men-at-arms took all the horses, and Enid was left to walk up the long flight of stone steps to the entrance, with Geraint at her side, and Lovell just behind.

Why did her throat feel so tight as she looked up? It was just a castle. People lived here, people who were no different than she was. But her palms were sweating, and she didn't feel like she could swallow. Surely she would trip on the gown.

Geraint glanced at her, and she met his gaze, lifting her chin with feigned bravado. He tilted his head, slight sarcasm in his smile, then held out his arm. She put her hand on it and allowed him to lead her up to her fate.

After they passed between double doors, the great hall opened up before them, massive in size, with a timbered ceiling high overhead. Tapestries lined the walls, and some of the battle scenes depicted seemed a bit . . . gruesome. There were hearths as tall as a man on each side of the room, and near one of them was a raised dais with a single gilded throne. King Erbin of Cornwall sat there, filling the chair with his broad shoulders and impressive presence. He must have been young when

Geraint was born, for he did not have the look of an older man, though his dark hair was gray at the temples. He was obviously still a proud warrior.

There were at least a hundred people within the hall, cheering and waving. They parted as Enid and Geraint walked forward, and then as if on cue, the sounds began to die away. She saw their puzzled looks, knew they were wondering at the respect Geraint paid her.

Even without her warrior garb, she looked different from them. So many were short and dark, and she had hair as yellow as the sun. She towered over most of the people, men included.

When they approached, King Erbin stood up and stepped from the dais toward them. To her dismay, Enid realized she was an inch or so taller than the king. Some men took great offense to that.

But though the king gave her a moment's thorough scrutiny, it was his son he studied. Was that skepticism he betrayed? Or perhaps just worry?

Geraint stepped forward, and Enid remained behind him.

"My king," he said simply, bowing.

The king's smile was slow in forming, but hearty when it fully appeared. "My son." He clasped Geraint's upper arms and gave him a little shake. "You were gone many months."

And then he hugged his son, and though she couldn't see Geraint's expression, she saw his hands stiff at his sides, as if he didn't know what to do with them. Slowly, he brought them up and patted the king's back.

"Father, you look well," he said, when they finally stepped apart.

"As do you. I missed you, son."

The king searched Geraint's face, but Geraint didn't seem to know how to respond.

"Of course I missed you, Father."

"Missed me? Bah. I doubt that you missed me standing over your shoulder. But I have received regular missives from the high king, and he is full of praise for you. You have done Cornwall proud, my son."

By the gods, Enid felt tears sting her eyes, even though she told herself she shouldn't care about Geraint's feelings. But it was obvious he did not have the best of relationships with his father, and this seemed to be a step forward.

And then King Erbin turned to face her with an assessing dark gaze. She wondered if he would be the kind of man who considered his daughter by marriage a threat.

"Will you introduce us to your guest?" the king asked without taking his eyes from her.

"Father, this is my wife, the princess Enid."

The hall was deadly quiet, as if all his subjects awaited King Erbin's reaction.

Belatedly remembering at least some of what she'd learned at Camelot, Enid performed a decent curtsy. The king openly studied her, and she waited, trying to appear serene.

Without looking at Geraint, he said, "My son, you did not wish to celebrate your marriage at Castle Cornwall?"

Geraint shrugged, but the tension in him was so very visible. "I did not wish to wait."

"What a surprise," the king said softly.

To her shock, Geraint seemed to flinch.

To Enid, the king said, "You are welcome in my home, Lady Enid."

"Thank you, sire," she answered.

King Erbin finally relieved her of the weight of his stare and glanced at his son, resignation and amusement warring on his face. "You have arrived in time to partake of the evening meal with us. We shall break bread while you tell us of the momentous change in your life. And of course, I have news of my own."

Chapter 9

• • •

WHILE the servants set up dozens of trestle tables throughout the hall and a long table on the dais, Geraint followed his father to a gathering of cushioned chairs before the fire. Geraint frowned at the pleasant grouping of furniture, one of many changes he'd already noticed in the brief minutes of his return.

The biggest change was his father. Much as Geraint was glad to know that his father had heard of the many services he'd performed for King Arthur, Geraint expected an angrier reaction to the marriage. He'd always accused Geraint of being too impulsive, and though Geraint might have lived down this reputation under the high king, to his father he'd just proved he hadn't changed at all.

Marrying Enid *had* been the most impulsive thing he'd ever done. And he hadn't needed to. She had offered herself regardless of marriage, as if where she came from, pleasure and need were all that mattered. But it had never only been a matter of lust between them. He'd wanted her to be his, body and soul.

He didn't feel like she was his at all.

"Lady Enid, do you wish to refresh yourself before the meal?" his father asked without subtlety.

She looked between them, and Geraint wondered uncomfortably what she saw with those intelligent, blue eyes.

"I am proud to meet my husband's family, sire. I would wish to know you better, if you do not mind my presence."

The king grinned with a bit too much eagerness, and Geraint knew how he relished a challenge. Enid should have retired, so that he could explain their marriage in private.

Geraint could have asked her to leave, and she might have done it—or maybe not. And how would that have looked? Much as he always told himself not to care about his father's opinion, he couldn't help himself. His father was the king, after all.

Geraint looked on his wife, so still, so serene, and he felt something in him reluctantly soften. In this old hall, with so many people as dark in coloring as he was, she glowed like a golden angel, her plaited hair weaving together many shades of yellow. Certainly no one could doubt that he'd been overcome by her appearance from the first. He was no different than any man here, he noticed, as his gaze searched the hall. People were watching them with curiosity, but men studied Enid's rare beauty with envy.

As if that were all that mattered.

The king seated himself, then gestured to the chairs on either side of him. Geraint and Enid sat down, and maidservants came with tankards of ale and goblets of wine and cider. Geraint and his father took the ale, and Enid chose cider. Did she want to be the one with the clearest head for this battle?

"Was your journey uneventful?" the king asked.

Geraint focused his attention on his father. "Aye. Usually there is the occasional attack by thieves beyond our kingdom's borders, but not this time."

"Maybe news of your accomplishments has spread farther than you know, my son."

Geraint blinked slowly, disbelieving his ears. Was his father complimenting him? "That does not seem possible, Father."

"King Arthur is quite pleased with your progress. And now to hear that he's begun to rely on you for counsel . . . well, I am amazed."

Geraint stiffened, but he detected no sarcasm in his father's tone. He felt off balance, as if the man had changed in some indefinable way.

"So tell me about this marriage," King Erbin said. "When did it take place?"

"Not quite a fortnight ago," Geraint answered.

The king turned a smile on Enid. "Ah, still a new bride then. I am glad Geraint brought you home to meet us so quickly."

"As am I, sire," she said. "It is good to have new family."

"And what about your own family? Who are your people?"

Geraint tensed and saw Enid hesitate. He couldn't risk what she might say.

"Father," Geraint said, "she is from a village a day's journey from Camelot, and her father is a well-respected knight."

He didn't know a damn thing about her father, but Enid was so gracious and poised that she had to have been raised well.

Her pale blue eyes flashed at him, but all she said was, "My father rules his land with a benevolence you would appreciate, King Erbin. I have a younger brother who will inherit someday, and my mother watches over us all. I also have two sisters."

The king sighed. "Siblings are a good thing to have. I always regretted that Geraint's mother died so young, leaving him an only child." He looked over Geraint's shoulder, then came to his feet and grinned. "But I am in the process of rectifying that situation."

Puzzled, Geraint glanced where his father did and saw a young woman descending the wide stairs from the second floor, surrounded by several ladies. Leading the way was her very pregnant belly.

Geraint's mouth fell open and he looked back at his father, whose new satisfaction now seemed justified. "I guess I'm not the only one with a surprise bride."

King Erbin strode to the base of the stairs, then reached for his wife's arm. She smiled at him and leaned on him gratefully. She was short and delicate, with a hint of dark hair beneath her headdress. The king led her to the chairs before the fire and seated her in his own.

He finally met Geraint's gaze. "My son, this is my

wife, Queen Portia. My queen, this is Prince Geraint, and his bride the princess Enid."

Portia's smile displayed dimples in her cherubic face. "Sir Geraint, it is a pleasure to meet one whom I would like to consider a son."

Surely she was younger than he himself, Geraint thought with amusement, but he only bowed. "I am glad my father has found a woman to make him happy, my lady. He has seemed lonely over the years."

His father frowned at him.

"But now he will be too busy for idleness," Geraint continued smoothly, "since you are soon to gift him with another child."

"But not one who could ever replace you in your father's thoughts," Portia said demurely. "Perhaps you and Lady Enid shall have a child soon, and our offspring could be raised together as playmates—though uncle and nephew, of course," she added with a smile. "Or aunt and niece? Good gracious, I am prattling on."

As the king reassured his wife, Geraint saw Enid put a hand to her stomach and look a little pale. Had he just assumed she would understand that a prince needed an heir? He wanted to groan at his own stupidity. The mystery of a comely, sword-bearing woman in need of protection had made him forget all else.

Enid remained a little apart from this new family, studying her husband's reaction to his new stepmother. It had been rather comical, his shock. Had he thought his father wanted to be alone for the rest of his life? Even Geraint hadn't wanted that, Enid knew. He had wanted the commitment of marriage more than just having her briefly to fulfill his lust.

Or maybe he'd wanted ownership.

But Queen Portia did not seem a woman to be owned, not with the way her husband waited on her. He guided her to the table, full of concern because of her delicate condition. He put choice meats on her plate, saw to the refilling of her wine, waved away her weak protests.

Portia loved every bit of this treatment, Enid thought with amusement.

Geraint didn't seem to know what to do with himself, so busy was he staring at his father. When Geraint would have ignored the maidservant bearing a cauldron of soup, Enid made sure that he was served. She would have worried, but Geraint's amazement was genuine, not full of jealousy. Many men did not like to lose a parent's attention, but Geraint was above that.

She was relieved.

She didn't have to make dinner conversation, because everyone was so distracted by their attention to the queen. Feeling at peace, Enid watched King Erbin's subjects. They had no problem enjoying themselves before their ruler; he was obviously a man who inspired loyalty and not fear.

But she had already known that, just from being with Geraint. Though she'd spent days thinking she didn't know anything about her husband, she had to admit that his actions spoke to the man he was.

She'd always thought his behavior full of kindness. He treated everyone with the same courtesy, from servant to high king. Couldn't she put aside her disappointment and try to trust him again? But he didn't want the same from her.

He had lied to his own father for her, answering the king's question about her family. He could have left her floundering, knowing she had to keep her secrets. Was he just trying to keep his embarrassment to a minimum?

Geraint and his father began to discuss the battles and skirmishes that Geraint had fought with King Arthur. Enid listened most carefully to glean anything that would help train her people. But they had barely begun to talk when the queen leaned forward and beckoned to Enid.

"Come sit by me, Lady Enid. We have so much to discuss."

Geraint may have been engrossed in conversation, but he sent Enid a small frown, and she gritted her teeth. What did he think she was going to do, attack his step-mother? Display her sword and challenge the woman?

After a serving boy brought her chair to the far side of Queen Portia, Enid sat down. A maidservant displayed cut fruit and cheese, and the women helped themselves. The queen took a healthy amount, and Enid found herself relaxing. Enid's own appetite had often been compared to a man's—at least by her proper sister, Cinnia.

After nibbling on cheese, Portia asked, "How long have you known Sir Geraint?"

Enid swallowed a grape. "We married but a few days after we met."

"Instant love," Portia said, laughing. "It is such a wonder when it happens. My own husband quite romanced me into marriage. I admit I was reluctant to marry a king, but he was persistent."

"As was his son," Enid said ruefully.

Portia eyed her with curiosity. "You would not have married so quickly?"

Enid hesitated. It was so awkward to speak to a stranger about such intimacies, but Portia seemed like a woman with a core of firmness beneath her fragility. "I would have been content to wait as long as Geraint needed me to." She would have done anything he wanted, she thought sadly, if only to be with him.

"We do what is necessary for our men," Portia said softly, her hand on her round stomach. She gave a little start. "Oh, this child is quite eager to play. He kicks at me constantly. Would you like to feel him?"

Enid was not used to women's ways, and she drew back wide-eyed. "Oh, nay, my lady, I am far too clumsy."

But the queen took her reluctant hand and put it on her taut belly. Almost immediately, Enid felt the child inside move. He was already his own person, with his own wish to move, as if not a part of his mother. She stared at her own hand, then up at the queen.

Portia smiled. "Is it not marvelous, to carry life within us? It makes us part of the future, does it not?"

Enid smiled wanly, knowing that she herself used a potion mixed by the women of her tribe to temporarily prevent conception. She was a warrior first, not a mother. Until her mission was over, she could not give up one role for the other.

Portia was a woman who had all she wanted, Enid thought, recognizing her own envy. Portia used her femininity to sway the king, not for any cruel purpose, but to accomplish her own needs.

If only Enid could be like that. But what she wanted,

she could not ask for. She could not have Geraint's help. She had never imagined regretting her vow of secrecy to her father, but more and more she was beginning to. But her regrets changed nothing.

Portia leaned toward her, her smile sympathetic. She put her hand on Enid's where it rested on the table.

The moment stretched out, and Portia's expressive smile slowly began to fade. Enid, who couldn't look away, found herself somehow connected to this other woman—her mother by marriage, though there could only be a few years between them.

Portia's head tilted, and she studied Enid's face as if memorizing it. Her expression was intent and curious. Then she looked down at her belly and moved her hand there, away from Enid's. She smiled again, but this time she seemed flustered.

"Ah, this child is so demanding," she murmured, caressing her stomach as if she already comforted the babe.

Enid frowned. "My lady, you seem pale. Shall I send for your ladies?"

"Nay, I would not want the king to worry. I shall eat and drink—I have had this hungry, faint feeling before, as if the child cannot get enough food. Can you reach the platter of bread?"

Enid leaned across the table and brought the platter near.

Portia sighed and shook her head. "Of course you can reach it. It must be wonderful to be so tall."

"Not always, my lady. Most men do not wish a woman to look down on them."

"Then it is a good thing you married Sir Geraint. I never thought he'd be that tall."

Enid paused, then looked the queen straight on. "But I am taller than the king," she said softly.

"He is a confident man, Lady Enid," the queen said. "And I am confident in him."

"It must feel good to be so confident," Enid murmured without thinking first. Then catching her breath, she looked at Geraint. He was still engrossed in conversation with his father.

Portia's smile was soft. "You have not been married long. Confidence will come."

"My lady, forgive me for being so bold, but you have not been married long either."

"Long enough," she said, her expression a shade wicked as she smoothed her gown over her belly.

Enid finally smiled.

• • •

GERAINT'S bedchamber was comfortable as befitted a prince, and Enid felt strangely at home there. A fire warmed the room. Cushioned chairs were grouped before the hearth, and a massive, curtained bed took up one wall. Enid quickly looked away from it. Their coffers had been brought in, and someone had hung her few gowns on pegs mounted on the wall. But the best thing was the bathing tub laid on towels before the hearth, steam rising from the water. She stared at it with longing, though she knew she had to bathe in a forest pond this night.

"You may use it first," Geraint said, coming up behind her.

She gave a start, even though she was always aware of his presence. She hadn't thought to bathe before him, something that had given each of them pleasure the morning after their wedding.

Now she felt reluctant to taunt him by brazenly bathing. Yet part of her stirred to life at the thought of his gentle touch, at the memory of the way he could make her skin shimmer as if it burned for him. After all the terrible things they'd said to one another, the awkward tension that was always between them, she still wanted him with a ferocity that frightened her.

At her long hesitation, he turned away. "I promise I shall not watch," he said darkly.

"You have a husband's right to do as you wish." Was she actually giving him the opportunity to demand such intimacies? It was as if she was making him take the first step toward what she desperately wanted. It seemed so long since she'd lain beneath him, since the joining of their bodies had made them one.

He glanced at her, his eyes narrowed. "And if I was to take advantage of 'a husband's right,' what would that make me in your eyes—or my own?"

She sighed. "I only meant that I would not force you from your own chamber with my need to bathe."

"Then bathe and stop talking about it."

He busied himself at his coffer with his back to her, and Enid quickly divested herself of her garments and sank into the tub. Usually, they only came to her waist, but this must have been created especially for a large man like Geraint, for she could sink up to her neck. Her appreciative sigh was a little too loud, but he said nothing.

The soft soap was fragrant with the smell of roses, and she rubbed it into a cloth and began to lather her skin. But her mind wasn't simply on her own comforts.

"Geraint," she said, "you seemed surprised by your father's warm greetings. Did you have a falling out before you left?"

Behind her, she heard movement, and after a moment he said, "Nay. But my father and I often did not agree on the decisions I made."

She held her breath, glad that he was actually confiding in her.

"He claimed me far too impulsive," Geraint went on dryly.

And then she understood why he was telling her this. Coolly, she said, "And you believe you married me impulsively, thereby proving your father right."

"I *was* impulsive," he said. "You were content to take your time, but I could not wait to have you."

Was he blaming himself? "Geraint, your regrets will not help the problems between us. And regardless of my hesitation during our courtship, if I wouldn't have wanted to marry you, we would not be here today."

"So we were both foolish."

It hurt her to hear him speak bitterly of their marriage. She had thought herself so in love with him, and he with her. Now she didn't know what they were but two strangers bound together forever.

To change the subject, Enid said, "The queen seems like a lovely woman." With a glance over her shoulder, she saw that her husband was staring out the window into the darkness, so she risked lifting her leg out of the water to soap it.

"He was never interested in another wife," Geraint said after a heavy pause. "They seem happy."

"They do. Queen Portia is intelligent, and she must love your father."

"I hope she did not upset you with her talk of us having children."

She fumbled with the cloth, and it slid to the bottom of the tub. She rolled her eyes. "I was not upset. It was a natural assumption."

To her surprise, Geraint approached the tub, and she sank in deeper, glad the soapy bubbles hid much of her body. She didn't want to tease him. He pulled up a chair facing the fire and sat down, not looking directly at her.

"Enid, I never even asked you whether you will be glad to have children," he said.

She studied his profile, and he seemed sad, as if his regrets about their marriage were a burden neither of them had anticipated.

"I did not enter into marriage with you lightly," she said, as she soaped her wet hair. "I gave consideration to the fact that as a prince, you would need an heir. It would be foolish of a woman not to understand that."

He sighed and slid lower, leaning his head against the back of the chair. "That is good."

"I am not with child now," she added. "Any decision you make in regard to me would not have to consider an innocent life."

He glanced at her, brows lowered. "Any decision *I* make?"

"You seem so disappointed by the woman that I am."

"I am disappointed that you do not trust me."

"You believe my loyalty is in question," she said, feeling her slumbering anger awaken, "but 'tis not."

"I had forgotten—'tis my *courage* that is in question."

She ground her teeth together and said nothing. She was finished defending herself against such a ridiculous accusation.

"If you were loyal to me," he said, standing to look down at her, "then you would not have needed me to lie for you about your family."

She gripped the sides of the tub. "I did not ask you to lie."

"But you would have lied to my father, the king."

"Aye, as you would have done for your father, were he to ask it of you. I am sorry that you are so embarrassed by me that you felt the need to deceive him."

"A king would not understand your need for subterfuge."

"Obviously neither does a prince."

She wanted to be done with this conversation, clothed so that she would not feel so vulnerable. She reached for the bucket of clean water next to the tub and lifted it on high to dump over her head.

Geraint took it from her hands. "Stand up," he said brusquely.

She glared at him.

"Do you want the soap rinsed, or do you want to leave half in your hair?"

She came to her feet, feeling the soap bubbles making their slow way down her skin. Then he began to pour water over her head. She ran her hands through her hair to remove the soap.

He was so close, and she felt like she was thrusting her breasts beneath his very nose. The warm water sluiced down her body, taking away the last of the soap.

She met his eyes, and he didn't relinquish her gaze as he set down the bucket. The very heat in his dark eyes burned as they moved down her body. She would not be embarrassed, because it had not been her idea to so wantonly bare herself before him. She reached for a linen cloth from the nearby table and draped it around herself.

When her husband turned away, the sadness clutched itself even tighter about her heart.

As she stepped out of the tub, he began to remove his garments.

"I shall call for clean water," she said.

"Nay, do not bother," he said impassively. "You bathed enough on the journey that you cannot have been *that* dirty."

She finished drying herself, not watching as he sat down with a splash in the tub. She had no night rail—she had not needed one in the first days of their marriage—so she donned a clean smock to sleep in. As she was pulling tight the laces gathering her neckline, Geraint suddenly spoke.

"I spent a week without anyone to wash my back. As my wife, you should do it."

Turning to face him, she found him watching her boldly. She arched an eyebrow, but rolled up her sleeves and approached the tub.

"Where is the cloth?" she asked.

"I know not."

His defiance was almost childish, and she had to restrain herself from smiling. As if she was going to search the water around him. She picked up a dry one from the table and dipped it in the water. He leaned forward in the tub, and she began to rub him, perhaps a bit too briskly. But he did not rebuke her.

The wide expanse of his back was familiar territory. She had explored it with her fingertips and her lips, and the memories were overpowering and raw. If he thought he was punishing her, he was not. He was only creating tears she had to restrain.

When she was done, she let the cloth fall into the water and stood up to turn away, grateful that he did not call her back. A maidservant had left a pitcher of wine and goblets on a low table, and she poured herself some nervously. When she could hear him stand, she tensed, waiting for him to ask her to rinse him, but he did not. And she found herself disappointed.

Next to the high bed was a little set of stairs that even she had to use to climb on top. It was a large, kingly bed, full of strange carvings on the wooden headboard, with four tall posts carved intricately like vines. She began to release the bedcurtains for warmth, watching as Geraint strode naked to the wine pitcher and poured himself a healthy amount. He looked at her, not hiding his erection, and gulped his wine down like it was an elixir to make him stop wanting her. Because want her he obviously did, and her own body answered, heating, moistening. She couldn't seem to breathe deeply enough as they stared at each other.

Would he demand his rights as husband in his own bed? She hadn't refused to wash his back, but this intimacy was surely different. It would be . . . cruel to misuse what had once been so powerful, so loving between them.

He didn't ask. He just climbed into bed beside her—

still naked, she realized, holding back a groan—pulled up the covers, and lay down, turning his back to her. Stiffly, she also lay back, but she faced him, watching warily.

The potion in his wine did not take long. Soon he was snoring, his body more than relaxed.

"Geraint?" She shook him, but he did not stir.

It was time to go. She had to find her water beneath the stars, and since they were sharing the same bed, she knew she could not risk trying to fool him again unassisted. The last time he'd caught her returning in the middle of the night, it had changed their marriage forever.

Even with her magic, she did not want to risk running into too many people, so she forced herself to wait several hours, until the castle was still. She donned her shirt and jerkin quickly, but she did not take her sword. There would be no practice tonight; she didn't want to risk someone discovering her. Once again she called the shadows to her, and she escaped through the great hall, knowing no other way to leave the castle.

Chapter 10

• • •

h OURS later, refreshed and calm, her powers replenished, Enid felt the tension begin to leave her
as she cautiously walked down the corridor leading to
their bedchamber. Though cloaked in shadows, she did
not move carelessly, but still she was surprised when as
she passed a large set of double doors, one opened. She
froze in shock as Queen Portia leaned out, her brows
furrowed, her expression alert. Enid didn't breathe,
didn't move, since they were but yards apart.

The queen did not retreat; instead she stepped bare-
foot into the corridor, her silken night rail fluttering
with a draft. She did not seem to feel the cold. Her head
was tilted as if she were listening—or sensing.

"I know you are there," Portia whispered softly.

Enid was feeling faint without air.

"Princess Enid?"

Oh, gods. Whatever fey senses the queen carried
could not be deceived. Enid took a deep breath, then let
the cloak of shadows fall from her.

Portia did not seem surprised, as if she knew exactly
where Enid had been standing. Her expression serious,
she murmured, "Enid, why do you disguise what you
are? Do such secrets not damage your marriage?"

To Enid's surprise, her throat tightened with the tears
that never seemed far from the surface anymore. "My
queen," she whispered and raised shaking hands to wipe
her wet cheeks.

"Wait here," Portia said and disappeared back into
her bedchamber.

Enid waited in despair for the appearance of the angry
king, but to her surprise, Portia emerged alone, wrapped
in a dressing gown. She took Enid's hand and pulled, and
Enid had no choice but to follow. Their pace was slow
due to the queen's belly, and Enid's guilt doubled. Then
Portia turned into a room filled with comfortable chairs
and rugs and cushions. This must be the queen's solar. A
loom filled one corner, and several pieces of embroidery
lay half finished on a table. The remains of a fire still
glowed in the hearth, and when Portia reached for the
wood beside it, Enid came out of her stupor.

"My lady, allow me," she said, stepping in front of
the pregnant woman to throw several logs onto the fire.
She pushed a chair near and motioned for the queen to
sit. "Shall I fetch a blanket for your lap?"

Shaking her head, Portia sat down, then looked up at
Enid with a smile. "You must sit as well, or I will hurt
my neck trying to see you."

Enid sat opposite her, but she could not meet the

knowing eyes of the queen. She rested her forearms on her knees and stared at the floor.

"Enid, I assume that your husband does not know of the magic that you hold."

Enid shook her head. "I cannot tell him," she whispered.

"You feel it is better to hurt your marriage with such secrets?"

Enid raised her desperate gaze. "I owe my tribe my loyalty, my lady. How can I turn my back on my family?"

"Yet you have allowed Sir Geraint to become part of your family," Portia said with gentleness. "Do you not think he will respect the truth?"

"It is not my decision," Enid admitted brokenly. "You see how I am dressed, the sword I carry at my side. He is embarrassed by my upbringing and wants me to be different than I am. Even if I were permitted to tell him everything—"

She couldn't go on, could barely control her weeping in the face of the queen's understanding and pity. And in that moment, she knew she could tell Portia everything, unburden herself to this woman who would understand.

Enid was suddenly shocked by what she contemplated. She had not confided in her own husband, yet she was suddenly willing to place all her trust in a stranger. The queen obviously had power of her own; was she manipulating Enid?

The queen sighed, as if sensing Enid's withdrawal. "I do not know your husband—but I know his father. They are men who value the truth, and yet are objective enough not to judge it."

Enid didn't believe that—she'd already felt Geraint's judgment. And because of it, her future was at a standstill, waiting for him to decide what to do with her.

But she still had her mission, her purpose. It might be all she ever had, and she would not abandon it. She rose to her feet.

"Queen Portia, thank you for this gift of your time. I will not ask you to keep your silence, because you must do as your conscience dictates—as must I."

The queen sighed and eased farther back into her chair, obviously feeling the discomfort of her child. "Put your mind at ease, Enid. For now I will say nothing, because I know little to actually say. I have a gift of understanding even the most hidden of hearts, and in yours I sense no malice, only confusion—and love."

Enid lowered her head. "Aye, I love him, my lady. And if love were all that mattered, the world would be a peaceful place."

She escaped the solar before the queen could see her break down in despair.

• • •

IN the morning, as they broke their fast in the great hall, Geraint studied his pensive wife. Since their arguments had begun, there was always a feeling of awkward tension between them, and it was difficult to pretend nothing was wrong. The queen was watching them a bit too closely, as if looking for something she suspected. And Enid never lifted her gaze, tolerating the scrutiny. He wondered what had happened to eliminate the serenity Enid had displayed the night before. His father looked between them all with a frown, but centered most of his imposing stare on Geraint.

Geraint knew that he and the king would be having a long talk this day.

The only thing that distracted them all was the curious behavior of Lovell the squire. Though he was a guest in Castle Cornwall, he kept taking trays of food from a maidservant named Fryda so that he could serve Enid personally. Geraint sighed as Fryda forcibly pulled back a tray, and half the sauce for the sliced lamb ended up splattered on the girl's gown.

All of this had his father's attention. The king said, "Lady Enid, this boy is with you?"

She nodded, glancing at Geraint for but a moment. "He is Lovell, sire, and he is my . . . servant."

Geraint was not going to be a part of any more lies than were necessary. "Father, in truth, Lovell serves as her squire."

There was an awkward silence at the head table, although his stepmother wore a satisfied smile. Perhaps she did not like secrets either, and they had more in common than just his father.

The king turned on Enid the forbidding gaze that had haunted Geraint's childhood.

"Your squire, Lady Enid?" the king asked.

She nodded, her back straight and proud. "I am training him, sire."

"Surely not in women's arts," he said, turning to smile at his wife, then frowning in confusion when Queen Portia only gave him an arch look.

Lovell backed slowly away, then went to help Fryda clean the mess that had begun their discussion.

Geraint felt his wife's curious stare, and he met it, giving her a shrug. She should explain whatever she wanted to.

"My king," Enid began, "I am a warrior woman of my people." And then she told the story he now knew, of her tribe and its unorthodox training methods.

The king remained silent through it all, his frown of concentration evident.

Enid finished her tale. "When Lovell asked to be my squire, he solved my problems of needing a training partner. So I accepted."

There was silence at the head table, although all around them the king's subjects continued to enjoy their meals and their conversations, enviably ignorant of the tension.

The king turned to look at Geraint. "And what do you think of your wife's abilities?"

"When I first saw her, she was wielding a sword, Father. I admit I was . . . intrigued."

Geraint could not remember blushing like this since his youth. The queen turned her head away, obviously hiding a smile.

"At first, I thought she had been forced to learn to defend herself," Geraint continued.

"And you wanted to be her protector," his father said dryly.

Surely Geraint's skin could not feel any hotter. He said nothing.

The king suddenly rose to his feet. "Come, my son, there is much to discuss about our kingdom."

And your marriage, were the unspoken words. Enid did not look at him, though she offered a smile to her mortified squire.

• • •

THE king's solar was normally a hive of activity. Geraint remembered coming here as a child just to sit in a corner and watch the running of the kingdom. Ministers and counselors and learned men all gave their opinions to their king, and Geraint had always tried to absorb their knowledge, and emulate the way his father gave everyone equal consideration.

But now the few clerks still writing on scrolls when they arrived were dismissed with a wave of the king's hand. He sat in a big comfortable chair, but did not offer one to Geraint, who waited with resignation.

"I received another missive from the high king today," King Erbin began.

Geraint was surprised at the subject, but he welcomed it with relief. "All is going well at Camelot, is it not? Such a missive could not have left much after I did."

"Nay, it did not. But it details the problems King Arthur noticed after your marriage."

Geraint stiffened.

"The king is gracious. He feels you are a man newly in love, that your lack of attention to your duties was just an aberration. You have not lost his favor, and your counsel will still be eagerly awaited."

Geraint let his breath out slowly.

"So you did not consult your father *or* the high king before you made this girl a princess, a future queen of my realm?"

"It is not as if I would ever allow her to rule in my place," Geraint said, narrowing his eyes. "Do you worry that she has an unnatural hold over me?"

"The hold of love is enough for men to do foolish things." The king shook his head. "I do not fault you for being struck by her unusual beauty—and the mystery of her background."

Was he so transparent? Geraint wondered. "She is a good woman, Father. You will see that."

"And you already know this after but a few days? Then why do you seem so uneasy? Surely it is not just the worry of introducing your bride to her new family. You have not even held her hand in my presence."

The king was getting right to the heart of his problems. Where once Geraint would have scoffed at the idea of confiding in his distant father, this new man—this new husband—seemed more open to confidences.

Geraint sat down across from him. A flow of words started that he had not expected. "I thought she needed me, Father."

"Has she said that she has no need of your love?" the king said ominously.

"Nay, 'tis not that. She claims to love me, but where I thought I had her trust, I have discovered it is not so. There are things I do not know about her—"

"And you think you should know everything in just a fortnight?"

There was a hint of amusement in his father's expression that made Geraint feel terribly young again. "Of course not. I thought I was looking forward to a lifetime of learning everything about her. But she is a warrior, Father, and apparently I have disappointed her with my own skills."

"That cannot be so," said the king. "No one doubts your training or your talent."

"She does. I thought I had her loyalty, but she holds the secrets of her family closer than she does me." He could not bear to reveal that he had caught his wife sneaking from their bed.

But what he had revealed seemed enough.

His father studied him thoughtfully. "I always knew that you had a gift for understanding people, my son. Just hearing King Arthur's praise for your skills of negotiation confirms that. You would not have chosen a wife as blindly as you seem to believe you did."

Geraint stared at his father in shock—was he being praised? Had the entire world shifted since he'd last been home?

"Yet I am concerned about your doubts," the king continued. "You must establish the truth your wife hides and make her prove her loyalties. She will be a queen, of great influence on a king. You have to determine if you can trust her."

"And if I cannot?" he said softly, bleakly.

"Let us not rush to judgment. Your impulsive nature has been tamed, but it is not gone, I see. Your wife brings this out in you."

Geraint sighed, too ashamed to be annoyed. "You cannot understand how full of sorrow I am that I have brought this strife upon you."

"Do not be sorry, my son. This gives me the chance to send you on a mission that I would have had to attend to myself. Now I can remain here with my wife in her time of need."

"I shall do whatever I can for you, Father."

"I want you to travel about our kingdom and mix

freely with our people, hearing their complaints and gathering their opinions."

Geraint frowned. "Such a mission seems like one for a king's councillor, rather than a prince."

"Ah, but you have not allowed me to finish," he chided.

The patience and diplomacy that Geraint so prided himself on seemed to fade away when he was back to just being his father's son.

"Lady Enid will believe this is your only mission, but she has not proven herself worthy of hearing the secrets of the kingdom. In truth there is a tribe, the Donella, on our northeast border who has always existed in peace with us. I have begun to hear rumors of their powerful magic, and I need to know if they would turn that against Cornwall. I cannot allow them to be a distraction, what with the rumors of the Saxons far to the east. If a Saxon invasion comes, I need to know that they're our only enemy."

"And what if I determine that this tribe is aligning itself against us?" Geraint asked. "Do I have your permission to begin negotiations?"

"After all these years of peace with the Donella, the fact that they might rise against us now convinces me that they have lost that right with Cornwall. You have my permission to annex their tribe and their land, if it keeps the kingdom safe."

Geraint felt a chill of recognition. This same sort of precarious situation had happened to him before, and with disastrous results. "But . . . is that not a hasty decision, Father? A discussion might clear the air between our peoples."

"I no longer trust that they would keep their word. If a fight is necessary, do it."

"I appreciate your trust in my experience, but I have worked hard to dampen my impulsiveness, as you have long requested. You wanted me to learn to think before I made a decision."

"And that is still what I want," said the king, rising to his feet.

Geraint remained seated, knowing that at this moment, his father might not appreciate being towered over. "I think before I do battle. Many a fight did I avert for our high king." He had never told his father about the battle that had changed him into a diplomat rather than just a warrior. It still caused him too much pain. "Give me the chance to do the same for Cornwall."

The king stared at him, and Geraint waited for his decision. He had risked much by speaking honestly to his father, and now he wanted back the trust he might have jeopardized.

King Erbin stepped back. "I have given you your instructions, Geraint. If they are dangerous, you know what I want done. But I trust you."

Geraint stood up. "And you know how I appreciate that, Father."

"And in the meantime, you have to learn if you can trust your wife."

Chapter 11

· · ·

WHILE her husband conferred privately with the king, Enid retreated to their room and waited, as if for a sentencing. She paced as long as she could stand it, then opened the shutters and looked out the window on the inner ward. To her surprise, she could see Geraint emerge from the great hall below her, and he disappeared inside the barracks against the far curtain wall. When he appeared minutes later, she could not read his expression, but behind him the building seemed to erupt with commotion. Soldiers stormed in and out, and she could see the stables taken over by the activity, with lines of grooms hauling saddles. Squires emerged from the barracks carrying loaded packs.

Enid watched for several long minutes, until finally the door opened behind her. She turned to see Geraint stride into the room.

He came to a halt and they stared at each other.

"Are you leaving?" she asked softly, when she really wanted to know if he were leaving *her*. Her throat tightened as if holding back sobs.

"My father is sending me and his soldiers on a quest," he said.

Blinking back tears, she saw her future stretching out before her, alone here among strangers, with no access to knights to continue her training, no way to complete her mission, yet trapped into remaining because of her love and her marriage.

"You are coming with us," he said impassively.

Her relief was so great she found herself trembling, but then his true reasons became clear. "You do not trust me to remain here without you," she said softly.

He shook his head. "Nay, it is my father's wish that you accompany me as a princess of Cornwall. We will be traveling the kingdom, greeting our subjects. It is a complex thing to keep the loyalty of a people."

And that was all? she found herself wondering with skepticism. Something darker was being deliberately left unspoken.

As if that was anything new within their marriage of late.

But she would not voice her suspicions, not when she was equally at fault. "I thought your father would be greatly displeased by your choice in wife," she said.

Geraint sighed. "He does not know you enough to be displeased. But he does want you to fulfill your duties as a future queen."

"Is this a . . . test?"

One corner of his mouth curved up, but he did not

look amused. "Call it what you will. But since you were not raised at court, he wants proof that you can play the part of my wife properly."

She winced as his words stung. "So it is a part I must play, not me that you want? Must I prove myself to you, too?"

He didn't answer, only turned his back to begin packing.

Enid went to her own garments, but she folded them away slowly as her mind hummed with thought. For just a moment, she considered going home, completing her mission for her father. Maybe she had enough skill to train her warriors. Then she could return to Cornwall, and she and Geraint could begin again with no secrets between them.

But—why was the king sending his son and a troop of soldiers to wander the kingdom? Surely this small country wasn't riddled with thievery. If discussions with innocent villagers were the only purpose, such a show of force should be unnecessary. Or perhaps King Erbin was the kind of man who was always prepared for any opportunity to increase his holdings. Could he be the king about whom her father had heard rumors?

Enid's mission yet remained—to protect her people. She would be vigilant and discover the true purpose of this journey. But was such a strategy on her part compatible with proving her loyalty to her husband?

• • •

ENID rode sidesaddle beside her husband at the head of a troop of twenty-five mounted men-at-arms. Far more than was necessary, in her opinion. How ignorant did the king think she was?

But she had to let go of this anger, at least toward her husband, or she'd be no good to herself, to her marriage. Geraint was following his father's orders, just as she was following *her* father's.

Lovell rode behind her, but at her side rode the maidservant Fryda, newly assigned to her by the queen. Enid did not think she needed a servant's help, except in lacing up her gowns. Normally she would have asked Geraint for such assistance, but now that might inspire thoughts that she did not wish for.

So she accepted Fryda's company, though she silently questioned the queen's wisdom when she saw how Lovell and Fryda glared at each other. But at least the girl was silent, leaving Enid to her bleak thoughts.

The entire troop was strangely quiet, and she found herself looking back at them in curiosity throughout the day. Were there worries in the kingdom of Cornwall that made them rightfully vigilant? She occasionally studied her husband, but he only looked out over the moorland, his face impassive.

As the sun set and the sky turned to light gray before twilight, the troop headed down from Bodmin Moor toward the valley below. Trees and greenery seemed to swallow them, and suddenly she saw an arrow shoot past her and imbed itself in a tree.

The moment's surprised silence suddenly became a cacophony of sound as the soldiers called orders, dispersed, and formed a tight circle around her. Enid felt for the sword at her hip, and knew the worst feeling of helplessness when it wasn't there. She had smuggled her own garments and weapons onto one of the carts, but that wouldn't help her now.

Tears streamed down Fryda's face as she fought to control her pony and remain by Enid. Lovell reached out and took the reins, earning the girl's weak glare, but Enid's gratitude.

Geraint pulled his mount to a halt at her side, even as the first clash of swords could be heard. "Remain here, Enid. Please."

She opened her mouth to protest, but he was already gone, maneuvering his horse between two of the soldiers' mounts.

This was little to ask of her—her obedience in a skirmish. Surely there were enough soldiers to counter the attack of one foolish band of brigands. And hadn't she wanted to feel feminine, to have Geraint treat her like a woman?

But from her position at the center of the melee, she could not see to the outside to determine the enemy's numbers. Horses wheeled, swords clashed, and men shouted. There was no break in the soldiers circling her, so she didn't think anyone was terribly wounded, but why were the brigands not fleeing at their obvious failure?

Suddenly a man on foot flung himself between two horses into the small clearing occupied by Enid, Lovell, and Fryda. The girl screamed as Lovell tried to turn his horse about in the circle that was rapidly closing in on them.

In one smooth motion, Enid pulled the dagger from her boot and flung it at their attacker, burying it in his throat beneath his bushy beard. Wide-eyed, he clasped

his hands about the hilt and pulled. Blood gushed down
his filthy tunic, and he collapsed unmoving onto his face.

As if his death was interpreted as a signal, the rest of
the brigands fell back, melting into the trees that had
hidden them.

From his place with his men, Geraint turned to look
at her, and the harsh lines of his face softened in relief.
She just nodded at him, knowing that he didn't see the
dead man in front of her horse. If he didn't mention it,
neither would she. All around them soldiers dismounted,
removing the bodies for burial. She was startled when
Lovell touched her knee, and then handed over her dagger, now spotlessly clean.

"My lady, you are not hurt?"

She shook her head, sliding the dagger into her boot.
Looking back at Geraint, she found that he was no
longer watching her. He was in command, sending pa-
trols into the woods in case the brigands lingered, gathering together the few wounded soldiers, and shouting
orders to make camp back above on the moor, where
they would take advantage of the visibility of the open
grassland.

An hour later, as the darkness became complete,
Geraint looked about at their small campsite, where
fires glowed between several groups of soldiers. He had
finished conferring with Ainsley, the captain of the
guard, and sent Tyler and Toland out to keep the good
spirits going among the rest of the soldiers. The men
had easily won their battle, but they could not be fully at
ease, knowing that poorly armed brigands had felt they
could attack a company of mounted soldiers so close to
Cornwall Castle.

Geraint found his wife sharing her fire with Lovell, Fryda, and Wilton. Wilton, the most talkative of any soldier Geraint had ever commanded, was making them laugh with another of his tales. Enid's lively smile faded when she saw Geraint, and he withheld a sigh. She sat upon a blanket, legs folded demurely beneath her, but she moved aside to make room for him.

Wilton passed around the fox meat when it was finished sizzling over the fire. Geraint ate silently and thought of Enid's behavior this day. She could easily have demanded to fight at his side, but he'd been relieved she'd acquiesced so easily to his request. He had been able to worry about her less and concentrate on the battle. She was a trained warrior, but these soldiers had to respect her as a princess. Otherwise, rumors that she could not conduct herself as a future queen would get back to King Erbin. Geraint felt like a little boy worried about being tattled on. His father had put him in a depressing predicament.

He watched Enid eat, saw the amusement in her eyes as she listened to Wilton. He wanted to experience the softness of her regard just for himself. Somehow he had to get over the wound to his pride she'd inflicted. But he wasn't sure he knew how to get past the anger. He was angry with himself for rushing into this marriage, angry with his wife for her secrets and her stubbornness, and lastly, angry that instead of serving King Arthur, he was touring fishing villages.

The wind across the open moor whistled as it wended its way through the clusters of soldiers. He saw Enid shiver and search about her. Her cloak rested in a heap just out of reach. Geraint settled it about her shoulders then moved behind her. She tensed as she looked back at him, but he stayed where he was, blocking the worst of the wind from her.

And when he saw her head droop, he slid his arm around her waist and pulled her back against him. He couldn't allow his wife to fall headfirst into the fire. She remained stiff, but she allowed the gesture. She was still angry that he hadn't allowed her to fight. There was always so much anger in their marriage now.

But the smell of her hair against his cheek made him ache for the peacefulness of their earlier relationship. He didn't know how to get it back, how to move ahead. When Fryda softly said that Enid's small pavilion was ready, Enid sprang up as if she'd been waiting for a reason to leave him. The two women retreated behind the canvas walls, leaving Geraint surprised to feel alone.

"Such a shame, milord," Wilton said.

Geraint frowned at the soldier. "What do you mean? We were victorious."

"Oh, o' course—as if I had any doubts about that! But nay, I be wonderin' whose idea it was to bring the maid along."

Geraint glowered at the fire. "My stepmother's."

Wilton laughed. "Too bad ye didn't bring *two* servants to keep each other company, while you remained with yer wife."

• • •

THE next afternoon, after a wet, foggy, uneventful morning's march, they reached the first village on Geraint's list. Several dozen thatched-roof homes were nestled in the cliffs beside the sea. The fishing boats were

out on open water, leaving the harbor strangely bereft.
Enid agreed to accompany Geraint and his four men-at-
arms into the village as an advance party, rather than
frighten the women and children with a whole troop of
soldiers. Or did they leave the soldiers on the outskirts of
the village to guard against attack, she wondered?

The few men still ashore met them at the village
green. Enid played the good little woman and allowed
Geraint to help her from the horse. For a moment, she
thought amusement had twinkled in his eyes, replacing
the anger she always sensed in him now, but it was
quickly gone.

After introducing himself, Geraint led her forward
by the hand. "And allow me to present my wife, the
princess Enid."

Every village man had to look up at her, and she
watched their mouths sag open in surprise. But the
dozen women behind them, most carrying babies or
with children tugging at their skirts, pushed their men
aside and gazed at her with eager curiosity.

"Come to the tavern, milady," said one robust woman,
who carried not one but two babes, "I be the best brewer
in Cornwall."

Geraint smiled, unleashing his full charm on the
woman, and Enid felt its effect as if the rain had come
after a long drought.

"We would be honored, mistress," he said. "Lead on."

The crowd surged around them, and though Enid felt
a little dazed at being the center of so much attention,
she tried to put her tumultuous feelings aside and join
in the spirit of the day.

The tavern had low ceiling beams, from which hung

dried meat and herbs and the occasional string of veg-
etables. The women smiled their amusement as Enid
and Geraint had to duck or be blindsided. While the
men pulled Geraint aside and gathered around him, the
women drew Enid into their midst and gave her a seat
of honor—the only chair in a room full of benches and
stools.

Enid forced a smile as she accepted their stares. The
children fingered the material of her gown in awe, and
finally one woman rallied her courage.

"Princess—milady—might I touch yer hair? 'Tis
like having a fine gift, that color."

Feeling foolish, Enid granted the request, and after
rubbing a yellow lock between her fingers, the brave
woman retreated and whispered something to the others.

The brewer gave Enid a gap-toothed grin. " 'Tis time
to be tryin' me beer, milady."

For several hours, Enid heard stories of village life,
of the lean or plentiful fishing years, of babies and the
newest weaving pattern. She listened politely, determined to make a good impression as the proper wife,
but she only knew the basics of needlework and could
not relate to the endless talk of children.

Occasionally she stole a glance at the men on the
other side of the room and found herself envying
Geraint. They would be discussing the safety of the village, something she could understand.

More men crowded into the tavern as the fishermen
came home for the night. Everyone gathered together to
share the evening's supper, and then Geraint and Enid
were offered the room above the tavern, the only "inn"
in the village.

When the door was shut behind them, the sudden silence was rather overwhelming. Even though Enid had shared a room with her husband for many nights, she still felt awkward and even a little guilty. He was a man, and she was his wife—those village women below would say she owed him her submission, regardless of whether he deserved it or not.

Her body longed for intimacy with Geraint as much as her mind did, and she shivered, wondering how much longer it would be before she could no longer control her need for his kiss. She was shameless in her wanting of him.

But she said nothing, simply strolled to where her bag had been laid across the bed. As she searched for her night rail, Geraint moved about behind her. He crossed to the fireplace, and she surreptitiously watched him lay extra logs on the fire to last the night. She appreciated even the width of his back, and the way his muscles flowed with his movement.

Someone knocked on the door, and Enid was startled from her reverie. Geraint opened it to reveal Fryda. The shy maidservant could not meet Geraint's eyes, as Enid followed her behind the changing screen.

"Do ye need me help bathing, milady?" she whispered, her shoulders hunched.

Enid wondered why the queen had sent the girl on a mission with so many men, if she was this shy. "Nay, Fryda, I shall be fine. Do you have a place to sleep?"

"A pallet in the kitchen with the other maids, milady." She smiled. "'Tis warm there, and the maids have been kind to me."

"Then go seek your rest."

They stepped out from behind the screen, and to their surprise, Ainsley was in the room, unbuckling Geraint's brigandine with his gnarled hands. Fryda gasped and threw herself before Enid, as if Ainsley had never seen a woman in a night rail before.

Ainsley was already turning away. "Milady, forgive me, we thought ye heard me come in."

Geraint started to apologize, but Enid waved it away.

"Please finish," she said. "I'll remain behind the screen."

When the door closed behind the two servants, Enid peered out, but this time she and Geraint were alone. He still wore a shirt and hose. His arms were braced against the mantel as he stared into the fire, but when he looked up and saw her, he straightened. And his gaze moved slowly down her body, setting her aflame.

Chapter 12

• • •

GERAINT looked upon the beautiful form of his wife, and was once again overwhelmed with an aching need for her. The night rail she wore hid much, but draped thinly over her curves. Her golden hair hung to her waist in undulating waves. She had a soft beauty about her that called to him, made him want to forget all of the anger between them.

And she waited, silent, as if she would welcome him.

Or would she be welcoming the distraction? Did she mean to keep the focus on the physical rather than their problems of trust?

He stiffened, determined not to give in. She lowered her head, and he thought he detected a soft sigh as she turned away to climb into the narrow bed. He eyed the low-slung piece of furniture dubiously. Two such large people were not going to easily fit in there.

He sat down before the fire and leaned his head back. He heard her moving about, as if trying to get comfortable. Then they both sighed together, and he shook his head in bemusement.

Glancing at the bed, he found Enid lying on her side, watching him. "You did not seem comfortable with the women today," he said.

She frowned, but he quickly raised a hand.

"I am not starting an argument. I know you were doing your best. Only I noticed your unease."

"Maybe because you know me well?" she asked dryly.

He groaned and turned away.

"Forgive me," she said. "I mean to start no arguments either. But aye, I am not used to being among large groups of women. Surely you noticed that at Camelot."

"But why? You have sisters, a mother." He could not sleep, so this seemed the perfect opportunity to learn some things he should have asked at the beginning of their brief courtship. "In my foolishness I did not ask before, but tell me about them."

She sat up, fluffed a cushion against the headboard, and leaned back. "I am the eldest. My sister Olwen is a year younger than I, and my sister Cinnia is three years younger. My brother, Dermot, has fourteen years, and will eventually become chieftain after my father."

"You must have been around women as a youngster; you yourself told me that women are not so very different in your tribe."

"They are not, but I am. My destiny was foretold before my birth, that I would be a warrior woman."

"You had no choice?"

"It was not a matter of choosing. I knew from an early age that the intricacies of defense were something I understood. Where my sisters wanted cloth dolls to play with, I begged for my own dagger. When we discussed boys, they talked about handsome features, where I wanted to hear about his fighting skills."

"So you accepted this destiny," he said, trying to imagine a little girl fitting into a warrior's world. It seemed very lonely.

"I never questioned it. I wanted to make my parents proud of me and play my part. Make no mistake, my sisters each had their own calling. Olwen is a gifted healer like our mother, and Cinnia possesses such a rare beauty that she will be able to make a fine match for the tribe's benefit. But from an early age, I spent time with other women warriors, where I commenced my training."

"You were fostered away from your family?" he asked, knowing that most children experienced that, including himself.

"Nay, but I was only with my family in the evening." She hesitated, looking away from him with a distant gaze. "I always tried to sew with them and listen to them talk. But they didn't understand what was important to me, and their growing impatience with my discussions of weapons and battle gradually pushed me toward my father. He was proud of me and encouraged my eagerness."

"Your mother was not proud of you?" he asked. "My own mother did not live to know me."

Her gaze met his earnestly. "My mother told me of her pride and love every day of my life. But I did not have much time to learn the ways of women, and I think she missed experiencing that with me. Luckily I was not her only daughter."

"More than once," he said softly, "someone would say that it was lucky I was not born a girl, who would know a deeper grief over a mother's death."

"You did not believe that!"

She sounded so defensive on his behalf that he almost smiled.

"Nay," he said. "I saw my father's grief, and it did not unman him."

She nodded as if in relief, and still he could not stop studying her, wondering about all the things he didn't know. Would they ever discover the deeper parts of each other?

"When that woman asked you to hold her child," he said, "I thought you looked . . ."

"Frightened? You would be correct. My sister Olwen is married, and just last year gave birth to a babe, a little girl. My niece looked so fragile that I didn't want to hold her, but Cinnia goaded me into it, then screamed to Olwen that I nearly dropped the babe. And the way little Bretta's head bobbled on my arm, maybe I almost did."

"Cinnia does not sound like she'll be my favorite sister," he said with disapproval.

Enid's eyes sparkled in the firelight. "Ah, that would be a clash worth viewing!"

For a moment he wanted to share her grin, to bask in the ease they had experienced from their first meeting. But their smiles both died as their troubled lives intruded on the fantasy.

Geraint turned back to the fire, and the awkward silence rose between them again.

Softly, she said, "You are not going to sleep in a chair, are you? You need your rest."

"Aye, discussing fishing with villagers is taxing."

He winced at the bitterness he revealed.

"You did not want this mission from your father? Did you only agree because of me?"

He didn't bother to answer. He just stripped down to his braies, slid into bed at her side, but kept his tense back to her. The blankets were warm from her body, and he was so very aware of her inches away from him. Surely he would get more sleep in the chair.

* * *

THE following day, they journeyed through a pouring rain that depressed the spirits of even Wilton. Enid rode hunched over her horse, her hood incapable of keeping the rain off her face. The sea breeze snatched at their clothing, and the smell of brine and dead fish rose up the cliffs. Two horses at a time, they followed a path overlooking the ocean. The care that had to be taken to ensure everyone's safety left them all on edge. A fight broke out between two soldiers at the midday meal, and by late afternoon, when they were looking for the best place to make camp, Geraint was obviously in a foul mood. He shouted rather than spoke, and his dark frown kept everyone out of his way.

Yet Enid hesitated to disturb him. They had dealt peacefully with each other all day, as if talk of their childhoods the night before had built a fragile bridge between them.

But somehow she had to be sure they were near a forest pond that night. Tiny streams would carry away her droplets of blood. Though she had never tried to use seawater to rejuvenate her powers, she sensed it would not be the same. She felt no calling deep in her bones for the sea, as she did near fresh water.

When Geraint talked with Ainsley about making their encampment on the cliffs, where a stream rushed over toward the sea, Enid interrupted.

"My husband, if we move into the woods, would we not have a break from the wind?"

He frowned; she had not once made a suggestion on this journey for fear he would assume she questioned his leadership. But her previous silence must have held her in good stead, because he nodded and had Ainsley send several men to look for a clearing in the woods.

Before she lost the light completely, Enid bade Lovell prepare for training. She would have to use the session to hide her true purpose.

He gaped at her, then looked around in guilt. "My lady, are you certain Sir Geraint would approve?"

She rolled her eyes, feeling itchy in her skin as she did on every third night. "He allowed me to take you as my squire, and he did not forbid our training on our earlier journey. We will just slip away alone where the other soldiers cannot see us."

When he opened his mouth, she interrupted him. "I will inform my husband. I would not do him the discourtesy of making him worry about me."

Lovell nodded. "Very well, my lady. What armor shall I bring for you?"

"Just my sword."

Lovell blanched.

"There will be no daylight left if I take the time to change."

"But my lady, what if I . . . hurt you?"

She smiled. "You will not. While you are building faith in yourself, you can have faith in me."

He returned her smile, but he still looked nervous.

Enid walked through camp, searching for her husband. She found him overseeing a group of soldiers who were doing some sword fighting of their own. She wished she could stay to listen to his instructions. By the gods, she wished he would take up a sword himself. The muscular line of his arm always made her feel—

She stopped her wayward thoughts in disgust. "My husband?" she called from where she stopped several feet away.

He walked toward her, his gaze still on his men. "Aye?"

"I am going for a walk with Lovell."

He frowned and looked across the clearing, where Lovell could be seen carrying something heavy. Fryda was glaring at him.

Before Geraint could speak, she said, "Aye, I will train with him. It is a duty you allowed me to accept. We will remain hidden from your men."

She could see his indecision. If he forbade her, what would she do?

But in the end he only nodded gruffly. "Do not venture far. Do you want the aid of another soldier?" Then he glanced at her. "I imagine not."

She grinned. "Lovell and I can handle anything we find in the woods. And I promise to remain within calling distance."

When Geraint nodded, she hastily left before he could change his mind. She gathered several torches, lit one at the fire, and caught up with Lovell.

Fryda approached them, looking confused. "Milady, they are preparin' our pavilion. Will ye not need my help to retire?"

"Thank you, Fryda," she said. "Wait for me there."

Lovell frowned as he glanced at the torches and fell into step beside Enid. "Are we going to be gone so long, my lady?"

She smiled grimly. "You never know what might happen."

By insisting that she was looking for just the right spot, she managed to get a good look at the surrounding forest. She found a small pond behind a thick copse of trees. It would hide her well.

While Lovell removed their swords and shields from his sack, she pulled the back hemline of her gown up through her legs and tucked it into the girdle at her waist. The squire looked up, blushing at the sight of her bare legs.

She shook her head. "Now, Lovell, when I wear my jerkin, surely this much is exposed."

"But . . . this is a *gown,* my lady."

Giving an exaggerated sigh, she withdrew her sword from its scabbard, glad for the weight of it in her hand. It gleamed in the setting sun when she swung it, and she complimented Lovell on the care he took polishing it.

And then she attacked. He was forced to back up until he ran into a tree, knocking the wind out of him. As he gasped for breath, she grinned, putting the point of her sword into the ground and leaning on the hilt.

"Do not let an opponent catch you by surprise," she said. "Never assume he will follow the same rules you've been taught."

He nodded as he hung his head and began to climb to his feet. She attacked again, although this time he fared better.

"Never assume your opponent will wait like a gentle knight."

He swung at her while she still spoke, and she laughed as she parried his sword away.

Geraint walked softly through the forest, not wanting to alert Enid to his presence. Though he knew her skill with a sword, he was uncomfortable leaving her alone away from the encampment.

He heard their laughter before he saw them, and at the last moment he ducked behind a tree instead of alerting them to his presence. Lovell held his sword with determination, although his cheek shown with a glimmer of blood in the growing dark. Enid faced the boy, her gown hiked to reveal her slim, muscular legs. Geraint paid no attention to her instruction, just watched her move.

The same fascination for the mystery of her warrior training still held sway over him. When a man attacked, Geraint judged his form, his skill; when Enid lunged at Lovell, driving him back, Geraint noticed none of this, because it was such a part of her. He saw the movement of her muscles, the grace of her straight back, the proud tilt of her head.

And her face alight with laughter, something he seldom saw anymore. They had made each other so unhappy. He felt . . . helpless, caught between his pride and his obsession with Enid.

She worked Lovell as hard as any knight would, and for the first time, it occurred to Geraint to wonder why she stayed in this marriage when she could survive easily on her own, and perhaps find someone who could make her happier than he did. She was not a woman trapped by her femininity, as so many others were.

Darkness finally settled all around them, and only two torches kept it at bay.

Enid lowered her sword and stepped back. "Enough for tonight, Lovell. You have done well."

Geraint couldn't see the boy's face, but he held himself as if full of pride.

Suddenly Enid turned her head. "Did you see them, Lovell?" she asked, pointing into the darkness.

Geraint stiffened, his every sense alert.

Lovell lifted his sword. "My lady?"

"Rabbits!" she said. "At least a half dozen. Go chase them toward our encampment. The soldiers always set up snares. I have such a taste for rabbit."

He grabbed up a torch at her bidding, took a few steps, then looked back. "I cannot leave you, my lady!"

"I need a bit of privacy, Lovell. Surely you understand."

Geraint watched the boy nod and hurry off. Thank God he himself was there to wait for Enid. Even a knight should not linger in a dark, unfamiliar forest.

Enid took the other torch and stepped behind some trees. Geraint waited, but she didn't reappear in a normal amount of time. Was she ill?

Suddenly, he felt an unusual tension in the night air. The hair on his arms rose; he thought he heard a static sound. And then a bolt of lightning shot from the sky behind the trees where his wife had disappeared.

Just like what had happened on the eve of their wedding.

Full of fear, Geraint vaulted over a bush, ran between the trees, and slid to a stop where the woods ended in a clearing. A waning moon peered out from behind dark clouds. Enid, nude and thigh-deep in a small pond, was already striding from the water.

"Did you see the lightning?" she cried when she saw him.

For a moment, she seemed to glow under the moonlight, and he forgot his fear for her, the lightning, everything but how he'd missed her touch.

"Enid." His voice was hoarse with need as he came toward her.

He splashed a step into the water, and their bodies met and merged with a fierce kiss. He lost himself in the taste of her, even as his hands explored her body as if it had never been his. Her skin was moist and hot, and her nipples pressed hard into his hands. As she moaned, he answered her in kind.

"My lady?"

As they heard Lovell's voice, they broke their kiss, but Geraint continued to shield her with his body. He looked down into her wide eyes, saw the wetness of her parted lips. Maybe if they were quiet, he'd just go away.

"My lady, where are you?"

Geraint was about to send the boy back, when Enid pushed at his chest. He released her.

"Lovell, I am with my husband," she called, and her voice shook. "We shall be with you in a moment."

Geraint frowned, his body aching with a need he'd denied for too many nights. "Enid—"

She gave him a sad stare, though she did not cover herself. "I will not have you like this, on a moment's whim when you have forgotten your mistrust of me and only care about your body's demands."

He felt himself redden with anger, but especially embarrassment. "You do not care that I still desire you?"

She arched a slim brow. "Still? As if you should not?"

"You know that is not what I meant."

She waded around him and stepped onto dry ground. She pulled on her smock and gown and then faced him. "Geraint, I would never deny you. I am your wife. But I think it is too easy to hide our problems if all we care about is our desire."

"You know 'tis not all I care about—and do you think I would force myself on you if you are unwilling?"

She lowered her eyes on a sigh. "You know I am not unwilling, Geraint. I cannot forget my feelings for you. But it is too easy for you to forget yours for me."

Before he could protest, she turned and walked back between the trees, toward her squire. And Geraint thought seriously about dunking himself in the cold water to chill his passion—and his anger.

• • •

THE next afternoon, Enid's already low spirits sank even farther as the welcome she received at the next village was less than gracious. Rather than greeting her warmly, the women sent her sidelong glances that marked her as foreign and not to be trusted. She was offered no babies to hold, for which she should have been grateful. While the men talked, the women simply waited, staring at her. Finally, she said she would walk about the village, and escaped the scrutiny.

She knew Geraint would not appreciate her leaving without at least Lovell as a guard, but she had Fryda with her, and the dagger in her boot for defense.

The village green was more brown than green. Sheep and chickens roamed at will, and their thinness bore testimony to the scarcity of food. The village was several leagues inland, and perhaps the villagers didn't have easy access to fishing boats.

While she thought, she walked, little realizing she'd left the small village behind until Fryda tugged on her sleeve.

"Milady?" the girl whispered, staring at the rugged rocks lining the lane. "Could we turn back?"

Enid walked several more paces, feeling reluctant to return to such an unhappy place. But if Fryda was frightened—

She heard a rider galloping down the lane, and turned to see Geraint bearing down on her, wearing an angry expression. He was impressive in his traveling armor, and he wore his shield on his arm instead of hung from the saddle behind him, as if he expected to do battle over her. Lovell rode behind him. Her squire looked red-faced, and she hoped he was not the recipient of Geraint's anger for losing her.

To her surprise, Geraint rode straight at her, then leaned over, caught her by the waist and hauled her up to sit across his lap. When she had to grab his arms to steady herself, she stared up at him.

He looked back over his shoulder. "Lovell, bring Fryda with you."

Enid leaned back to see behind Geraint, trusting him to hold on to her—and he did, with his solid arm behind her back. Lovell was atop his horse, reaching down to Fryda. They were obviously arguing, although Enid couldn't hear them. Finally Fryda took Lovell's hand, and he lifted until she could reach the stirrup and swing her leg up behind him to sit astride. Lovell said something, then firmly placed the girl's arm around him, as if she would have let herself fall off before touching him more than she had to.

Enid tried to hide her smile, and found Geraint watching her impassively.

"Did they find common ground?" he asked.

"Barely."

"They are jealous of each other over you."

He made it sound like he couldn't understand it, and she found her response to his nearness cooling. She would not think about his hard thighs beneath hers, or his broad chest pressed to her shoulder.

"They should not be jealous," she said. "I make time for them both."

"Like they are your children?"

When she didn't answer, he tipped her chin up until she met his gaze. "Surely you understand that as a princess, you cannot wander off alone anymore—and do not say you were with Fryda," he added sternly. "Even Lovell is not enough protection for a princess."

"I've been careful. I've only seen farmers in this village, and they cannot harm me."

"Nay, but your beauty could give a farmer ideas that could get him killed, were he foolhardy."

"My supposed 'beauty' would never make men do such things."

He shook his head. "Do you not think I feel bewitched by your face at times?"

That saddened her, because he did not mean it as a compliment. And she could not refute his statement, because she'd been given the ability to be more appealing to men to help her complete her mission.

To her surprise, he lifted her hand in his. In the first days of their marriage, they'd held hands almost constantly. Now she wished she could still relax into the comfort of his touch.

But he had other intentions, as he lifted her hand palm up and frowned at the web of small scars, some newer than others. What must he think? How could she explain?

"Your skills with the dagger are not what I would have thought," he said.

She bit her lip, but didn't try to pull away.

"Your work with Lovell is not helping you, can you not see that?"

"It is helping him," she said.

"Every time you go off on your own, trouble follows you. Mayhap I arrived in time to prevent some today."

"Last night *you* were the trouble." Her simmering anger began to rise.

He dropped her hand. "Regardless, you must remain with my soldiers at all times."

"I am allowed no woman's privacy?" she demanded, angry more at herself. If she'd just stayed in the village, he would not be issuing ultimatums.

"Not if I deem it unsafe."

She clenched her teeth and remained silent, knowing childishly that what she did not promise, she would not keep.

Another stone went up in the wall between them, and her throat tightened with sadness. She wanted to be a true wife to him, but her beauty was false and her instincts to protect herself were overpowering. Was she deluding herself that she could somehow fit into his world?

Chapter 13

• • •

THIS time, the mercenaries attacked before dawn, and Geraint was prepared for it. His men reacted like the trained soldiers they were. He'd assigned his four men-at-arms to guard Enid's pavilion with Lovell, and the rest defended the encampment.

The shouting and the clash of arms were deafening, and in the distance, he could see the hobbled horses panicking. But the assigned soldiers soothed them. Geraint joined in the melee, determined to discover who was provoking these attacks, because again, it seemed foolish for these mercenaries to battle a troop of trained soldiers.

This time their attackers were the ones mounted, and Geraint found himself jumping sideways to avoid being run down by a frothing horse. He swung his shield at the horse and caught it in the flank startling it so much

that it threw its rider. Geraint killed the brigand with a
blow to the head and moved on to his next opponent.
Within minutes, the attackers were unseated and fighting on the ground, where they were swiftly outnumbered
and outmatched. Some ran, some died, but Geraint
knocked one unconscious and kept him alive.

This time, one of his own men had died. The rest of
the soldiers, looking for vengeance, gathered angrily
around the captive as Geraint tossed water on him. The
man sputtered as he awoke, then gaped at the murderous
faces all around him.

The man pulled a knife from within his tunic.
Geraint lifted his sword and realized too late his intention. The captive stabbed himself in the throat and
slumped back to die. The information Geraint had
hoped to gather died with him.

Angrily, he ordered the dead buried, while the rest of
the soldiers were to prepare to march. Looking toward
Enid's pavilion, he saw her standing just outside it, Fryda
hugging herself at her mistress's side. He glimpsed a
dagger in Enid's hand, but when he came closer, she
was standing serenely waiting for him, her hands empty.
At least he knew she could defend herself on this dangerous journey, he admitted reluctantly.

She studied him. "The brigand died before he could
tell you anything?"

Geraint nodded.

"Their coordination betrays them," she said.

He glanced at her, not surprised that she understood
what was happening.

"Do you have any idea who would deliberately orga-
nize attacks on the prince of Cornwall?" she asked.

"So far the attacks have been from Britons, not Saxons."

"Hired mercenaries?"

"I suspect so, aye."

"Is there anyone with a motive for hiring soldiers?"

"Anyone who wishes to topple the kingdom of Cornwall."

A corner of her mouth turned up. "And such men could be legion?"

He just shrugged and glanced once more at Enid's trembling maidservant. "Did your guard protect you?" he asked in a softer voice.

Enid nodded. "Your men are brave and well trained. Fryda has never been away from the çastle, let alone on a long journey. She is handling herself admirably."

Geraint saw the grateful look on the girl's tear-stained face—and Lovell's dramatic eye rolling.

• • •

WITHIN an hour's march, Enid began to suspect that there was more than just a band of mercenaries after them.

They were traveling down a steep road leading toward the sea, which was yet a few leagues' distant. A stiff, salty wind was blowing directly at them, growing colder by the minute. She wrapped her cloak more tightly about her, even as she fought to keep her seat riding sidesaddle on such a steep slope. How could women be thought of as fragile if they could master this?

The first flakes of snow caught her by surprise. Her home was not so distant from here, and she had seen snow but once or twice in her lifetime, and that was during a rare storm in the dead of winter after the New Year.

At her side, Geraint raised a hand to call a halt as he studied the ever-darkening sky. His horse danced beneath him on the dangerous path. "This does not seem right."

She was about to agree with him when she felt the first seeking tendril of magic rise up off the ground around them. Catching her breath, she froze. She wanted to use the gift of sensing magic given to her by the Lady of the Lake to determine if good or evil was at work here, but she could not tell. She was frustrated by her lack of skill with the magical arts, for she'd only been taught just what she needed to complete her mission. She continued to concentrate, but the chimera of magic was elusive.

"Enid, what are you about?" Geraint demanded.

Opening her eyes, she found him frowning at her uneasily. Then she gasped as the sight of the clouds above them going black and unleashing a heavy fall of snow. The wind drove it into their faces, and Geraint turned away from her to issue orders.

"We cannot halt here!" he told Ainsley, his captain, shouting above the rising moan of the wind. "We are too exposed on the side of the cliff. We aren't far from the village. Tell the men we press on."

Enid wondered if he could sense the magic that seemed so obvious to her. She promised to tell him the moment they were safe from the storm. Pulling the hood of her cloak low over her face, she felt her bare hands gradually going numb as she held the reins and fought her horse down the path.

Behind her Fryda shrieked, and Enid whirled in her saddle to see the girl's horse sliding uncontrolled

toward Enid herself. Geraint was suddenly there, pluck-
ing the girl from the back of the horse and almost tossing her to sit behind his saddle. As she clutched him,
burying her sobbing face in his back, he caught the reins
of the frightened horse and guided it toward temporarily
level ground.

The snow struck Enid's face in stinging pricks of
cold, but she gave Geraint a grateful smile.

"Can you yet ride?" he shouted at her, his hair covered in flakes.

She nodded and guided her horse ever downward. It
took all her concentration. Wet snow clung to her face
and froze her skin. She had to squint to see through the
fury of the snow as it swirled about her. She wouldn't
even have noticed that the terrain had flattened out, if
Geraint had not ridden back to her side. Fryda was no
longer with him, but she saw the girl clinging to Lovell's
back.

"Follow Ainsley while I see to the rest of the troop!"
he called. "The village is just around the bend."

The magic seemed to crawl up her horse, wrapping
about her legs, winding like a vine even up to her throat.
She gasped, sensing no menace, but she could no longer
afford to wait.

"Geraint!" she cried, grateful when he rode back toward her. "Do you sense it?"

He frowned, snow clinging to his lashes and eyebrows. "It is a snowstorm. What is there to sense except
nature's fury?"

"But 'tis not a natural storm, not for Cornwall. Can
you not sense the magic?"

She did not think his frown could have grown darker,

but it was suddenly menacing, even though not directed at her.

"Magic?" he demanded. "Explain yourself!"

She shivered and huddled in her cloak, blinking at the snow as the wind drove it into her eyes. "I can sense magic. It drives the very storm itself."

"It is an attack?" he demanded, unsheathing his sword. But he stared at her as if he'd never seen her before.

She was frightened of the implications of that look, for she would have to answer to it later. Right now she wanted to tell him that a sword was no weapon against magic, but he was King Arthur's knight, and it was how he fought all his battles.

"I sense no malice," she said hesitantly. "I think the storm is but . . . a distraction. Nay, that is not right."

She closed her eyes, at last giving herself over to the magic itself. As it seemed to sense her surrender, it intensified, but still it was not an evil thing. Its very intensity allowed her to comprehend even more, and she saw a presence behind the storm itself.

And in that moment, the howling wind ceased, and the snowfall lessened, finally fading into stillness. Enid opened her eyes to find Geraint staring at her in astonishment. Lovell was seated on his horse at Geraint's side, and the boy almost looked frightened—of her?

"I swear I did not cause the storm to subside," she said, flinging off her hood so that Geraint could see the truth in her face. "I have no such magic. But I gave myself over to experience it, to sense what was behind it, and it just . . . stopped."

"And what did you sense?" he asked skeptically.

She preferred that emotion to fear, although he studied her as if she were something new he needed to comprehend.

"Someone, something guiding the storm, delaying us for a time, but not with any evil intent." She shrugged. "That is all I know."

"Then we go forward and confront this . . . thing," he said, whirling his horse about.

Her trepidation didn't ease as she watched him move among his troops, easing their fears. He would not be telling them about the magic, of that much she was certain. Soldiers solemnly donned their helmets and drew their swords. Would Geraint lead an attack against what he didn't understand?

Lovell watched her without speaking, and Enid didn't know what to say to him. Since their first meeting when she'd laid hands on him, he had known that she was not a normal woman—could he yet be surprised when unusual things happened to her?

Fryda, back on her own horse, rode up beside Enid. "Milady, why is Lovell givin' ye such a rude look? Shall I box his ears for ye?"

Enid blinked and looked away from her squire to smile at the maidservant. " 'Tis not rudeness, Fryda. He is curious about the snowstorm, as we all are."

"My lady," Lovell said formally, "might I have a private word with you?"

Fryda scowled, but guided her horse away, glaring back over her shoulder.

Enid waited calmly for him to speak, but inside she panicked and prepared persuasive reasons why he should remain her squire.

He bowed his head. "My lady, this . . . gift you have . . ." Then he looked up at her with shining eyes, his adoration restored. "'Tis wondrous! Your ability with magic can only help the prince!"

She smiled with relief. "Please, Lovell, do not assume any usefulness from such a meager gift. Sensing magic is not the same as combating it."

Geraint had returned. "It needs combating?" he said dourly.

"Nay, not this time, I think. I was simply explaining to Lovell that what good is sensing magic, when you do not know how to fight it?" She leaned over and put a hand on Geraint's arm. "But there is no need for battle, not this time."

"Why am I not relieved," he said, raising a hand to signal the march of their troop. "But my men will remain alert. Ride behind me." And then he slid home the visor of his helmet.

Enid prayed that he would at least speak with the village elders before he attacked.

Though the snow had ceased falling, and the air was beginning to warm, there were still dangerous drifts of snow that forced the march to move slowly. Geraint was almost glad for the distraction, because it was difficult to think about this newly revealed dimension of his wife.

She could sense magic.

What else did she know about such things? And how could he have been stupid enough not to realize that she might have something more than other women—besides her sword fighting skills?

Telling his father such a thing would not be easy, not

unless he could find a way to know the exact extent of
Enid's abilities. Discovering that would mean finding
the correct questions, because she didn't seem to know
what to reveal voluntarily.

The wisdom of his quick marriage grew ever dim-
mer, he thought, holding back a sigh. But whenever he
looked at her, remembered their moments alone, he
didn't remember hastiness, only need.

The seaside village came into view, and it was surely
the most prosperous one they'd seen yet—and miracu-
lously free of snow. Dozens of homes and buildings,
decorated with flowers, lined the harbor. As he watched,
the last of the clouds dissipated, and the sun shone
down with a dazzling warmth, reflecting off the waves
and the shining paint of the well-cared-for fishing boats.
He used his own senses now—senses honed in battle—
but there seemed to be no danger, not in this peaceful
place.

He shrugged his cloak back off his shoulders and
motioned for his soldiers to follow behind him, instead
of remaining outside the village as they'd done in their
travels up until now. Perhaps soldiers couldn't combat
magic, but Geraint wouldn't take a chance.

They rode down the lane between houses, and although the occasional head peered out from behind a
door or shuttered window, no one came to greet them
except one lone man, who waited for them near a large
tree on the village green. Sheep grazed around him, ignoring everyone. The man wore a long tunic, but carried
no obvious weapons. Geraint could not believe that only
one man would greet an entire mounted troop.

"Geraint," Enid said warningly.

He glanced back at her, but she, too, was staring at the lone man.

"*He* is the source of the magic."

Geraint rested his hand on the hilt of his sword, but did not draw it. He was not unfamiliar with the consequences of magic, having ridden the kingdom for King Arthur. The high king's own sisters were sorceresses. But so often it was a matter of luck, to be able to defeat someone with skills one could not match—or even imagine.

The man spread his arms wide. "Welcome, visitors! Welcome, prince of Cornwall. We greet you in peace."

"He already knows we mean him no harm," Enid said. "The magic must have found us for that purpose."

After signaling his soldiers to remain as they were, Geraint removed his helmet and looked at Enid. "You remain with me."

They rode forward alone, and the man waited for them, a peaceful smile on his face. He was in his middle years, his beard beginning to go gray, but his eyes were alight with intelligence.

Geraint reined his horse to a stop, but did not dismount. Coldly, he said, "Who are you, and why did you use magic against us?"

The man bowed. "I am Ossian of Tregarian, the healer of this village. And I did not use magic *against* you, as your wife can attest."

"Do not play with your words," Geraint said. "You used magic, when a simple party of greeting would have told you all you needed to know."

"And you might have killed them, if you were of a mind," Ossian said in a gentle voice. "Each man here is like a child to me. You resent the way I contacted you, but there are many who are frightened of mounted soldiers. So come, Prince Geraint, accept my apologies for our first contact, and my hospitality for you and your men."

Geraint glanced once more at Enid, whose face remained neutral. Reluctantly he dismounted, then helped her from the saddle.

"You are at peace with this?" he asked softly against her ear, knowing that the wizard could probably hear everything they said.

She frowned. "He means us no harm, my husband. But his purpose eludes me."

As if the wizard had given a signal they could not see, the village houses opened up as women and children poured out, carrying dishes of meat and fruit. Geraint had never seen such a small village willingly feed a troop of hungry soldiers without first asking for payment. He frowned at Ossian, but the wizard turned away and directed the few men not out fishing to set up trestle tables to bear the food.

Ossian walked to the milling soldiers and invited them to feast. When the young women shyly offered their help, Geraint could see that his men were already looking forward to a fine afternoon.

Ossian returned to him and bowed. "My lord, my lady, would you care to dine in my home?"

There were things to be said in private, Geraint surmised ruefully. He accepted the invitation, then turned to give instructions to Ainsley. He and Enid followed Ossian across the village green to a humble home. Inside they found but two simple rooms: a living area, and a curtained-off bedchamber. Ossian bade them sit and brought forth wine.

The wizard smiled at Enid as he poured it. "Since you sensed my goodwill earlier, you know that I am serving you only the best wine."

She tilted her head and smiled. "It would seem purposeless to poison your prince, when the king's wrath would be great. No magic is involved in that simple deduction."

Geraint hid his smile behind a sip of wine.

"And your village seems far too cozy for you to want to abandon it," she continued.

Ossian sat down across the table from them. "But you have been under attack more than once on your journey. You do not consider it to be under my orders?"

"Nay," Geraint said shortly. "But I seek to play no more games. Why do you live among these simple villagers?"

"It has always been my home, my lord. I did travel to study and perfect the arts I was born with, but I returned here many years ago to find peace. And I have it. And in exchange, I grant the villagers—many my own family—the security of my healing, the location of fish, good harvest for poor soil, the birth of healthy calves and lambs—and warning about the purpose of intruders."

"Quite indispensable, aren't you," Geraint said dryly.

With a modest bow of his head, Ossian said, "I try to be."

"Then tell me what you know of these attacks on my company."

Ossian considered his wine. "I know they happened leagues from here, my lord, and outside the humble scope of my powers."

"Then how did you know they happened at all?"

"Because I could sense your worry that it was about to happen again."

"You can read my thoughts?" Geraint demanded.

"Not quite." He frowned. "I do have a small gift of information for you, in hopes it will keep me at peace with the future king of Cornwall."

Geraint studied him. "Then tell me."

"There is a man of magic stalking you."

"We have seen no one but the mercenaries, who did not use magic."

"It is a small gift of magic this man bears, and it has not been used against you. But it will be. There is nothing you can do to avoid him, but I suggest he be dealt with to avoid future heartache."

"So we're going to meet an enemy with magic, and we're supposed to kill him." Geraint spoke dubiously.

"I cannot predict your actions, my lord, or what the correct path is. I only know what I know because I receive impressions of emotions." He glanced at Enid. "Impressions of power."

Geraint watched her stiffen.

"Then your gifts fail you, Ossian," Enid said. "I have no great power."

"Not great, no, but some small abilities. You are more—and less—than you seem."

Enid set down her wine.

Geraint stiffened and said, "Your riddles do not amuse me, Ossian."

"I intend no amusement, my lord. I only wish to help heal a marriage. Now let me bring you nourishment."

Geraint watched his wife, but she looked absently at

the hearth instead of at him. That fact that she had secrets was no secret to him, but hearing a stranger verify
that embarrassed and dismayed him.

"We will talk tonight," he said softly, for her ears
alone.

She bowed her head and nodded.

Chapter 14

• • •

OSSIAN bade them make camp on the hillside above the village, where he assured them there would be plenty of grass for their horses and plenty of wood for their fires. Enid stood on the hill overlooking the harbor and the village, the encampment at her back. There had been no battle, and she was weak with relief. Geraint was a man who could be reasoned with.

Yet when Ossian had offered the hospitality of the village to her and Geraint, her husband had declined. He wanted her alone when he interrogated her.

She shivered in the breeze and drew her cloak tighter. What would she tell him? She could not betray her father, her people, or her mission. But how would she answer the charge of being "more and less" than she seemed? Wasn't that a riddle that all could claim for themselves at times, regardless of any magical gifts?

Fryda brought her back to their fire when the freshly caught fish—a gift from the villagers—were roasting. They feasted for the second time that day, and she knew that the soldiers were enjoying themselves. But Geraint sat across from the fire and just watched her. Surely he was sorting through his questions even now.

When he was finished eating, he rose to his feet. "Fryda, your mistress and I need privacy for an hour or so, so she won't need you tonight. Lovell will amuse you until we're finished talking, and then you can find your pallet."

Enid blushed as her husband's twin soldiers elbowed each other and grinned. There would be no pleasure for her in that pavilion. But she led her husband there, ducked inside the opening, and watched as he followed her inside. He had stopped to light a candle from the torch outside, and set that meager light before her pallet.

She had a morose urge to moan as if in pleasure for the benefit of the whole camp just to spite him. Gods, she was becoming so childish in her sadness.

"You can sit," he said.

So now she needed his permission? But she sank down amidst her blankets and waited for what seemed like a death sentence. Surely not the death of her marriage.

He knelt across from her. "If you would have told me of your magic, you could have helped us."

She winced. "As I said, it is little magic, and the moment I was able to use it—today—I told you. I would not allow harm to come to us or any of our people if I could help it."

"Is this another gift that separates your people from mine?"

"Only some are granted it, Geraint," she said earnestly, "and I was not so blessed until I was setting off alone into the world outside our village. My father wanted me protected."

His face was so unreadable, even the stillness of his body closed to her. She almost wished for more magic, so that she could understand his heart, and see if she'd lost it forever. But she only had a woman's intuition for that, and it was proving useless.

Geraint tiredly ran his hand down his face. "You have so many secrets, Enid."

As do you, she thought, thinking of the mysterious purpose of this mission ordered by King Erbin. There was no point in asking, because he wouldn't betray his father's confidence—and she wouldn't betray hers. They were at an impasse, as far as missions were concerned.

"Do you have other gifts of magic that I should know of?"

She hesitated, but he had chosen the correct question, because at least this she could answer—somewhat. "Before my journey, I was given several small, temporary gifts of magic to aid me. I was trained by the Lady of the Lake."

Geraint betrayed surprise. "Sir Lancelot, one of King Arthur's knights, was raised there. Did you know him?"

She shook her head. "I only lived there for half a year before I met you. To help me outwit my enemies, since I would be traveling alone, she taught me to cloak myself in shadows, so that others cannot see me."

"That is how you moved freely at Camelot when you wanted to train," he said, his face and voice once again impassive.

Nodding, she let all her wistful feelings of regret echo in her voice. "I did not want to draw attention to myself—nor the censure of kings down on you."

He looked away. "Is there more?"

"Aye. Though the battle skills are all mine, I was given the strength of ten men to aid me. You have no reason to risk your men in worry for my safety."

In a low voice, he said, "But I worry, Enid. I am your husband."

Once again, she was close to tears. "And your care for me moves me, Geraint. Before you, no man had ever treated me as anything but a warrior. I have not always been this beautiful," she added hesitantly. "I think that's what Ossian meant when he said I'm less than I appear."

"These sorcerers changed your very features?" His expression was aghast.

"Nay, nothing like that, but another way they protected me was making me more appealing to men. It is not my magic, but theirs."

To her surprise, he traced the features of her face.

"Is this your nose?"

She bit her lip. "Aye."

"And these are your cheeks?"

"Aye."

"And the brilliant blue of your eyes is yours?"

She could only nod.

His thumb brushed across her mouth, hesitating as if he would dip inside her. She closed her eyes and shivered.

He whispered, "And these are your lips, that work such magic?"

Oh, she wanted his kiss. She was about to kiss him

first, when he said, "Then perhaps what they gave you was confidence in yourself, in your womanliness. You have told me you were only treated as a warrior. Mayhap they gave you the ability to see that you are more than that."

She pulled her head back and stared at him in surprise. As a warrior woman, she'd been able to give men the confidence they needed. Had the Lady of the Lake done the same thing for her? Was it truly her own beauty shining through?

"Geraint, can you accept that I have meager powers that aid me?"

After several moments, he said, "I cannot say that I am unfamiliar with magic. It is a two-edged sword and can be used as easily for evil as for good. At the high king's court, I have seen Merlin aid the king with magic, and all benefited. But the king's sister Morgause, queen of Lothian, uses her gifts only for great evil, and many live in sorrow because of it."

To her surprise, he reached for her hand, and seemed to absently rub her fingers as he thought. She stared wide-eyed, grateful for his beloved touch.

He met her gaze solemnly. "I do not believe you mean harm, Enid. And I am grateful for what you've told me tonight." His voice dropped to a whisper. "I wish you could tell me more."

The first tears fell from her eyes and she did not try to hide them. "I wish *you* could tell me more. But we cannot break vows to the other people we love."

Geraint saw heartbreak on Enid's face, and the last of his anger toward her faded away. They were both caught in situations not of their making, and the trust that they wanted to share was yet so elusive.

He wanted to prove to his father that he had chosen right, that Enid was a good wife—and would make a good queen. And if he could get her to soften toward him, maybe she would finally reveal the rest of the secrets that kept them apart.

He looked down at their joined hands and thought of the strength in her fingers, the strength in every part of her being. Her bravery could not be feigned. She was a lone woman given gifts to help her battle a dangerous world.

He met her eyes once more and saw her longing. He sighed.

"Fryda is waiting for her pallet," he said softly.

Her gaze dropped to his mouth. "Aye," she whispered.

He leaned forward and kissed her gently, once, twice. "Until the morrow."

For the first time, he sensed hopeful possibilities.

• • •

EARLY the next afternoon they toured a seaside village that owed its prosperity to the mining of tin. The people lacked an abundance of good farmland, but were able to barter for what they needed. They treated Geraint and Enid to a feast, and sent rations to their encampment for the soldiers. Enid walked among the women, listening to them point with pride to their meager vegetable gardens. She admired their skills with the needle.

One woman plucked Enid's sleeve, desperation evident in her eyes. Enid allowed herself to be drawn a little away from the group. "Aye, mistress?"

"Milady, ye must come see me loom. 'Twill be the

pride of the village, but none will believe me. If ye look upon it and say 'tis fit, the rest will believe."

Enid didn't have the will to resist such heartfelt pleading. She followed the woman to her home, on the edge of the village farthest inland. Inside, there were only two windows, and although the shutters were closed, there were enough cracks for her to see the gloomy clutter of the place. Crates were piled high on either side of the door, and the place smelled strongly of fish. Where was the loom?

A tingle crawled up her spine, so faintly that she did not recognize it until the door suddenly slammed shut behind her, and a loop of rope dropped down over her head and shoulders from behind one set of crates. Now that the rope was touching her she sensed its magic, tightening around her like a snake. She tried to lift her arms, and they wouldn't move. She turned toward her attacker, only to feel another length of rope twined her about the knees. Now even her legs were frozen. Was this the magic that the wizard had warned them of?

"Who are you?" she demanded, turning her head side to side trying to see into the shadows behind the stacked crates. "You do yourselves and your village great harm by attacking the future queen of Cornwall."

On her right, a man stepped out from behind the crate. As he walked in front of her, he moved in and out of beams of sunlight. He was bearded and long-haired and wore a rough tunic and wool hose. He had no magic of his own; it was in the rope.

"I be offended, girl," he said mockingly. "Do I reek of fish? I be not of this village."

He came closer to her, and she saw the spiked club

he walked with, using it almost as a cane, though he did not limp.

"Milady, I be here for you," he said, twirling the club absently on the earthen floor.

The other man scuttled out of the shadows and almost hid behind his partner. He was shorter, thinner, but dressed much the same. "We should leave, Hartun," he whispered, cocking his head at the shuttered windows as if he could see between the slats.

"Aye, Bureig," said Hartun. "Ye take her feet, I'll take her shoulders."

Bureig held back. "She has strong magic."

"The rope has tamed her."

"Where did you get such a thing?" Enid asked, trying to stall for time. Surely Geraint would miss her soon and come roaring after her, thinking she'd left on her own again.

Hartun smiled, revealing several brown teeth. "I had a fight with a troll. I won."

"You mean you stole his property. He might already be after you."

Hartun shrugged and came around behind her to grip her shoulders. "He will not be leavin' his cave, not to come so far south."

Enid turned her direct stare on Bureig, who shrank away from her legs. "And how do you know what magic I possess?"

"We seen it," Bureig said softly.

"You haven't been following us," she shot back.

Bureig lifted his chin, obviously trying for courage. "No, we been attackin' ye."

"Bureig!" Hartun hissed.

The littler man dropped to his hands and knees, like dog sensing it would soon be kicked.

"You are with the mercenaries," Enid said slowly. "Has your leader sent you on such a dangerous mission without support?"

Hartun laughed. "Not so dangerous. And he wouldn't listen to me. I knew gettin' ye away was the key to gettin' yer man away, too. But that's not how *he* wanted to play it. I'll show 'im. I'll bring yer mate to him, and then I'll get me reward." He stuffed a dirty rag into Enid's mouth.

"Me, too!" said Bureig.

This seemed to embolden the little man, for he grabbed Enid about the calves just as Hartun tipped her backward.

Where was Geraint?

Enid tried to fold in a heap to the floor, but the two men dragged her toward a window at the back of the cottage. After opening the shutters, Hartun climbed out, and between the two of them, they maneuvered her through, with much soft cursing and heavy breathing.

She tried to call out, but any noise was muffled by the gag. The cottage was the farthest from the village green, and it hid their escape. They had two horses waiting. After throwing her over the back of one, stomach first, Hartun climbed up behind her, and they were off. Enid turned her head, trying to see behind them, but the road took a quick bend around the base of a cliff. They picked up speed, following the ocean to the east. The pounding against her stomach was fierce, but that was nothing compared to her rising fear.

She was being used as bait, and Geraint, ever her

protector, would take it. Though in the midst of problems with their marriage, she knew he would do anything to rescue her, even if it endangered himself.

She felt a tug on her skirt, heard the sound of tearing. By the gods, what was this villain trying to do to her on a horse?

She saw the fabric flutter to the ground behind them.

"Won't take yer man long to find yer trail," Hartun said with satisfaction.

They rode for another hour, and by the end of it, Enid was hoping to pass out just to avoid the ceaseless pain. She didn't think she'd ever be able to draw a deep breath again.

But after a last climb up a steep path, the horses drew to a halt. The sky was darkening with twilight, as the sun sent its last rays arching overhead. Enid was pulled off the horse, and she groaned as the men dumped her onto the ground. She blinked up at them, dazed and unable to swallow.

Bureig looked fearful. "She had that gag in her mouth a long time."

Hartun looked about. "Go ahead and take it out. No one's behind us yet. Surely her man will find the clues we left."

Bureig knelt beside her and reached toward her mouth. Enid gratefully opened wide, but even then, the fabric stuck to her, peeling away some of her skin. She moaned, but instead of scurrying back, Bureig hovered over her with obvious concern.

"Are ye thirsty?"

She restrained her sarcasm and nodded frantically, trying to look helpless. It wasn't very difficult to let tears glisten in her eyes when she was so worried about her husband.

Bureig held a horn over her face, then tipped it slowly, letting water run into her mouth. She drank it frantically.

"Not too much," Hartun cautioned. "She'll sicken on us."

Bureig backed away. Now that one need was met, Enid turned her head to watch Hartun. He was taking several torches out of a bag attached to his saddle. He lit them by striking sparks with flint and steel, then drove them into the earth at intervals. She couldn't quite follow his every movement from her position on the ground.

"What is he doing?" she asked Bureig.

"Lightin' the pit."

Her mouth sagged open. "Pit?"

"Roll 'er in!" Hartun yelled.

Bureig's worry was evident. "Can't we lower her in gently?"

"If you harm me," Enid said forcefully, "my husband will see that you both die. If you want mercy—"

"Ye'll be the one cryin' fer that," Hartun said. He gave her a shove, and she rolled once. "Bureig, help me! None o' yer slobberin' over her."

After the fifth roll, she felt the earth give way beneath her shoulder. She cried out and hung there, suspended, knowing that with one more push, she would fall into the darkness below. What awaited her down there? She struggled once more against the ropes, but they held her immobile.

Hartun squatted above her, peering into her face. "I

don't have to send ye down there, if ye decide to be nice to me."

She glared at him. "I would rather face the pit."

With a grimace, he gave her a final shove, and she fell. Her shriek was short-lived, for the depth of the pit was not too great. She landed on her back, with the wind knocked out of her, gasping for air as she gaped up at the purple sky. The depth couldn't be more than twice her height.

Hartun peered over the edge. "Ye alive?"

She licked her lips and debated not answering. But all that would get her was Hartun clambering down after her, and in his anger he might do worse.

"I am unharmed—I think."

"Good. Rest ye well, milady. Maybe we'll let ye see yer man before we take him away. And then it's off to the captain, and he'll decide what's to become of him. And give me my reward," he added gleefully.

"Our reward," Bureig whined.

As they moved from the pit, their bickering faded away.

The hard, uneven earth beneath Enid's back was damp, and soon she was wet and chilled through. She tried not to think about how thirsty she was, how her stomach growled, and how her muscles ached. She screamed for help, but when they laughed, she realized it only played into their game. Geraint would come running frantically if he heard, rather than taking the time to create a sound plan.

To keep her mind occupied, she considered how strange it felt to be waiting for another person, helpless and dependent. She'd begun to take her magical gifts for granted, and had thought nothing could harm her. Now she was totally dependent on Geraint to rescue her. She would hate the mere thought if it were anyone else. But with her husband, she appreciated his protectiveness. It didn't make her feel inferior to need him. It made her feel . . . loved.

Another hour passed, and the sky turned to black. Still the torches blazed at the corners of the pit, and for that she was grateful. Something crawled slowly along her neck, and she held her breath, praying not to be bitten. She wanted to shake until it was off her, but didn't dare. At last it crawled away. Was it in her hair?

She was going to drive herself crazy with these thoughts. She was trying not to think of what was on her skin, when its itchiness took on new meaning. The moon was calling her, although she couldn't see it. It was the third night since she'd renewed her magic. If she didn't perform the ritual, she would lose everything. She would be useless to her mission—useless to Geraint in her own rescue, should he be able to free her.

It was still early, she told herself, trying to remain calm.

Chapter 15

• • •

AT first, Geraint thought his wife had merely wandered off again, and he was angry and offended. Fryda had come to him, near tears, unable to find Enid. But after searching the village, he realized she was gone. Her horse was still there, so he couldn't believe she'd left voluntarily.

Someone had taken her.

A chill swept through him, and he found that he, always so logical, was having trouble thinking about anything other than setting off after Enid, heedless of the danger. The fact that she seemed unable to have used her magical strength gave him a terrifying feeling of helplessness.

"Milord," Ainsley said, "what are yer orders?"

Geraint watched the milling soldiers talk in low, angry tones. "Ainsley, my first thought is to go alone.

Maybe the presence of a group of mounted men would get my wife killed."

"Ye don't know that, milord."

"We know nothing. Is she with an army? Is magic involved?"

"We can only find out by chasin' 'em," Ainsley said. "And if ye want my opinion, we should all go. If ye need to leave us behind at some point, ye only have to say so."

"Very well. Let us leave this cursed place."

When the soldiers were all mounted, and Geraint about to lead them away, they were called back by two of the village elders who supported a sobbing woman between them.

"Milord," the village bailiff said, "Mistress Ailith has confessed to aiding the two men who took the princess."

"Only two?" Geraint said harshly, looking down on the woman from his horse.

Her knees buckled and they let her sink to the ground. She raised her tear-stained face. "Milord, they threatened to kill me babies if I didn't help them."

Geraint sighed. "What can you tell me?"

"I only saw two men, both dressed poorly, though armed like soldiers. They bade me bring yer wife, and she came willingly, because I—lied to 'er." The sobs began anew.

"Mistress, we must hurry!" Geraint said.

"When I got back to me cottage, the back window shutters were broken, so I think they took 'er out that way. They—they said I should tell ye to come alone. They'll be able to see your soldiers, and will kill 'er if you disobey them." She bowed her head. " 'Tis all I know, milord. Please believe me."

"I do. You do not know which way they went?"

She shook her head, and he could hear her mumbling, "My babies, my babies."

Geraint looked at the bailiff. "Do not deal harshly with her, for the fault is not hers."

The woman collapsed onto her face, sobbing her thanks.

Geraint looked at Ainsley. "Two men."

"They could be meetin' others."

"Mayhap, but since they want me alone, I doubt it."

Ainsley frowned. "Ye can't be thinkin' to go alone, milord."

Geraint looked to the west, where the sun was already falling. "They must *think* I'm alone."

"Very well," Ainsley said, beginning to smile. "They won't even know we're behind ye."

"And you will stay behind, but for a trusted scurrier to watch for my need of you."

"Aye, milord."

"Then let us go."

At first following the trail went slowly. The ground was rocky and hard, and the earth had earlier been trampled by Geraint's soldiers. But there were only three paths away from the village, and Geraint now knew that he was meant to follow, so they would have left a marker. It made him feel better about Enid's condition—they needed her alive, didn't they? He couldn't let himself think anything else.

The main road went north, up the steep cliff path. Surely they wouldn't have used this—they might easily have been seen. So it was either path along the ocean, east or west. He rode a hundred yards to the west, but the horse had to go slowly, picking through rockslides and boulders and places where the trail just gave way. This would be too difficult for an easy escape, so Geraint turned back. He didn't see any sign of his soldiers as he crossed the main road again and headed east. This path was wider, obviously well used. It wasn't long before he found a ragged piece of fabric fluttering among an outcrop of rocks.

"It is hers," Geraint breathed, feeling exhilarated and determined. He had found the path.

Soon, as the sun began to set, the road was harder to follow. Storms had washed boulders down from the cliffs, forcing Geraint to travel slowly. He found himself leaning forward in his saddle, as if that would make the journey faster.

Within an hour, he saw man-made light flickering in the distance, higher up. As he got closer, he could see that torches ringed a deserted hill overlooking the sea. The paths to the top were treacherous and narrow, hugging the hillside above the crashing ocean. There was no movement on the hill, certainly no army, as Geraint had feared. But then he couldn't see his own soldiers either.

He left his horse tethered by the side of the road and began a cautious climb up the twisting path that hugged the cliffside. He could have ridden, but he was hoping he hadn't been seen yet. The sun had already set, the sky was dimming from gray to deep purple, and the streaming shadows were confusing, but he struggled on. As he neared the top, he quietly drew his sword. It looked like this might be the only way up, which would be perfect for his soldiers to trap the villains.

He hunched behind a boulder. All he could see were the torches, two horses tethered near the wall, and a yawning darkness in the center of the open hilltop.

His stomach tightened. It was a pit.

There was a sudden tumble of pebbles, and something long and light dropped on Geraint from above. His instinctive reaction was to duck and roll away, right onto the open hillside. Out of the corner of his eye, he saw a piece of rope being pulled back. They had meant to capture him, not kill him, which was important to know.

He sprang to his feet, just as two men jumped from the cliff above him. One raised his sword threateningly, but the bigger man only grinned as he held up a spiked club. Geraint attacked. They seemed stunned that he came after them both, because they stumbled back toward the cliff, then separated, so he'd be forced to face them on each side. He slashed at one, was parried, felt the other coming at his back, whirled and just missed being slammed in the head with the club. He turned and vaulted over the pit to the far side.

"Geraint!"

He heard his wife's scream, and his relief was so great he almost fell to his knees to peer down at her. But instead he held his sword menacingly, looking back across the pit at the villains.

"What do you want of us?" he demanded.

Enid shouted, "They're with the mercenaries!"

The taller, broader bearded man scowled down at her. "I woulda told him! Ye give away no secrets, girl."

He glanced back at Geraint. "Ye come with us peaceful-like, and she goes free. I don't need her."

"I'm bound with magic rope!" she cried.

"So how was she to go free in your little scheme?" Geraint demanded.

"I woulda given her a knife."

Geraint considered his options. He tried to appear hesitant, let his sword drop a bit, as if he didn't know what to do. But behind Enid's captors, he saw the first of his men creeping up the cliff trail, two at a time. They passed the boulder he'd hidden behind, hugged the cliff wall—and dislodged a rock, which skittered away down the side.

The kidnappers turned to look over their shoulders just as Geraint leaped across the pit again.

The smaller man cried out, and together the two villains stumbled back toward the cliff. All was pitch dark behind them, but Geraint could hear the roar of the ocean below as the waves crashed into the rocks.

Geraint put out a hand. "We will not harm you. You only have to talk to us."

Both men took another step back, and the smaller one gave a squeak of fear. The bigger man searched behind him, then to Geraint's shock, he grabbed hold of his friend and yanked backward. They disappeared over the cliff with only a single shriek.

Geraint rushed to the edge, but he could see nothing in the darkness. The sound of the waves crashing on the rocky cliff made him shudder. What a terrible way to die.

"Milord!" Ainsley called. He came over to stand beside Geraint. "They do much to protect their secrets, these mercenaries."

With a nod, Geraint turned away. He pulled a flickering torch out of the ground and held it over the pit. "Enid?"

She lay bound on her side, but she lifted her head. "Aye, Geraint, I am well. But this magic rope—" Her arms suddenly broke free as the rope shredded from her strength. She snapped the second rope with her hands. "It's become normal! Why would it lose its magic?"

"Perhaps with the death of its master, the magic is gone."

She looked unconvinced, but she slowly stood up, then groaned, rubbing her arms. "I have been frozen in that position for hours."

"I shall come down."

"Nay, just send down a rope. 'Tis not far."

"Do not protest. You are weak with exhaustion."

Ainsley produced a rope, knotted it around a boulder, and Geraint climbed down it easily.

Enid smiled at him softly. By torchlight, he could see that she was spotted with mud, but there were no obvious injuries.

He put his arms around her, and she swayed against him.

"I so feared for you," he whispered into her hair.

"And I for you. They wanted to take you back to the main body of the mercenaries, to use you to win their own reward."

"It sounds like they were working on their own."

"They were. They thought they were so clever. But they are dead?"

He nodded. "They jumped into the ocean below rather than be taken by us."

"That is dedication—or fear of their master." She shuddered. "I wasn't sure if they needed you dead or alive."

"We are both very much alive, and I am grateful to God for that."

She pulled back and looked into his face. "I had no doubt you would rescue me. With anyone else, it would gall me to need help. But with you, I only feel protected."

There was a softness inside him he'd never felt for another woman. Regardless of their secrets, he was glad he had married her.

"Come, Enid, let us be away from this place."

He helped her from the pit and down the steep path to the seaside road below, where the rest of their men waited. Though they had to use torches to travel west again, toward the main road, no one wanted to linger near the cliffs.

Geraint rode with Enid in his arms. The horse plodded on slowly; men talked around them in low voices. It was peaceful.

Enid stirred, though he'd thought her asleep.

"Do you think that was the magic that the wizard warned us about?"

"I know not, but it seems likely."

"He told us to deal with it now, to avoid heartache later. Surely we did that."

"The villains did it themselves."

He didn't want to talk about danger anymore. He tipped Enid's chin up, and kissed her.

She whispered, "Though I yet have secrets that belong to another, I want you to believe you have my trust. I have something to show you."

"Do I have to wait until we make camp?" he growled, nipping at her lower lip.

She gave a throaty laugh. "Aye, my husband, I want to be away from here."

• • •

WITH the threat to his wife still fresh in his mind, Geraint demanded that his soldiers travel several more leagues before they made camp for the night.

He couldn't stop watching Enid, who looked excited and far too pleased with herself. He was in for another revelation.

He should be worried—but he had been able to accept everything she had already revealed. Her very differences were what had attracted him to her from the beginning, and he could not forget that. Surely she was trusting him more and more each day. He shut out thoughts of the disapproving world back at Camelot or Castle Cornwall, and thought only of the mysteries of his wife, revealed one by one, as if she were shedding garments.

It was uncomfortable to ride when he was picturing his wife shedding garments.

He spent their midnight meal watching her, and she was watching him. He noticed most gave them plenty of room, as if whatever was between them could not be interfered with. They didn't speak as many around them gradually found their pallets. Enid's maidservant started toward their pavilion hesitantly, and Enid told her to go ahead.

Enid turned back to Geraint. "Shall we go?"

He picked up a torch. "I have men stationed throughout

this small woodland, up to a league away. We'll be safe, I promise you."

She gave him a saucy grin. "But can we be alone?"

"They have orders not to disturb us. And I promise I can be very quiet."

Side by side, they walked away from the encampment.

After a while, Enid said, "You have probably noticed that I've been following the stream. Surely it must widen out to a pond somewhere."

He had been paying so much attention to the needs of his body that he hadn't understood her confused expression. "Enid, most of these streams end in the sea."

By torchlight, he watched her wide eyes show the first hint of worry. "Then we need to go upstream, to find its source."

They reversed course, walking back the way they'd come, skirting the quiet encampment, and reassuring the sentries. As the forest closed around them again, the stream narrowed, forcing them to work harder to stay by its bank. The eager tension Geraint had earlier felt in Enid now drained away, and she seemed more and more panicked.

In her haste to continue upstream, she walked into a branch that cut the smooth skin of her upper arm. Even the welling blood did not halt her.

"Enid, stop," he called.

"But we have to keep going," she said, turning frightened eyes on him.

"What are you so afraid of?" he asked.

He tried to touch her, but she ducked aside, hugging herself forlornly.

"Dawn is only hours away. I can feel everything draining away already."

"What do you mean?" he asked patiently.

"My magic gifts."

He frowned at her. "Why would they suddenly do that?"

"I have to renew the magic every third night, or it will leave me completely. But I need a pond!" she suddenly cried, whirling around, ducking beneath the low branches of a tree, and starting away into the dark.

"Enid, wait, you need the torch. You cannot see much by the crescent moon."

She didn't stop, and he hurried behind her, bringing the light, but not any comfort. The stream was not fading, but it was not getting any larger either. She pushed aside branches frantically, and when he heard her sob, he caught her arm. He thrust the torch into the soft earth of the embankment, then put his arms around his squirming wife.

"Enid, calm yourself," he murmured into her hair, feeling the tension that stiffened her body. "The world will not end should the magic leave you. It wasn't part of you to begin with. And as your husband, I will never let you come to harm."

"Nay!"

Her voice was low, hoarse with desperation, and she pushed at his chest until he released her. The tears in her eyes made the need to help her rise into an ache. If only he could understand the mystery of her.

"Geraint, I cannot let this go! I am the last resort of my people."

"Let me as your husband be their last resort."

She shook her head. "Your father has your loyalty, and although I know you want to be loyal to me, too, I fear in some things that can never be."

She was right, he thought with despair. Always in the back of his mind was the worry of his father's reactions to her abilities and to her mysterious mission.

"I have to find a pond," she cried.

She would have thrown herself into the dark, overgrown woods, but he stopped her, grabbing her upper arms and pulling her to him. He had never seen his wife in such a state.

"Enid, please, I will help you, but you must calm yourself."

She trembled against him. "I can feel it fading," she whispered forlornly against his neck. "'Tis calling to the moon, and there is no answer."

He looked into her grief-filled eyes. "Can we build our own pond?"

She stared at him with incomprehension.

"Is there any rule that says it must be a specific-size pond?"

"I know not."

"Then let me try to help you," he said, hoping his patient tone would calm her. "Find all the rocks you can, and we shall dam the stream right here, where the water comes down the cliff in a little waterfall."

She latched on to his idea with desperation, dropping to her knees to begin her search. They worked quietly to gather rocks, then discussed the best place for the dam. After another hour's work, they'd created a small pond, several yards across, no more than six inches deep.

"Will this do?" he asked, stepping back to look on their creation with satisfaction.

But she wasn't looking at him anymore. She was staring at the water, and the small reflection of the moon within it.

And then she began to remove her garments. He could barely keep his mouth from sagging open.

He made no move to stop her; with every item that dropped to the ground, he felt the tension in his body wind higher. He watched the thrust of her breasts, and the smooth slope of her stomach leading to blond curls. Her hips cradled the deepest part of her, where he ached to be. The last thing she removed were her boots, and as she tossed them aside, she was suddenly holding a dagger that gleamed in the moonlight.

Before Geraint could move, she made a small slice in her finger. He realized at once that what he'd thought was the work of an opponent's sword on her hands was actually self-inflicted. She even bore pain for her tribe's benefit. He had never known such a woman.

She held her finger over the small puddle of water, and the moment the first drops of blood hit the surface, he felt something in the very air around him, an awareness, a waiting. The blood sank instead of being carried off as it would in a stream.

Then she lifted her arms to the night sky and called out in a language he didn't understand. But the woods understood; he was surrounded by trees that began to sway with a wind that had not been there a moment before. Enid moved in time to it, her hair whipping and flowing. After several minutes of harmony with a wind that Geraint could see but not comprehend, she took a graceful step into the water.

The very air seemed to crackle around her, and he saw sparks of light rise between her upraised arms. She suddenly seemed the embodiment of lightning that went up *toward* the moon, instead of coming from the sky. He lost his breath, lost all sense of reality as the body of his wife seemed to glow. He knew he should be afraid for her life, but his emotions seemed so remote.

She turned toward him, and a gust of wind blew out the torch. They were left with nothing but the small crescent moon to see by, but it seemed to shine down on Enid with abnormal power.

She was the focus of the lightning he'd seen twice before. She was in her element, a woman of the night sky, a goddess, with the majesty of the forest all around her. Her expression was serene and relaxed as she watched him, and in that moment, she embodied the seduction of every mystery of the earth. How could a man dismiss that?

It was as if he were truly alive for the first time in his life, aware of all that was around him, things he never saw, never thought to understand. All that mattered was that she was his wife, in union with only him. He wanted her, and he had to have her now.

Chapter 16

· · ·

THE power still tingled within Enid even as her joining with the moon faded away. She realized that the torch had died out, but she could still see Geraint by the light of the moon. He was watching her, and she waited for his condemnation or his acceptance. Their whole marriage hinged on this moment.

His face was full of shadows lit from above. She could make out the jut of his nose and chin, and strangely even the hollow of his dimple, but not his eyes, in which she had hoped to read his emotions. His hands were fisted at his sides, and before she could wonder if he harbored anger, he came toward her.

He tilted his head up, eyes closed as if in reverence, as if in longing.

"Geraint," she said with a gasp.

Then he swept her into his arms, lifting her off her feet

like the lightest flower. He pressed his face between her breasts, murmuring her name in a voice hoarse with need.

She wrapped her arms about his neck, her legs around his strong waist, and with both hands lifted his face for a kiss. The joining of their mouths was full of a hunger long denied. She could not get enough of the taste of him. She moaned her desire into his mouth, then took his tongue into hers. It was a mimicry of mating that only made her need him more.

Suddenly she found herself falling backward as he lowered her to the large, flat rock that rested next to the base of the small waterfall by their dam. He straightened and put his hands to his garments, then froze, slack-jawed as she arched her back, accepting the mist of the falling water on her skin. Her hair had come down and now cushioned her head, spreading out all around her.

She watched through lowered eyelids as Geraint yanked off his clothing as if he were afire. When he was naked, the moonlight bathing every warm curve of muscle, he knelt between her thighs and put his hands on her knees. Slowly, he slid them up her body. She shuddered when his thumbs met in the curls hiding her sex, but he did not stop. He rubbed the skin of her stomach, now damp from the waterfall's mist, but stopped just at the lower curve of her breast.

She could not bear the separation another moment. She rose up and took him by surprise, lifting him and turning so that he was the one beneath. He stared at her wide-eyed as she moved above him. When he would have reached for her, she held him down with a grip the likes of which she'd never used on him before.

He was helpless beneath her, and in their shared

gaze, she saw that he recognized it, accepted it, even enjoyed it. Only then did she mount him, taking him deep within her, controlling every movement of their mating.

She released his arms, and his hands came up to knead her breasts. Throwing her head back, she arched, taking him in ever deeper. As she lowered herself over him, hands braced beside his shoulders, she began to move in earnest, raising herself up and down. He came up on his elbows and took as much of her breast as he could within his mouth. The movement of his tongue, the pressure of their joined bodies, even the power of the moon shining down on her back, all combined to raise the threshold of her desire. It felt like magic once again, only better, suffusing her, surrounding her, taking her higher than she'd ever been.

And then it crashed over her in ever rising waves. She shuddered beneath the battering of it, and through slitted eyes watched the passion take Geraint, too. He arched back on the rock, thrusting up inside her with a movement that rippled every muscle down his damp torso.

At last she fell against him, her hair wildly covering him, and he caught her in a hug. Gasping for breath, she let him ease her to his side, though she regretted the loss of him inside her. With her eyes closed, she let the mist of the waterfall soothe her.

He lay against her side, his thigh over hers. When he slid his arm beneath her head, she curled into him happily.

In her ear, he whispered, "I have so longed to be one with you again, my sweet Enid."

She rubbed against him like a cat. "I, too, my husband."

She didn't want to think of the problems of the world yet awaiting them, so she took his hand and held it to her breast.

"I was so afraid what you would think of this magic," she whispered.

"When the lightning consumed you—"

"Consumed me?" She turned her head to stare at him in puzzlement.

"For just a moment, I thought you could not survive such a thing."

He kissed her shoulder, held her breast, caressing it gently.

"And I thought if you died," he whispered, "I would die with you."

"Oh, Geraint." She did not think her body could contain her feelings of love for him. Did he yet feel the same?

"But that was only a fleeting thought, for you stood so tall and proud as if you battled against the moon with your own power."

Her laughter was soft, happy, relieved. "I know not what it is that the moon and I do to each other. The Lady taught me, and I simply accept it for the lifesaving gift that it is."

"So that you can walk in my world, among my people, and not be harmed."

She nodded hesitantly, still watching him. His brows furrowed in thought, but she could not fear his condemnation, not after everything they'd just shared.

"You know we must keep this a secret," he finally said.

She could feel his sorrow as if it were alive. "Aye, that I surely know. After all, I even kept it a secret from you, my beloved husband."

"My father could not accept such a thing in a future queen of Cornwall."

Deep inside, the tension she'd thought gone began to stir.

"He would believe that I could be manipulated by this magic of yours," he continued, "that the very kingdom itself could be jeopardized."

"But I would never do such a thing!"

"He does not know that. There is always the worry that a woman's wiles can affect a man, but this . . . this wouldn't be understood."

She found herself imagining a future where her magic was revealed before all of Cornwall. As if in a play, she could see Geraint forced to choose between the sorceress they'd call her, or his very kingdom.

Or would she be the one asked to give up everything that she was, in the quest to be his perfect queen? It always came back to her not knowing how to be the proper wife for him.

But right now, he did not say such words. He only held her in his arms, until the evening air finally chilled them both. They rose to cover their damp skin with clothing. With flint and steel, Geraint relit the torch, and they returned to the encampment, where all was quiet at each fire. She watched him look about with relief.

"Did you think something had happened while we were gone?" she asked, as they stopped beside her pavilion. They held hands like young lovers, and she didn't want to let him go. "Thieves? Mercenaries? Wizards?"

He grinned. "This journey has been so eventful that there's always the chance for more."

"But not tonight," she said with a smile. "Tonight the only magic was between us."

He kissed her lightly. "Sleep well."

She leaned against him for a moment. "I will miss you beside me."

"When we return, I shall tell the queen that she disrupted our marriage with a maidservant."

"And not to do it anymore?"

He harrumphed. "I imagine that she has her way as much as she wants."

Amused, Enid bit her lip to hold back her comment—that surely a woman's wiles were already affecting the king of Cornwall.

•   •   •

AFTER their morning's march toward the northern coast of Cornwall, they stopped for a midday meal. All heard the pounding of a horse's hooves, and Enid, surrounded by men with their hands on their sword hilts, watched with curiosity as a lone man came into view from around a bend in the road.

Laughter and relief moved through the soldiers, and she realized that the man was one of theirs. She had been talking to Lovell about the training he was doing with the other soldiers, but now she made her way to Geraint. Her husband did not see her approach as he waited. The messenger dismounted and bowed to him.

"My lord, I come from your father, the king of Cornwall."

She could just see Geraint's smile.

"I know his title, Chatwyn," he said.

Chatwyn ducked his head. "Forgive me, my lord. But the king wanted you to know that the rest of his army has returned from Camelot and will be ready for the invasion at your word."

Invasion? Enid felt as if a cold wind swept around her, filling her with ice.

Geraint, still unaware of her presence behind him, sighed. "Tell my father that I deemed this amount of soldiers all that is necessary."

"But, my lord, he said that when you move against the Donella tribe—"

Enid could not help the gasp that escaped her lips. Geraint turned to face her, and she saw his confusion.

"Enid?" he said in a questioning voice.

"You are attacking?" she whispered, backing away as if she'd never really seen him before.

"I am *not* attacking anyone."

But it was too late; she had heard the truth. "My father was right. There is a greedy king."

The confusion in his expression turned into dawning surprise. He looked between her and the wide-eyed messenger, then with a growl of frustration turned to speak to the messenger.

She ran back to her horse. She had to escape, to warn her father that what they'd feared was about to come true.

Instead of some nameless tyrant deciding to gobble up their land, it was her own husband and his soldiers, these men she now knew by name.

She'd let her guard down at Castle Cornwall; she'd seen a king newly married, with another child on the way, and thought he was a man of peace. And she'd foolishly waited, telling herself she would discover what the king was up to. But all along, she was more concerned about earning her husband's love, instead of returning at once to warn her people.

She almost wished for the release of tears, but she felt dry and barren. Her fury now consumed every other emotion.

All along, she had been traveling with the invading army, and they were soon to join with another one. It would not take so many men to slaughter her small tribe, especially since she had not returned in time to train them. She had selfishly put her marriage before their lives; she had failed them.

"Enid!"

When she heard Geraint's shout, she began to run. She was still wearing a ridiculous gown, but she refused to ride sidesaddle. Grabbing up a soldier's saddle, she threw it onto the back of her own horse.

Lovell was suddenly there, helping her straighten the saddle. "My lady? Tell me what has happened!"

Geraint's hand gripped her arm a moment before he turned her to face him. It hurt too much to look at him. She shoved him hard, and he landed in the dirt. Lovell gaped between them. She no longer cared who saw what she truly was.

"Do not try to stop me, Geraint!" she said, turning back to finish saddling her horse.

She heard him get to his feet.

"Enid, do you want listen to what I have to say, or do you wish to run off without the whole story?"

When he would have touched her, she jumped away, startling the horse, who pranced between them, separating them farther.

"Lovell, I'll need supplies for a week's journey," she commanded.

To her relief, the boy did not question her; he ran off to do her bidding.

"You are not going anywhere," Geraint said firmly. "We shall discuss this."

"What is there to discuss?" she demanded, facing him defiantly. Maybe the hurt would go away, and she would see him for what he was. "Your father sent you on a mission so terrible that you had to keep it a secret."

"You have been a part of every step of this mission," he said, his face reddening with anger. "I was to meet with my people, as my father does on a regular basis."

"And then invade a land that is not yours?"

"Your land, you mean? With that little bit you just overheard, how would you know what I am charged with doing?"

"We may be a small tribe, but my father is no fool," she said, pointing into Geraint's chest. "He received word that a greedy king wanted our land."

He wiped a hand down his face. "My father is not greedy, and he does not want your land."

"We have been circling each other for weeks, each concerned with protecting our own people," she said. "I was ignorant of the truth, but did you know all along that your father meant to invade the Donella?"

"Enid, I had no idea which tribe you are from, because you would not tell me. Only now, seeing the betrayed expression on your face, do I know the truth."

"And do I not have a right to feel betrayed?"

He took her arm again. "Let me tell you everything, but not here in front of the men."

"You don't wish them to see you bested in a fight?" she cried heatedly.

He looked down at her, the eyes she thought she loved now cold and impassive.

"It has come to battle between us?" he said softly. "When we know not the full truth of each other?"

She could barely fight the ache in her chest or hold back her tears. Where had her fury gone? All she was left with was a terrible sorrow. She tried to imagine lifting a weapon against him, bloodying the flesh she'd just kissed last night, and the image was too terrible to contemplate.

"We shall talk," she said heavily.

He nodded and motioned her away from the soldiers, who were watching silently, warily. The moorland they traversed was barren except for piles of rock in tall, uneven formations. She marched around one to put it between them and his men. With her hands on her hips, she faced him and waited.

Geraint sighed. "My father heard rumors that the Donella tribe—your tribe, you now inform me—is beginning to use great magic."

She rolled her eyes. "We are doing nothing more than we've normally done."

"Giving warriors unearthly strength is normal for your people?" he said sarcastically.

"Of course not! The Lady does not bestow her power indiscriminately. I was one of the rare chosen, and only for this great mission."

"This mission you keep mentioning but not explaining."

She glared at him. "You first, since your mission is full of bloodshed."

"Have you seen any blood spilled that we were not forced to shed?"

"Not yet, but you are not finished, according to your father."

"My father has always dealt peacefully with your tribe, but now we have a constant threat of invasion from the Saxons to the east. There is talk that your father will side against us."

"We are a peaceful people! We would not go to war against Cornwall—unless attacked first. Make no mistake, when you attack, the soldiers I trained will be ready for you." She kept her face impassive, but inside she was wailing over her inability to finish her assignment. Her people would be slaughtered by Geraint's mounted, armored soldiers.

"My intention is not to attack, but to talk."

"And that is why your father wants to send an army."

For the first time he looked hesitant, and she knew true fear.

"The king has put me in command. He worries for our people, the distraction of a second battlefront. If your tribe cannot be reasoned with, I am to do what's necessary. But Enid, I refuse to let it come to that! I will not allow this to happen again."

"Again?" she echoed, wondering how many innocent people her husband had gone against in battle. She had thought him the gentlest of men, and now he was revealed as a stranger.

"Enid, your expression—" He faltered, looking bereft. "I thought by now you knew me, trusted me."

She looked away. "I had thought so, too, but this—" She broke off, angry that she'd begun to cry.

"Let me explain to you why I do not rush headlong into battle, why my every instinct cries out for negotiation, for a peaceful communication. Will you listen and not interrupt with questions until I'm done?"

Mutely, she nodded.

He sat down on a rock and looked up at her expectantly, but she didn't join him.

He sighed. "Several years ago, when I was first awarded the honor of serving as a knight to King Arthur, there was a tribe far in the north constantly attacking, as a flea attacked a dog. They were little skirmishes, and we were ordered to put them down as they happened, but not to bother with diplomacy. They were barbarians, so I was told, and not worth negotiating with. I was young, and ever the good knight, thought it my duty to obey my superiors in everything, though my instincts told me otherwise. The skirmishes went on for months, and eventually this northern tribe broke their pattern, organized into one large group, and set a trap. We went in with confidence, because we'd always defeated them easily before."

He looked away, and she saw the sorrow he didn't bother to hide. And her traitorous heart began to soften for him. Using all her willpower, she shored it up.

"Most of my men were slaughtered," he continued. "And I blamed myself, although no one else did. But from the beginning I would have talked before fighting. It is far too easy to underestimate an opponent. They might have wanted something as simple as water rights. In my report to King Arthur, I explained my position, my failings, and what we *should* have done." A corner of his mouth turned up, but not with amusement. "The king was convinced I had learned from it, and began to include me in his diplomatic missions."

"I am glad you profited from the misery of others," she said.

He frowned at her. "Profited? My friends died! I learned the hard way that talk is more important than foolhardy bravery. And I told my father this, and I intend to keep my word. My father can send all the armies he wants—he's only proving to me that he still does not trust my judgment. He thinks I act in too hasty a fashion, but doesn't see that in this instance, *he* is the one not thinking clearly. And whom could I consult, who would not think I was setting myself against the king? But I cannot go against my conscience. There will be no battle, because I will not begin one. I sent the messenger back with that exact message." With tired eyes he stared at her. "But if your father attacks, I cannot guarantee what will happen."

"Then I will warn him."

"So he will attack?"

Geraint rose to his feet and stared down at her, one of the few men who could.

"Do you want a battle between our people, Enid?" he asked softly. "Because by rashly riding off, you will start one."

She couldn't look at him anymore, so she turned and stared off across the moor, where the horizon seemed to last forever.

What should she do? Leave her father ignorant, risk that her people would be unprepared?

Or remain with the invading army, hoping to stop a war before it starts? She wanted to despise herself for feeling compassion for Geraint because of the way his father treated him.

"I have told you everything," he said. "Is it not time you told me why you left your home?"

If he knew the truth, maybe he would believe the peaceful nature of her people. She faced him, her chin raised in the air defiantly. "You will listen and believe me?"

"I have never thought you a liar, Enid," he said quietly. "But you have held on to your secrets."

She stared into his face—it was the same as just last night, when she'd made love to him, when she'd thought they'd finally found trust in each other. Could she risk everything by telling all the truth? Would her father understand if she broke her vow of silence? Regardless of what she believed about the king of Cornwall, she could not imagine her husband as a man who would indiscriminately slaughter a helpless tribe. If he knew everything, could he stop his father? Or could she?

Chapter 17

• • •

THEIR entire marriage rested on these few minutes. Geraint knew a panic that he'd only ever experienced in battle. He loved her; he wanted back the
fragile trust they'd begun to rebuild last night.

With reluctance in her voice, she finally said, "I told
you that my father sent me on a mission, and saw that
I was given gifts to aid me."

"You were chosen instead of a man because you are
a warrior woman?"

"Aye. And since I do not regularly defend our villages, I could be spared. And it was I who proposed this
mission, I who most wanted to see it done. I was to master the fighting techniques of the Britons and bring them
back to train our people."

He clenched his jaw. "For battle?"

"Nay! To promote peace. If we are strong, no one

will dare give challenge, because we could finally defend ourselves."

"Of course these skills you would train your soldiers in could also be used against Cornwall."

"My father is chieftain, and he is nothing like *your* father."

He told himself not to react; she was so angry that she wasn't thinking clearly. Yet he found himself taking an aggressive step toward her, as if she were already the enemy. "And what do you mean by that?"

"He wants peace!" she cried, pacing away from him as if she would explode by remaining still. "We want to live our lives as always, to marry, and to raise our children free of fear."

He thought of marriage—their marriage, and a sudden sick feeling swept through him. Their wedding night had revealed more than just mutual passion. "You were no virgin when you came to me. Was part of your mission to find a gullible man to marry?"

Her eyes went wide. "Nay!"

He grabbed her upper arms, shaking her though he had had no intention of doing so. "Was I just a pawn in your mission, to be used to get into Camelot, to help you spy on my high king?"

"Geraint, what are you saying?" she cried, fisting her hands in his garments. "I did not seek you out—you sought me! You romanced me, insisting that we wed. I could have refused your courtship and remained at Camelot studying the training of your knights. I didn't need you for that."

"But you admitted that they gave you powers to make you appeal to men. Was I bewitched?" He'd thought himself so in love with her, so quickly, that he had ignored everything else—his duty, his honor, his destiny.

Tears flowed freely down her face. "Nay, never, Geraint, my husband. I loved you."

"Loved? Is all we shared gone now, even after last night?"

When she closed her eyes, sagging in his grip, he let her go.

"I thought we had begun anew last night," she whispered. "You had heard of my powers, seen my renewal, and you accepted it, accepted me. I knew there were secrets yet between us, but I thought we were almost ready to share them. And this is the result, isn't it?" she said bitterly. "But you have to believe that I did not mean to use you. I only wanted to learn, and to be with you. I have changed myself for you, but nothing I do seems to matter. You could not tell me of your father's intentions; I could not tell you of mine."

There was a chasm between them, and until their respective people met, nothing could be decided. Could he believe his own accusation of spying? Where had their trust gone?

She met his gaze. "You mentioned our wedding night now in anger. You wanted nothing of my past when I came to you, no explanations. Do you want them now?"

He didn't know how to answer, torn between wanting to know and afraid to find out.

She took his silence for assent, because she said, "I am a warrior woman, Geraint. I give young men the confidence to succeed in life. I train them, not only in battle, but in the intimacies between men and women."

He could barely stop his mouth from sagging open

like a gaping fool. "You've been giving yourself to men?"

Her eyes flashed. "Did you not listen to me? I have been taught to bring young men into adulthood. Warrior women are revered as teachers, as the guardians of the future of our tribe. And if you must know, I am yet young in my profession, and have only trained three men in the art of love."

He choked on a bitter laugh. "Profession? You mean that of a whore?"

Instead of the slap he had expected, she punched him hard in the jaw. He slammed into the earth, and for a moment he saw flashes of light instead of the sky as he rolled onto his back.

She stood above him, nursing the hand she'd hit him with, righteous and beautiful in her fury. "I do not sell my body for money! When a young man has eighteen years, he is deemed ready for his first woman. Rather than have him ignorantly take the virginity of his future bride, we guide and teach him. The men trust us, because we have been their instructors for four years already. Should not we be the ones who teach men how to treat a woman? The women of our tribe are grateful that we teach their men gentleness and pleasure. Can you say that all of your knights treat their women like that?"

He knew they did not, had heard of more than one young bride traumatized by the ignorance of her groom on their wedding night. But just because he could understand the function of that sort of teacher did not mean he could easily accept his wife as one. He lay on his back, looking at the sky, feeling dazed.

"What say you, Geraint?" she asked coldly. "You

wanted to know nothing of me in courtship, now you might believe you know too much."

He sat up slowly, rubbing his jaw, and thankfully the world did not spin around him. "You've almost made sure I cannot speak."

"You deserved it."

"I did."

"You know nothing of my tribe's ways, yet you deem yourself judge—" She broke off as if it took her a moment to hear his response.

He rose to his feet. "I apologize for my crudeness. You are right, I do not know your tribe. In some ways I do not know *you*."

She winced, but said nothing.

"What will you do now?" he asked. "I stopped you from leaving earlier."

"You are not forbidding me to leave?"

"I think leaving is ill-advised, especially after all the danger we have encountered. I am going to speak to your father. You could travel safely with me."

She looked him in the eyes for several minutes. He wondered if she had no faith in him at all—if she thought he'd use her as a hostage. Geraint wasn't capable of that, but maybe she no longer knew what to believe of him. How could he expect to make diplomacy and compromise work with her father, if he couldn't succeed with her?

Finally she nodded. "I will remain with you. For now."

Geraint watched as she walked back toward his men. He thought of his father's insistence that Enid prove her loyalty to her husband; instead she was more worried about her people.

But was he any different? This might be his only chance to prove to his father that his own instincts were right. Diplomacy should be the rule before battle.

Yet in his mind lingered the worry that Enid had used him for her own gain.

• • •

WHEN Enid returned to the resting soldiers, they regarded her with curiosity and even wariness—after all, she had knocked their beloved prince onto his ass.

She stood in their midst, feeling restless and frightened and confused—and so sad, that everything she'd worked so hard to accomplish in her marriage over the last few days had fallen apart. She had tried to become what she wasn't for Geraint—or maybe for his father, a king who used battle to subjugate, regardless of who was in his way. King Erbin did not deserve her attempts to honor him.

Lovell ran to her, his expression full of concern. "Are we still leaving, my lady?"

"Nay. I am sorry to abandon a task that I ordered you to work on."

He shrugged sheepishly. "I thought it might be a lover's quarrel, and since you love each other, you would make up rather than leave."

Did this boy really think that she and Geraint loved each other? Even she didn't know anymore.

She gave him a tired smile. "So you did not pack supplies?"

"Nay, my lady."

"Would you mind finding my clothing and my weapons?"

He frowned. "But you said—"

"Nay, I'm not leaving. But I am finished pretending to be what I am not. My own garments are more comfortable, so I will travel in them from now on."

Her husband must have been mulling over their discussion, because by the time he returned, Enid was dressed in her shirt and leather jerkin, with her own boots laced up her calves. Her sword was back on her hip, and she felt . . . no, not whole. Not when she saw the bleak look in Geraint's eyes before he masked it with impassivity. And there was a growing bruise on his jaw.

He stood before her, and every soldier remained silent, deliberately looking away as they prepared to leave.

He gestured at her clothing. "Are you making a statement?"

"Only that my own garments are easier to travel in. This is who I am, Geraint. I do not need to prove anything to a bloodthirsty king."

He narrowed his eyes. "My father is a good ruler."

"That remains to be seen."

She turned away from him and met Lovell, who was leading her horse. She mounted as a man would, saw them all stare.

"Have none of you ever seen a woman's knees before?" she demanded.

She regretted her childish outburst immediately. She looked at Geraint, but all he did was shake his head and turn away.

As they set out, she felt very alone near the front of the column, as Geraint made his way back to talk to his men. The twins, Tyler and Toland, fell into place on either side of her. Wilton rode up next to Lovell at her back. Even Ainsley stayed just before her guiding them all north. In the land of the Britons, these men were her first companions beside her husband; they had known what she was from the beginning. She tried to relax.

Wilton called from behind her, "So milady, are ye going to train with us again now, too?"

The twins laughed, and Enid felt some of her terrible tension dissipating as she turned in her saddle to face Wilton.

"Do you have a wish to meet me across swords?" she asked sweetly.

"Not in the mood ye're in today, milady."

She saw Lovell's troubled look, and she found herself wanting to reassure them all. "It is just a quarrel, boys. Do not worry yourselves."

But no one was convinced, least of all herself.

•   •   •

FOR several days, they traveled to the northern coast, then turned east, stopping at villages along the way. Enid found herself stared at, but the villagers were always gracious, and some even impressed that a woman dared display a sword.

She watched Geraint carefully, and as usual he impressed her with his ability to relate to the villagers, to be a help to them rather than simply a ruler. Once or twice someone belligerently voiced a complaint, but always he was able to handle the situation, to leave people feeling helped rather than ignored.

On the night of the new moon, Geraint silently followed her to a small pond away from the cliffs at seaside, watching her back as she renewed herself, though she had not asked him for assistance. Without moonlight it was dark, but the moon was only asleep, waiting for her, and still her energy was fed by it.

The following morning, they had not ridden far when one of the troop's scurriers returned from his advance scouting and drew up beside Geraint.

"Milord," the soldier said, "we're seein' signs of an encampment where a mounted party stayed but a night or two ago."

Geraint looked at Ainsley. "We have heard nothing from the villagers about such a thing."

Ainsley shook his head, looking dour. "Nay, milord. They might o' come from the south or east, and are now headin' away from us."

"Are they afraid we'll see them?" Geraint mused, his brow furrowed.

Enid leaned on her pommel and simply watched, needing to see how her husband handled this situation. She had to be able to predict his every action before they reached the land of the Donella.

Geraint looked back at his scurrier. "Range farther today. Look for signs of them, even get close enough to discover their identity. Remember, they will have men looking for us, too."

The scurrier grinned. "No one sees me 'less I wants 'em to, milord."

After that, the mood was sober, quiet, as if all were waiting to hear something in the distance. But it wasn't until the evening that the scurrier returned with news.

Enid was eating with Fryda, Geraint, and several men around the fire at twilight, when the scurrier found them.

"Milord, their camp is but two leagues' distant," he said, breathing heavily. "They be well armed and well mounted, but not knights."

"How did an entire army get this far west?" Geraint demanded of no one in particular.

"Oh, 'tis not an army, milord," the scurrier said. "Just a small party—six men at most."

Geraint nodded. "But they are on Cornish land. And since this is the western edge of England, no one can just be passing through. We have to determine their mission. Ainsley," he said to his captain of the guard, "I need ten stealthy men. We are going to say hello to our temporary neighbors."

Enid put down her meat and started to walk toward her horse.

Geraint followed her. "You should not come."

She turned around and faced him. "I want to. If this is the beginning of your feared Saxon invasion, I need to know. I do not need a guard."

"These are not Saxons." He sighed. "I will not forbid you. But you will obey me in all things, as if you were one of my soldiers."

"As long as you do not indiscriminately kill these men."

He clenched his jaw, and a sudden sensation of guilt made her feel ashamed.

"That was unworthy of me," she said softly. "You would not kill a man for no reason."

He arched a dark brow. "That is almost a declaration of trust, coming from you."

They rode off in the dark, with only a crescent moon to see by. Enid found herself behind Geraint, and it was almost amusing that he thought he was protecting her, when she was guarding his back.

Within a league of the campsite, they left their horses behind and crept through the forest, glad the enemy had left the openness of the cliffs above the sea. For the last hundred yards, they moved from tree to tree, until they could see the flickering of a small campfire and hear the murmur of men's voices. Through the trees, Enid saw the men lounging by their fire, with no guard to watch for intruders. Their clothes were ragged and stained, as if they'd been traveling a long time.

Geraint gestured for half of the men, including Enid, to circle the encampment, while he and the other soldiers confronted the intruders. She obeyed his command, moving until she had a good viewing position on the far side of the campfire. Toland, Tyler, Wilton, and Lovell remained close to her, and she accepted it grudgingly.

Geraint suddenly stood up, along with five of his men, appearing as if from nowhere. The intruders scrambled to reach their weapons, but Geraint and his men swept forward, their own swords raised.

"Please remain still," Geraint said pleasantly, as if he wasn't a large, well-armed, threatening knight.

Five of the six obeyed, so one of the Cornish soldiers hit the sixth man over the head with the hilt of his sword.

When all was quiet, Geraint's smile grew even more relaxed. "And who is your leader?"

That man stood up, arms raised to show he carried no weapon. "Milord Geraint," the man said, bowing.

Geraint frowned, and then his puzzled expression turned to disbelief. "Redley?"

Enid exchanged looks with Lovell, who stared at her wide-eyed.

"Aye, 'tis me, milord," Redley said.

"Were you not stationed with my father's army?"

"We be on 'signment," he said.

Enid saw the way the travelers gave each other frightened looks, and she knew the truth immediately—deserters. Such men, cowards and traitors that they were, usually deserved death.

But Geraint did nothing but frown. "Do not insult me, Redley. The king knows that I am in this part of the country. He would not send you. And certainly he would have sent you better provisioned than this."

"But we were to bring ye a message—"

"I received my father's messenger just a few days ago. You are not he. You have deserted the army."

Several of the prisoners had a restless look about them, as if even now they thought they could escape. But their fate was sealed, Enid knew. Even among the Donella, deserters were not tolerated.

But Geraint continued to stare at Redley. "Do you want to return?" he asked softly.

Enid withheld a gasp. Would all Geraint's talk of negotiating rather than fighting matter even in these circumstances? Was he truly so different than his father?

Chapter 18

• • •

GERAINT looked at Redley, desperation evident in the man's face, and didn't see a deserter, but his childhood friend, the boy with whom he'd fished, chased chickens, and stole tarts from the kitchen. Geraint had to give him a chance.

Redley's mouth sagged open. "Return to Castle Cornwall? But—"

Geraint saw the other deserters looking about them, could see them calculating the odds of getting away from what they thought were only six men. But Redley only looked sad and resigned, as if he'd made a terrible mistake he now regretted.

"My father deals harshly with deserters," Geraint said, "but if you repent, perhaps I could speak—"

And then everything went to hell. Redley's hopeful expression turned to despair as his own men began to fight the soldiers all around him. One of the deserters cried out to Redley and tossed him a sword. For just a moment, Geraint and Redley faced each other across the clearing, but then a soldier attacked Redley, who turned to defend himself.

Geraint fought back earnestly against another man whose face he recognized. Had he trained this one himself years before?

And then he saw Enid, a warrior woman lit by flickering firelight, her hair bright as the flame itself, her sword moving with a speed and precision that didn't seem of this world.

From behind, Geraint was caught around the waist, and the gleaming edge of a sword appeared at his neck.

Another man beside him cried, "If we hold him captive, they'll have to let us go."

They might as well have dug their own graves. Geraint would not allow such a thing to happen. He was about to deal with his captors when something flew through the air before his eyes, striking the two.

It was a dagger, used with such force that it went through one deserter's throat and imbedded itself in the chest of the other. Wide-eyed, they both fell to their deaths.

Geraint looked around to see that his soldiers were already victorious. All six deserters lay dead, Redley included. Geraint stared at his old friend's body, feeling guilt that he knew he shouldn't feel.

Enid appeared at his side. "Had you fought beside this man before?"

"Nay," he said in a low voice, "but we spent our

boyhood together. His mother was a dairymaid at Castle Cornwall."

She hesitated, then put a hand on his arm. "It is a waste."

He turned away. He didn't know what to make of her kindness, not when she'd been so angry with him only hours before.

From behind him, she said, "You claim to be a man who gives thought after battle to what he could have done differently. What are your conclusions?"

He turned to find her studying him gravely, as if he needed to pass some sort of test to determine his worth in her eyes. Shouldn't it be the other way around, after how she'd been able to use him to spy on King Arthur's men? He grimaced and closed his eyes. He was the one who'd pushed for marriage, not her. But perhaps she could have accomplished the same goals without marrying him. He could question himself forever like this. They had both made mistakes.

Somehow he had to let it go.

"Diplomacy did not work with deserters afraid of a death sentence," he told Enid, "but I do not regret the effort. I had to take the chance to save him—them."

She nodded and walked away.

He ordered the bodies to be grouped together and covered with rocks. While his soldiers worked, to his surprise they kept stealing glances at Enid. She was gathering up any useful weapons and supplies, nothing out of the ordinary.

Then he remembered that she'd been battling alongside him. And that thrown dagger—who else had the strength to kill two men with one blow?

Back at the encampment, word of her prowess in battle circled among the men before the sun had even risen the next day.

As Geraint huddled in his cloak against the cold morning dew and broke his fast with dried beef, Ainsley came to him.

"Milord, the men are curious about yer wife. What should I tell 'em?"

Geraint debated letting the captain handle everything, but wouldn't that look as if Geraint couldn't be bothered to offer them some sort of explanation?

Geraint sighed. "Gather them together, Ainsley. I shall speak with them."

Enid was off for a woman's privacy, and it seemed the perfect time to Geraint to look out over the sea of expectant faces and try to explain it all. But . . . what to say?

"Half of you saw my wife in battle last night," he began slowly, "and the other half heard about it. She is of a tribe where some women are trained as warriors. Her skills are as great as those of any man I've trained—"

"Better!" yelled Manning, looking about at his fellow soldiers. "I saw her put a dagger through two enemies! Killed them both with one stroke."

The men murmured, and as Geraint waited for condemnation of her talents, he prepared what he'd say to protect her.

But instead, all the soldiers were intrigued. He heard more than one young man laughingly talk about challenging her when next they trained together.

"That is enough," Geraint said sternly, capturing their attention once again. "Lady Enid is your future queen, not a sparring partner. We will accept her assistance when she gives it, but we will also treat her as a noble-woman whom we are escorting."

At that moment, he saw Enid emerging from behind a jumble of high rocks. She came up short when she saw everyone gathered together, her expression wary. As she approached, the men gave her curious looks, and she glanced at Geraint in confusion.

When she came to his side, he said, "The men were quite impressed with your abilities. I was explaining to them that although you are a trained warrior, you are also their princess."

"I understand."

One soldier called out, "Are you in hiding, my lady? Is this a silence you need of us?"

Geraint watched her but said nothing.

Enid took a deep breath. "Although I am proud of my skills, I do not regularly display them. There are those who would not appreciate how different I am from your women." She hesitated. "But I wish to live in peace with you."

She wished to live in peace with them, Geraint thought darkly, knowing she'd tried to leave them all just last night. She could have started a war. Now she believed that she was the only one who could stop one—as if he wasn't capable of it.

"But I will not ask for your complete silence," she continued. "Mayhap your . . . discretion."

A rumble of laughter and approval swept through the men, and they all dispersed to load up for the day's march.

• • •

TWO days later a scurrier again returned with news—accompanied by a stranger. As Geraint continued to ride toward them, he studied the newcomer even as he fought the wind generated from the sea. The man couldn't be many years out of boyhood, and he wore a simple traveling tunic that bore no indication of where he came from.

Geraint didn't notice Enid's reaction until she reached across and put a hand on his arm. He glanced at her and found her expression full of shock and worry.

"Do you know this man?" he asked.

She nodded. "He is Druce, one of my people."

Geraint frowned, then lifted a hand to halt the column until the two men could approach. He noticed that Druce was watching Enid. The man wore a look of pleasure and expectancy, but no fear. Geraint tried to tell himself to relax, but something just felt . . . wrong.

Enid dismounted and walked forward, and Geraint did the same out of concern for her. What if her tribe considered her a traitor now that she'd married the son of their enemy?

Druce grinned, but prudently looked to the scurrier for a nod of approval before he vaulted to the ground.

To Geraint's shock, Druce embraced Enid, holding her so tight that her toes only brushed the dirt. Apparently not all thought she was a traitor.

"Enid," Druce said with satisfaction and relief when he finally stepped back. He looked her up and down. "You appear well."

Geraint cared little for the informality with which this man addressed his wife. He moved to Enid's side and arched a brow at her. She grinned, wearing a look of relaxation he had not been privileged to see much of lately.

"Allow me to introduce Druce, a member of the Donella tribe. Druce, my husband, Prince Geraint of Cornwall."

Druce's smile was wiped away in an instant, replaced by shock. "When I saw you traveling with these men of Cornwall, I thought—" He broke off, looking to Geraint hesitantly.

Geraint remained silent, allowing Enid to respond. After all, it must be difficult to explain that you've married the enemy.

She gave Geraint a grateful but wary look. "Neither of us anticipated the marriage, Druce, but we felt it would bring us happiness."

She should be a diplomat herself, Geraint thought wryly. She didn't exactly say what either of them felt about the marriage now.

"Why are you here?" she asked.

"I had been ordered to follow the men that your husband fought several days ago. They traveled too near our land, and we knew they had once been members of the Cornish army."

Geraint narrowed his eyes. "And why would Cornish soldiers concern you if there is peace between us?"

"We discovered they were no longer your loyal soldiers," Druce calmly answered. "We needed to discover their motives, to determine if they intended harm. They did not confront us, but I was to continue to watch them." He glanced at Enid and smiled. "And then I saw you, Enid, fighting against those men in all your glory."

With a sigh, she waved away his words as if they meant nothing. Geraint almost put a stop to this reunion, but hesitated, knowing his only motivation would be jealousy. Who was this man to Enid? He was almost afraid to find out.

Just to end the awkward conversation, Geraint said, "Come share our fire and our meal this evening."

He took Enid's arm and led her back toward their horses. The other soldiers were already dismounting and preparing their encampment.

For her ears alone, Geraint said, "Be careful what you say to him, Enid. You cannot reveal our mission."

She stiffened, but didn't pull away.

"If you tell him," he continued, "I will be forced to keep him with us as a prisoner. I cannot risk that he might twist your words and imply to your father that things are worse than they really are."

"He will tell my father that I am married to you. He'll testify that I am here of my own free will. Surely my father will be inclined to wait patiently to talk with you. Is that not enough?"

"But if Druce says I am coming specifically to deal with the Donella, will not your father see that as threatening?"

"Like I do?" Enid pulled her arm away, talking through a false smile for Druce's benefit.

He opened his mouth to protest, but she sighed and raised a hand.

"Forgive me. My behavior is not helping anything."

She left him to renew her conversation with Druce, while Geraint took care of her horse as well as his.

It was difficult not to watch Enid and Druce together. They were so at ease with each other, like friends more than comrades. Geraint felt unsettled.

It didn't help that Druce was a pleasant companion. As if being alone on his mission had stifled him, he did most of the talking that evening, praising the Cornish land, their harbors and fishing vessels. He sat around a fire with Enid, Geraint, Lovell, Fryda, and Ainsley, eating roasted fish. They licked their fingers and listened to him, and Geraint even found himself nearly laughing at Druce's amusing tales of his journey.

Druce glanced at Enid. "Continuing my training is the hardest thing when I'm on a mission alone."

"I remember that dilemma well," she replied. "It sometimes helps to be set upon by ruffians."

Lovell laughed loudly, as if she were joking.

Enid smiled at her squire. "That is what I was doing when I met Sir Geraint."

"Fighting for your life?" Lovell looked embarrassed.

"You have seen her fight," Geraint said dryly. "By God's Teeth, you've experienced it first hand. Think you one thief would be enough to defeat her?"

"No one can defeat her," Lovell said reverently.

Druce grinned. "Enid, is this lad another of your students?"

Geraint's slumbering unease only intensified.

"He is my squire," Enid answered after a moment's hesitation. "We train together."

If Geraint hadn't been studying his wife so closely, he wouldn't have seen the move at all—but in the meager firelight he saw her kick Druce in the ankle, while wearing an expression of innocence.

Druce didn't even act startled. "You have a good teacher, boy."

The sick feeling in Geraint's stomach blossomed into a jealousy he'd never experienced before. This man, this soldier, had lain with Enid before Geraint had. She had "trained" him, taught him the intimate arts that Geraint had shared with her in their marriage bed.

Geraint forced himself to participate as the discussion meandered through various training exercises. But it was difficult when he was fighting self-pity. He told himself that Enid had married *him,* had chosen his life over that of a warrior woman.

But she was already regretting those choices after the revelation of Geraint's mission. Had she changed her mind? Did she wish to return to the Donella now that she had Druce as a traveling companion? Geraint didn't want her to go—had recently convinced her not to—but short of tying her up, he didn't see how he could stop her. And she could probably break the ropes with ease.

Ainsley finally showed Druce to a fire where he could spread his pallet to sleep. Fryda went to the women's pavilion, and Geraint kept expecting Enid to follow. But she waited until it was just the two of them at their fire, awkwardly silent. Off in the distance, they could hear the howl of wolves. Sentries guarded their perimeter, and the quiet of the soldiers' voices as they passed one another sometimes carried on the wind.

And still Enid sat there.

"Do you not have something you wish to ask of me?" she said quietly.

He sighed. "Do you want me to?"

She stared at him with serious intent. "I wish for no more secrets between us, my husband. I told you that."

"Very well." Keeping his voice as neutral as possible, he asked, "Did you train Druce?"

"Aye."

"In everything?"

Without hesitating, she nodded, and his fears were confirmed. It seemed so much worse to meet a man that Enid had lain with, rather than just imagine it. When Druce looked at her, did he remember the beauty of her nakedness? For all Geraint knew, women of the Donella might give themselves to any man, regardless of their married state.

Enid sighed. "He was the first young man to whom I taught the arts of love. I was as nervous as he."

She watched him solemnly, with a shine of tears in her eyes.

"Is this too much for you to bear? Will my past always be between us, as well as our people?"

At least she cared how he felt. On his knees, he moved the short distance around the fire until he sat beside her. "Make me understand, Enid. This is so very foreign to me. How can you look at him and not remember what you were to him?"

"I do not forget that I was his teacher, Geraint," she said, hugging her knees to her chest. "But that's all it was. There was no emotion invested between us. We shared respect, and an eventual friendship, but it is not always that way. During all training, there is a distance that cannot be crossed. I was a mentor to him, not a lover. Even now, when I look at him, I remember our sword-fighting exercises more than the physical intimacy we shared for only one night."

"One night? That is all?"

She nodded. "If you'd like, I could explain how we trained them."

He held up a hand. "Nay. This was enough."

"It is difficult for you with Druce here, I know. But he will be gone tomorrow."

He hesitated. "And you will not leave with him?"

"I have given you my word!" she said, eyes wide. "I will go with you to see my father, and stand between you and him."

"We are civilized people, Enid. It will not come to that."

"Can you promise me that?" she whispered, her eyes again filling.

He cupped her cheek in his hand. "I do not wish there to be a lie between us. All I can promise is that I will do everything in my power to settle peacefully with your tribe. Can you trust me?"

"I hope so."

• • •

IN the morning, as the day dawned beneath gloomy clouds, Enid met alone with Druce for one last time to give him a supply of rations.

Druce nodded his thanks, then hesitated. "Enid, what do you wish me to tell your father? Have you already sent word of your marriage?"

She shook her head. "I had no one to trust with such news. You can be my messenger."

"I would be honored."

"Tell him that I fell in love with the prince of Cornwall and married him, but I have not forgotten my mission. I will come to see him as soon as I'm able. Everything is under control."

•   •   •

A day after Druce left their party, they traveled across the open moor, craggy hilltops etched against the sky in the distance. They passed a standing circle of stones, obviously put there with great care and deliberation. Enid, who'd been plodding along, lost in her thoughts, felt a whisper of magic.

She pulled her horse to a stop and stared at the stones, chipped and weathered and covered in moss. Several had fallen down, but they still formed enough of a circle to be used.

And they'd been used recently.

She looked for Geraint and found him guiding his horse along the line of soldiers, but his gaze was on her. She gestured for him, then dismounted and went to stand near the stone circle, but did not go in.

She felt him at her back.

"Enid?"

"Someone has done magic here recently."

"Can you tell what was done and why?"

He no longer even hesitated at talk of magic, and a small feeling of amusement moved through her.

She forced away thoughts of her husband, took a step into the circle, and closed her eyes to concentrate. It was like stepping beneath an invisible waterfall. She gasped at the sensation of magic all around her, bathing her. It pressed against her skin, crept into her ears and up her nostrils. She batted at the air before her as if the magic were a living thing.

She heard Geraint's voice from far away, but she could not heed it. The magic crawled on her skin like a million skittering bugs. She was swatting at it, scraping it out of her hair, feeling its corrosive evil as a sickness. It would never end—

Until someone grabbed her arm and pulled, and she emerged from the spell of the stone circle. She collapsed to her knees, nauseated, but at least the terrible feeling of invasiveness was gone. Only the hum of power nearby remained, a silent buzzing in the background. If she had not been rescued, she would have lingered there until the spell faded, and that could have been a long time.

"Enid?"

She felt Geraint's hands on her arms. She patted his fingers tiredly.

"Are you well?" he demanded. "Is there yet magic I need to combat?"

He put his arms around her, and she clung to him gratefully.

"I am fine," she whispered. "There was much magic in that circle, and not for good." As her thoughts cleared, she struggled to make sense of the fleeting impressions that had assaulted her mind.

Then she turned and stared up at her husband's face, so close to her own. "They have cloaked themselves so that we did not realize their nearness. They're coming!"

Chapter 19

• • •

TO Enid's relief, Geraint turned to Ainsley, his captain of the guard, and ordered the troops into a defensive position. Thank the gods he believed her.

Only then did he turn back to her and ask, "Can you see who it is?"

She shook her head. "I can only sense their evil intent. They've shielded themselves from our scurriers by using the magic. They are not great practitioners of it themselves, but this circle is ancient, and they used its power."

"Mount your horse, Enid, and stay behind the line. Take your maidservant with you."

She bit her lip but did as he asked, knowing that it was instinctive for him to shield a woman, especially his own wife. He'd only wanted to protect her from the moment he'd met her, and she loved that about him, even though she knew how impractical it was. She could be one of this troop's greatest assets. And she would be, if they needed her.

It was hard to believe that she could love him and still not trust him.

Their enemy was spotted almost immediately to the east by the cloud of dust raised by their galloping horses. The scurriers would have sounded the alarm much earlier, but for the magic used against them. As it was, Enid knew she'd given her husband's soldiers time to prepare. Helmets had been donned, shields and swords at the ready. Fryda found a hiding place behind a tumble of rocks, and Enid reluctantly joined her.

The enemy carried no banner, wore no uniform tunic, just like the mercenaries who'd attacked them twice before. There were more of them this time, and she realized that her husband's twenty-four soldiers were now outnumbered. But with their shields held before them, they kicked their horses into a gallop to meet the charge. The air was filled with the roar of men about to do battle, and she could not sit behind and wait.

To Fryda, she said, "I will be back for you," and began to slide down a tumble of gravel to the ground below, where her horse waited impatiently.

"Milady!" the girl cried. "I fear for you!"

Enid gave her a reassuring wave and mounted her horse. She followed behind her husband, determined to guard his back. Lovell, white-faced and brave, had waited nearby, obviously knowing her well. He rode up beside her.

"You must not fear for me either!" she shouted to him. "Take care of yourself!"

The clash of shields and weapons was almost deafening. Horses went down, pinning some riders, leaving others to fight on their feet. One of the enemy came through the line unscathed, still mounted. When Enid would have taken care of him, Lovell shouted a cry, kicked his horse into a gallop, and met the enemy. She was frightened to death for him, but she had trained him well, and she had to let him grow up.

Sword at the ready, she glanced between Lovell and Geraint, hoping neither of them would have need of her. Her husband fought at his men's sides, inspiring confidence and camaraderie, but the Cornishmen were outnumbered. She saw several of their soldiers lying still on the ground.

More of the enemy broke through the defensive line, and Enid was forced to leave off hovering over Lovell and charge into battle herself. She'd never fought on horseback, but it was what she had started out this whole mission to learn to do.

And with the help of the gifts she'd received along the way, she succeeded. She killed two men without having to dismount, and the second had fought quite skillfully. But the power that infused her arm made her invincible, and she found herself galloping into the melee itself. All around her men and horses screamed. Weapons crashed together. The very air seemed thin with the heat of battle, and men groaned just trying to breathe.

But Enid was in her element, using her every skill to help her husband and his men.

When Geraint called for them to fall back and regroup, she obeyed immediately. Both sides retreated, keeping the ancient standing stones between them. Their renewed power was fading fast, and she no longer heard the hum of energy. The injured and the dead, men and horses alike, lay strewn on the battlefield. She counted quickly, and saw that four of their men were no longer with them. Were they injured, dying, even one of the dead?

The soldiers were well trained, and gathered around their prince to listen to his instructions. Enid remained on the fringes, watching the enemy, who had lost even more men. Now their numbers were more even with the Cornish soldiers.

"My lady!"

She turned to see Lovell, blood running down the side of his head, approach her.

"You are wounded!" she cried, reaching to examine his cut.

He waved her away, and she knew she was behaving more like a mother than the master of a squire.

"We need your help," Lovell said in a quiet voice.

"I would do anything for my husband," she answered.

Lovell shook his head. " 'Tis for one of his men, the youngest but for me."

"Severin?"

"Aye. This trip is his first experience in battle, and when we had sufficient numbers, he felt confident in his prowess. But today . . . my lady, I worry that he will allow his fear to keep him from the next attack—to embarrass him beyond what he can stand. The king would insist that he never be allowed to travel with the prince again. Will you help him as you helped me?"

Enid hesitated only a moment. If her warrior woman abilities could help, she must use them. She followed

Lovell past the soldiers who guzzled water, even while they searched the ground for abandoned weapons to replace the ones that were broken or lost.

They found Severin with his back against one of the standing stones, his knees drawn up, his head cradled in his arms. Blood dripped from several small wounds, and he was breathing far too fast.

Enid went down on her knees. "Severin, can you hear me?"

But he didn't answer. He was shivering so hard that his teeth chattered. When Geraint called them to reform, if Severin was able to respond at all, he might get himself—or others—killed.

She put her hand on his shoulder, and he flinched as if she meant him harm.

"Severin, it will be all right," she whispered.

And with her thoughts alone, she called to her abilities as a warrior woman. Through her hand, confidence surged into Severin, and with a gasp, his head dropped back so that he could gape up at her. Where they touched, the faintest glow emanated, and without the sun, it was far too noticeable.

Guiltily she looked around and saw no one watching—except Geraint.

He had already accepted her magical gifts, and this was a lesser thing: courage when all seemed bleak. She turned away and looked into the grateful eyes of Severin, whose face had grown calm.

"Milady . . . what have you done to me?" he whispered in amazement.

"Only given you the strength to believe in yourself," she replied.

And at that moment, exhaustion swept through her, and she knew that although she'd given aid to one soldier that would last the rest of his life, for this next hour she'd taken away another soldier from the battle—herself.

Geraint watched Enid, feeling resigned rather than angry. He approached the two soldiers and his wife, and to his surprise, she couldn't get to her feet quickly. He took her elbow, and she lifted her grateful gaze to him.

"Enid?"

Earnestly, Lovell said, "My lord, she but helped Severin."

"And why did he need help?"

Lovell's gaze was stark with worry and hesitation.

"I don't need to know," Geraint said, sighing. He looked down at Enid. "This is the trait of warrior women you told me about?"

She nodded and spoke in a husky voice. "It has been a part of me since girlhood."

"I understand."

Even speaking made her seem paler by the moment, and he found his concern growing.

"Does it tire you so much?" he asked in a soft voice.

"I shall be fine in an hour or so," she said. "But I fear until then I might be useless to you."

"Not so invincible in battle right now?" He hoped he didn't sound sarcastic.

She answered seriously. "I know not. If called upon, I could defend myself, Geraint. But I would not trust myself to guard your back."

Ainsley called that all was ready, and Geraint found himself torn. Was his wife truly so defenseless?

"I will stay with her, my lord," Lovell said. "We will hide with Fryda."

Though Enid was a fool for making herself weak, he knew that she was a selfless woman who would do anything to help another.

Even marry the enemy? a dark part of him whispered.

He watched her until she was truly hidden with her maidservant and Lovell, and then he and his men remounted to make another charge.

They faced even less men than he'd surmised, and he realized that many of their enemy were beginning to slip away in the face of defeat. The battle was over almost before it had been renewed.

At last he stood victorious on the battlefield, watching the last six men of the enemy flee, some on foot, others on horse. Several of his soldiers gave chase, and the rest began to deal with the dead and wounded.

Wilton came running to him. "Milord, someone has slit the throat of each of the enemy casualties. There is no one left for us to question."

Geraint stared after the twins, who were racing down the moor in pursuit. "They certainly want to remain a mystery. Or perhaps the person who hired them insists upon it." He turned back to Wilton. "Search the bodies, and not just for weapons."

Geraint went to see to his own casualties, and grimly stared at two dead soldiers. Both of them had served with him for many years. The waste of it all infuriated him, and he longed to have someone to punish.

Enid approached him and stared at the bodies as Ainsley closed their sightless eyes.

"Oh, Geraint," she whispered. "I broke my fast just

this morn with Addis. He was going to be married when we returned home."

Geraint put his arm around her, and he was surprised to find her trembling. Surely only her magical exertions earlier made her seem so frail.

"Milord!"

Both Geraint and Enid turned at the sound of Wilton's voice.

"Milord, we've found Saxon gold on several of 'em."

Enid stared up at Geraint, and he gritted his teeth.

"Now we know who has been hiring the mercenaries for these attacks," he said, then looked directly into her eyes. "These assaults must be a precursor to a Saxon invasion. They could be landing here in the west to surprise the high king on two fronts."

"If the prince of Cornwall and his company are killed," Enid said, "the king of Cornwall will not only be distracted by grief, but will have lost some of his best knights, and might be of little use to King Arthur."

He nodded. "This changes everything, Enid. We can no longer afford to stop in villages just to meet with my father's subjects. We'll send word to King Arthur and my father to prepare for an invasion. On our way to rejoin my father, we will visit your tribe and make sure that the border of Cornwall is secure."

The tension between them rose again, as each remembered their argument.

Solemnly she said, "Trust me when I say that my father is Cornwall's ally against the Saxons. If you treat them fairly, he will do all he can for you. And he'll offer help."

Geraint hoped she was right.

It took him the rest of the morning to oversee burying the corpses of men and horses alike, and to reorganize the troop. One horse pulled a litter for an injured soldier, but they were still short a mount.

"Fryda is the lightest among us," Enid said as she stood beside her horse. "I will take her up behind me."

"Of course, milady," Fryda said, coming to stand beside her mistress.

Lovell, always at Enid's side as if she might yet faint from her ordeal, said, "My lady needs to recover. The maidservant will ride with me."

Geraint realized how much Lovell had matured in Enid's service during the several weeks that Geraint had known him. And he knew it had probably begun when Enid had "helped" Lovell fend off a bully at Camelot. Surely the boy had been the first Cornish recipient of her warrior woman gift.

Fryda's expression was comical as she fought to withhold her protest to Lovell's offer of a ride. Several of the soldiers chuckled, and Geraint was grateful for the moment of levity.

Finally the maidservant stamped her little foot. "Milady, 'tis certain am I that Manning will allow me to ride with him."

Lovell rolled his eyes. "Manning is too old for you."

"And now ye're me brother?" she shot back.

"You must not have had one, and that's the problem."

"Enough," Geraint said, no longer hiding his laughter. "If my lady Enid will consent, she can ride in my arms and sleep. Fryda, for now you can ride alone, but later I'll pair you with Lovell, where obviously your innocence will be safe."

Enid's eyes widened, and in that frozen moment between them, he wondered if she would refuse his offer. They were heading for her tribe, where the fate of their marriage would be decided once and for all.

But she gave a weary nod. "I accept, my husband."

It was difficult for her to find a comfortable position, and there was far too much squirming in Geraint's lap for his own peace of mind, but in the end Enid lay across his thighs facing him, curled against his chest, and fell asleep almost immediately.

• • •

AFTER the previous day's battle and march, Geraint knew that his men needed a day to recover. The tedious journey on horseback gave a man too much time to think about the dead left behind.

They had made camp near a stream, so most took the opportunity to wash garments and lay them out over rocks to dry. At first men dozed in the sun, or played dice games, but eventually some began to spar.

Enid and Fryda spent the morning together, and whenever Geraint's gaze strayed that way, he saw Fryda patiently teaching her mistress the art of embroidery. It was amusing to see the delicate maidservant and the tall warrior woman with their heads together over cloth and thread.

Geraint walked among his men, talking, encouraging, and listening. The sun arched in the sky and began the slow fall on its way to evening.

Manning, the soldier Fryda had befriended, was a mountain of a man, but when he talked about women, he pulled his cap from his head and twisted it between

his fingers. Geraint saw the telltale signs and wondered
what the man would say about Fryda.

"Milord Geraint," Manning finally said, " 'twas gen-
erous of ye to allow yer wife to bless us."

Taken aback, Geraint frowned. "Bless us with her
presence?"

"Nay, bless us with the gift of her magic."

Geraint closed his eyes for a moment, then looked
about for Enid. She was still sitting beside Fryda, but
now two young soldiers were squatting nearby, talking
to her. Geraint couldn't help wondering if his God-
fearing father would think this a pagan ritual to be
condemned—especially coming from a future queen.

Lovell approached Geraint and Manning, gesturing
toward Enid. "She is a popular lady today, my lord."

"So Manning tells me."

Manning's eyes widened, and he hastily left.

"Are they bothering her?" Geraint asked. "Those
men have enough foolhardy courage to start their own
war. They do not need her kind of help. Surely she'll
exhaust herself."

"She knows that, my lord, and she tells them so. But
they just . . . feel better with her simple blessing. Shall I
take her away, so it doesn't look like you disapprove?"

Geraint smiled at the squire. "You become more intelligent every day, Lovell." As Lovell started away,
Geraint caught his shoulder. "And I do not disapprove. I
only worry for my wife."

"Of course, my lord."

Geraint looked at Enid, and his voice became soft as
he said, "I need to protect her, boy, even though she
doesn't need that from me."

"She might not need it, my lord, but mayhap she wants it."

Geraint glanced at him in surprise, but Lovell walked away and went to Enid. Geraint couldn't hear what was said, but he saw Enid smile and get to her feet. When she strapped her scabbard about her waist, Geraint's own smile faded. Training wasn't the way to get Enid away from the soldiers. They'd only be curious enough to—

"Train with us, milady," Wilton called. "Now that we all know yer talents, there be no reason to hide."

Geraint narrowed his eyes, saying nothing.

Enid glanced at him, but to the gathered soldiers she said, "Very well. There seem to be no large rocks to hide my training behind."

"And if there were," Wilton called, "there might be Saxons hiding behind 'em!"

Several of the men banged their swords to their shields menacingly, and everyone displayed grim smiles.

"Let them try to get near us," Toland called. "We 'ave our princess to give us warnin'."

A cheer went up, Enid blushed, and Geraint told himself to relax. How could his father not approve of Enid earning the loyalty of hardened, cynical soldiers? Maybe Geraint could downplay the part about her giving blessings . . .

He moved among the sparring soldiers, answering questions, giving advice. But more and more, men took to watching Enid rather than training. A keg of ale was tapped, and torches were lit to extend the performance as dusk fell.

She was as graceful as a dancer, but lethal; watching

her was like seeing the beauty of a war tapestry come to life. Yet in her eyes burned the intelligence of a warrior, and more than once Lovell found himself on his ass. Soon the boy was so winded he staggered when he tried to stand.

Wilton stepped between the squire and his master. "'Tis enough, Lovell. Ye'll be useless to us if ye hurt yerself. But the lady is hardly winded."

Enid set the point of her sword in the earth. "Oh, nay, I'm finished."

"Nonsense, milady. Among us poor soldiers, there be only one man who can challenge ye—in bed and out."

There was a great roar of laughter as Enid blushed, but when she met his eyes, Geraint felt the usual spark of awareness, of power, between them. He had never imagined raising his sword against a woman, even in practice. But the thought of meeting her strength with his own, straining against her . . . well, it spoke of thing better left to the bedchamber. And perhaps she didn't wish such intimacies now, not when she didn't trust him.

She lifted her chin. "Afraid of a dare, my husband?"

This was met with hoots and cheers, and Geraint felt relieved at her playfulness even as all eyes focused on him. Could this be the beginning of a new start for them?

He boldly looked her up and down, from the tips of her toes to her crown of hair, burnished gold by torchlight.

Then he withdrew his sword from its scabbard and held it high. "I accept your challenge, my wife."

Chapter 20

• • •

ENID watched the challenge in her husband's eyes, saw the way he flourished his sword, and felt a thrill of hunger that spoke more of a bed than a battlefield. In all of her years training young men, she'd never felt like this—eager and thrilled and aware that this man was her equal in every way. Once they could get past the meeting with her father, things would be better. She had not hoped that he would be able to tease her like this, so soon after hearing every detail of her past.

By the gods, she hadn't thought she *wanted* to be teased like this again. But even when she was angry with him, he had a physical power over her that drew her to him. She found herself remembering the waterfall and the rock and the way she'd held him to it. When had the thought of a battle made her think about lovemaking?

Since Geraint had made her his. She lifted her sword

and shield. The shield was still unfamiliar on her arm, but she'd been practicing with it.

The soldiers began to call out wagers, but Geraint held up a hand for their attention. "This is a friendly sparring match, not the subject of gambling. Would you gamble on your princess?"

Money pouches were put away sheepishly, but Enid had to withhold a smile as the men began to whisper, as if she didn't know what was going on.

Then she concentrated on her husband, who began to slowly circle her. She did the same, keeping away from him. The torches cast uneven shadows that flickered in the night as they moved.

"Any rules?" she asked sweetly.

"Just that you don't hurt me," Geraint replied.

The men guffawed as she grinned.

"I shall try not to hurt you—but I know not my own strength."

"I do," he said softly, his voice deeper, rougher.

Though inside she shivered with delight, when he stepped closer, she raised her sword and kept it between them.

"You are trying to distract me," she said.

"Is it working?"

"Nay."

But she wondered if he was distracted in another way. He kept circling her as if looking for an opening, but he never struck at her. Even though he knew of her powers and her skill, perhaps it was not easy for a man to aim a blow at his wife.

She would have to break him of that. She lifted her

sword and slashed at him. He easily parried away the stroke.

She grinned. "Better?"

He cocked his head, but said nothing. He began to advance, swinging cautious blows that she met time and again.

When they stepped away from each other, she shook her head regretfully. "You are not trying very hard."

"Neither are you."

He came at her unexpectedly, swinging low at her legs so that she had to jump over his sword. She used the leverage of his shoulder to vault over him, and were he an enemy, she could have killed him.

Instead she let herself stumble, so that he had time to face her again. In that moment, she knew that although she could defeat him—and he knew it, too—she could not do so in front of his men. They needed a leader, not a man who was bested in battle by his wife.

Distracted, she almost missed Geraint's shield, aimed at her face. She ducked and twisted, and as she fell, she swept his legs out from beneath him.

She delayed her reaction enough so that he was upon her, his sword near her throat.

His teeth gleamed as he grinned. "You're finished."

"I am?"

He hauled her up and tossed her over his shoulder to the cheers of his men. "If you will excuse us, men. What needs to be done next is not for innocent eyes!"

Enid laughed along with his men, even though she wasn't quite sure they should forget all of their problems by making love. But for effect she pounded on his back and kicked at his chest. He slapped her rump playfully, picked up a torch, and began to stride into the darkness.

As the firelight faded behind them, Geraint lay her down on the ground. He propped the torch between rocks before it could start a grass fire. He loomed over her, and suddenly they paused, their hunger rising.

"We shouldn't do this," she whispered. He'd only just met Druce, was still coming to terms with the men she'd known before him. "And the men are so near."

"They won't listen. And I shall be very quiet."

On his hands and knees he crawled over her, and she waited, breathless, uncertain.

There was a sudden rush of air, and something hit Geraint in the head so hard he was flung off her. Before she could even move, it struck her, bringing blinding pain and the sudden darkness of unconsciousness.

• • •

GERAINT came awake to the pounding gait of a horse beneath him. But he wasn't sitting—he was thrown across the saddle, facedown, his legs and arms tied in place. He couldn't move. He could barely breathe because his ribs screamed with pain.

Geraint gasped and tried to lift his head, but the world was upside down to him. It was daylight—how many hours had he been held captive?

As the nausea receded, he twisted his head left and right, and he could make out another horse galloping next to his. There was a person tied to the other horse just as he was, and it took his befuddled mind a moment to realize that those legs belonged to his wife. Was she alive?

The pain brought another wave of sickness that made

lights sparkle behind his closed eyelids. But he still retained enough awareness to know that there was a sharper pain in his thigh. He was wounded.

How badly wounded was his wife? He tried to turn his head to see her again, but then he lost his battle for consciousness.

• • •

WHEN Geraint next awoke, he was lying on the ground, still bound, but mercifully still. Every muscle in his body ached, and taking a deep breath proved impossible for his abused chest and stomach. He panted and forced his eyes to slowly open.

Night had come again; a fire burned in the center of a clearing. Beyond the trees he could see the swell of hills.

Two men were seated on the ground nearby, eating noisily. They were shadows in the night, unrecognizable.

Where was Enid?

Panic and fright warred inside Geraint as he lifted his head. But he saw her not ten feet away, bound as he still was and lying motionless. Her eyes were closed, but she was breathing.

Geraint let his head sag back to the ground in relief.

His movement alerted the men. One threw his bone into the fire and rose to his feet, then walked over to squat down beside Geraint.

"Are ye awake?"

The firelight caught his face, and Geraint recognized him at once: he was Enid's kidnapper, whom she'd said was named Hartun. When Geraint had last seen him, he'd jumped off a cliff into the roaring ocean.

"You lived," Geraint said.

Hartun grinned.

Geraint struggled to sit up, but the ropes held him firmly in place. His right thigh burst into pain and he gritted his teeth, hanging his head to his chest until the dizziness passed. What had happened to him?

The second man, smaller, more timid, came closer. Enid had said he was called Bureig.

Hartun reached to Enid and prodded her legs. "Wake up."

She groaned and rolled onto her back, her hands bound in front of her. Hartun loomed over her, and when her eyes opened, she gave a startled cry.

"Are you all right?" Geraint asked her.

Enid glanced toward him and nodded. "But they have used more of the troll's magic rope, and I cannot move."

Geraint licked his dry lips and looked at the two mercenaries. "Why did you take us?"

"Don't ye want to know how we jumped from a cliff and lived?"

Bureig shuddered.

Hartun gave his partner an impassive glance. "*He* almost didn't. I told 'im to trust me, that the rope would not let us fall."

"You had secured magic rope beneath the cliff to climb down?" Enid asked.

"Aye," Hartun said. "Bureig panicked and would 'ave let himself fall to his death, but I caught him and held on."

"My congratulations," Geraint said dryly, trying to ignore the burning pain in his thigh. "I ask you again: why did you take us? Is this another attempt to retrieve a reward?"

Hartun's face darkened, and Bureig's shoulders hunched.

"Can't go back," Bureig said plaintively.

Hartun spat on the ground. "We don't need 'em."

Geraint lifted his head. "You have no need of Saxon gold?"

Hartun glanced at Bureig slyly. "Told ye he'd figure out who paid them. Ye're smart like me, prince o' Cornwall."

"They will not *have* you back," Enid said shrewdly.

Bureig sighed. "We failed. They said we were deserters, that if they ever caught us again—"

"Shut yer mouth!" Hartun said in a hiss. He trembled with anger, and he looked off to the south. "I got friends in the north. I don't need them that loves Saxons." His burning gaze focused on Geraint. "But I don't forget those who cross me. And now ye'll pay."

Geraint gave him a cool stare.

Hartun suddenly kicked him in the thigh, and the pain made lights dance behind Geraint's closed eyes as he writhed.

"Feel that?"

Panting, Geraint squinted at the kidnapper, who lifted up his club and twirled it in the firelight. The metal spike was coated in blood.

"I didn't wash it yet," Hartun said gleefully. "Wanted ye to see what I done."

Geraint forced a grin. "I'm impressed that you could so skillfully swing a weapon at an unconscious man."

Hartun scowled. "I could do it again."

"So what *do* you mean to do with us?" Enid interrupted.

Hartun slowly turned to look at her. "How do ye know I don't mean to kill ye?"

"Because you would have done it already," she said, "rather than go to the effort of dragging us across country. It must have been difficult to keep us hidden."

"And to outwit my men," Geraint added.

"They think ye're dead," Bureig said apologetically.

Hartun straightened with importance and started to pace back and forth in front of them.

"There are no bodies, so why would they assume that?" Enid asked as calmly as if they debated military strategy safe in the great hall at Castle Cornwall.

Geraint could only hope delaying the kidnappers gave Enid and him more options for escape.

"I left a lot of yer man's blood," Hartun said, twirling his club again.

"And some chewed bones," Bureig offered helpfully. "I saved them special."

"But they only saw the bones after they followed the trail of blood left as if ye'd been dragged away." Hartun arched a brow at both of them, obviously waiting for praise.

Geraint clenched his jaw, but Enid said, "Nicely done. Since you have gone to all this trouble to only make it appear that we're dead, might we bandage my husband's wound so that he will not bleed to death?"

"That don't matter," Hartun said. "Ye'll be dead soon anyway." He stood over Enid. "Think ye that little pit I threw ye in was bad? Wait until ye see the big pit— and the troll whot lives in it."

Chapter 21

• • •

AFTER hours of lying vulnerable on a horse, going higher into the hills, her ribs bruised with every pounding hoofbeat, Enid must have finally slept. When she awoke, shivering with the cold, the sun hid before dawn, but the sky was gray with the promise of daylight. Beneath her, the horse trembled with exhaustion, and she pitied the poor animal who'd been pushed past his limit.

Hartun dragged her off the horse, dropping her onto the ground. She rolled over and groaned. Glancing at Geraint as he landed on his back beside her, she saw his wince of pain. His thigh was wet with a continuing ooze of blood. How much longer could he go on?

She was counting on her strength with the troll—if she could be released from the rope. But what about Geraint? What if she couldn't protect him? She didn't

yet know if their marriage could survive the schism between their peoples. But she wanted to try—she knew
he wanted to try. Had she finally relearned to trust him,
here where they might yet die?

It would be so easy to panic, to let her love and worry
for him reduce her to helpless tears. But she refused to
give up. Surely they'd be able to save themselves.

All around them dark woods cut into the mountain-
side. Frost etched the ground. Though there should be
birdsong this early in the morning, it was as if the whole
world hushed in fear of the troll.

Hartun pointed behind them, and they twisted their
heads to see a dark slash in the ground.

"He's waitin' in there," Hartun said cheerfully.

Bureig remained behind him, peering out.

"He just sits in a hole?" Geraint asked with doubt.

Enid heard the exhaustion in his voice.

"The hole is just the beginnin' of his caves," Bureig
said softly, as if telling a fairy tale. "They go on forever,
and he has magic that makes ye get lost instead of
findin' him."

Enid exchanged a significant glance with her husband. This was a good development. If there was a series of caves, then there had to be another way out.

"Does that mean you will untie us?" Geraint asked.

"Not until ye're inside," Hartun said. "I'm offerin'
the troll a hunt, ye see. And what fun would it be if he
couldn't chase ye?"

"I bet he'd prefer his magic rope," Geraint said.

Hartun grinned. "He'll get pieces of it back." He
looked at his partner. "Help me roll 'em in."

Enid did not trust that they would be freed. She tried

to catch her foot on a root or something—but there was nothing. Once again she was dropped into a pit, and this time the fall was several yards farther. When she hit the ground, soft dirt gave way beneath her. Her husband landed next to her with a groan and didn't move for a moment.

"Geraint?" she cried frantically.

"It be no fun if he's dead," Hartun called.

Geraint groaned again and opened his eyes. "I'm not dead. So what about the hunt? You promised to free us."

A dagger fell and bounced between them.

"Hope ye can reach it," Bureig said. "This will help, too."

Several torches rained down on them.

"Bureig!" Hartun cried. "Ye wasted our light on them."

"But I thought it was a hunt! How else would they see to get away?"

Enid barely listened to them bicker. She concentrated on squirming in the right position to grab the dagger. When she finally had it, she was able to turn it inward between her wrists and cut the rope. The blood rushed back into her hands and her flesh felt pierced with needles. But once again, the magic in the rope died. After she was unbound, she sliced through Geraint's bonds. He stretched his hands, moved his feet, and when he tried to stand up, his right leg almost buckled beneath him. She caught him.

"Ooh, ye won't be much of a match for a troll," Hartun said with feigned sympathy. "Now don't ye be gettin' any ideas about coming back out this way. We'll wait here a long time to make sure. And to hear any screams, o' course."

Enid ignored him to look about the cave. It led into a small, too-short room with walls damp and mossy. Bones lay scattered about, as if more than one animal, or human, had fallen in. On one side, where the gloom seemed to thicken, she could just make out the opening of a tunnel.

"Enchantress, do you have a plan?" Geraint asked, leaning against a wall and rubbing his leg again.

She gave a thin smile. "To avoid the troll, of course, which may be difficult if he can change our perception of the caves. Or do we find him, and bargain for our escape?"

"We have little to bargain with except some cut pieces of an unenchanted rope."

"I have no magic to summon that would help us. If we got close to him, I could cloak myself in shadows, but that would not protect you. Perhaps you should wait here."

"I will not allow you to go in there alone," he said with conviction.

A handful of rocks pelted down on them from above. Hartun stood at the edge, leaning over them. "Go on with ye!"

"Someone is getting impatient." Wearing a white grin in his dirty face, Geraint produced flint and steel from the pouch at his waist and lit a torch. He limped farther into the cave, bent over because of the low ceiling.

The closer they got to the enclosed tunnel, the more she felt uneasy. The very floor under her feet seemed to prickle her awareness.

"Magic," she whispered.

Geraint stared at her. "You have thought of a way to use it?"

"I sense it, very far away. Bureig said the troll had

enough magic to keep someone from finding him, but maybe it will help us avoid him."

He held the torch ahead of him into the tunnel. Nothing but blackness as far as they could see.

"So you shall sense when he comes closer?" he asked.

"Aye, I believe so. I did when we dealt with the wizard."

He smiled and handed her the dagger. "With such talents, you shall have to go first."

"Wait." She lifted up her jerkin at her thighs to reach her shirt.

"Much as I appreciate the view—" he began.

She rolled her eyes at him. With the dagger, she cut several long strips from the hem of her shirt. "Sit down and I shall try to stop the flow of blood."

The wound in his thigh was a puncture several fingers wide from the spiked club. The bone did not seem to be damaged. But there was an angry red stain all around it that alarmed her. She said nothing, because certainly his eyes told him the same thing. She cinched the bandage as tightly as she dared.

He met her gaze. "Ready?"

She leaned in and kissed him. For a moment, she let the warmth of his lips soothe her.

"Now I'm ready," she whispered.

He cupped her face with one hand, his smile tender. She thought of his life's blood leaving him, weakening him every moment he walked. They had to escape quickly.

As the leader, Enid carried the torch in one hand and the large dagger in the other. Geraint followed behind

with the unused torches. She could only see the ground
for a short distance before her. All was darkness beyond
the limited range of the torch. Cobwebs hung from the
low ceiling and clung to her hair. She did her best to
singe them with the torch wherever possible. But she
couldn't afford to take her time; after all, how long
could these torches last?

Rats skittered by her occasionally, but since she
sensed no magic as they approached, she ignored them.
When Geraint gave a disgusted sound, she looked over
her shoulder at him.

He grimaced. "It ran over my foot. I hate rats."

Biting her lip to keep from smiling, she turned away
and continued to walk, bent over. They came to a fork in
the tunnel, and she hesitated only briefly before going
to the left. In the right tunnel, the troll's magic called to
her, dark and small and nasty.

She had no idea how much time passed. She kept
taking turns away from the troll, but he always seemed
to be ahead of her. Their torch sputtered, and they got a
new one lit before the first went out. Gradually, the tunnel began to slope upward, which seemed to indicate
they were going higher up, deeper into the hills, which
couldn't be good.

She turned a corner, and suddenly the low ceiling was
gone, and the walls of the tunnel widened out. She could
hear the sound of running water, as if an underground
river flowed somewhere nearby. She straightened in relief and Geraint came up beside her. She didn't like the
way he was perspiring—it was not that hot.

"Is he here?" Though he spoke softly, his voice
echoed into the distance.

"Nay, he has come no closer, but we have not left him behind. I wonder how large this room is?"

"And where the other side is."

They started walking to the left, staying near the wall. When they came to the edge of the river, they saw that it tumbled down rocks above them in a waterfall, but they couldn't see where it entered the cave above them. They couldn't cross it either, for it was wide and swift, with an unknown depth. They followed the river bank itself, and within an hour ended up on the far side of the cave, where the water disappeared beneath the low lip of a tunnel, leaving little room for even a boat to pass beneath. The wall took them back to where they had first entered the room. There were no other tunnels.

Geraint leaned against the wall, breathing unevenly. "Do we attempt to ford the river?"

"And mayhap die in the attempt." She shook her head. "Though it is what he wants us to do, I sense him not that way."

"And now we're looking for him?"

"What choice do we have?" she asked. "Avoiding him is taking us deeper into the hills."

"So I noticed."

"And our torches will only last so long. I say we look for him and face him."

"Says my fierce warrior."

She shrugged. "I do not want to fight. After all, he knows the way out." She looked in the direction of the waterfall, which was hidden in darkness. "He is up."

"Up?"

"We climb the river bank where it first enters the

cave." With concern she touched his cheek and found it warm to the touch.

He pulled away from her. "Next to the waterfall?"

"It is only a small waterfall." She hesitated and lowered her voice. "Will such a climb be too much for you?"

"I am not at my best, but until I slow you down, I will follow you, my sweet."

Her chest tightened with worry, but all she did was smile. "You like the view from behind."

His laugh was tired, but he pushed himself away from the wall. "Lead on."

They returned to the head of the river, and she stared upward as the boulders disappeared into the darkness. If they accidentally fell in, they would be swept to the far side of the cave, where the ceiling met the river. They had to be very careful.

"It will be difficult to keep the torch dry," he said, coming to stand beside her. "And what if the troll waits above for us? We will be vulnerable on these rocks, unable to help each other."

"He is not near, not yet. I sense the flexing of his magic. He knows of us, and perhaps thinks he can defeat us. We will plant a little doubt."

"And doubt could make him even more dangerous."

"Mayhap," she said. "But for now, our only advantage is foreknowledge. We have to press forward quickly. I will climb first, and try to lead the easiest path for your leg."

"You worry too much, Enid."

She bit her lip but said nothing.

"Yet it gives me comfort," he murmured.

She watched him adjust the torches in his grip, trying to keep one arm free to aid his climb.

"Geraint, let me carry them."

"Nay, you need to wield a weapon and a torch. I will manage."

But as she began the climb up the rock-strewn incline, the dagger belted at her waist, she noticed how slowly he moved behind her, how much the torches—and his wound—impeded his progress. Whenever she found easy purchase, she held the torch behind her, trying to light his way until he could move nearer. Soon she could no longer see the ground behind them, and lost track of the time they climbed. Her world narrowed to the circle of misting torchlight, the roar of the falling water, the wet, slippery rocks stretching higher above her—and Geraint, struggling behind her.

She heard the crash of a torch and whirled around to see him leaning out into the darkness.

He cursed, but called out, "It is not far. I can reach it."

"If it's only the one, then leave it."

"Nay, we have need of every one."

"Shall I climb back down to you?"

"Just hold the torch toward me."

All was darkness where he reached down beneath the rock he stood on. She saw his legs tremble, and worried that in his weakness, he would fall headfirst. She climbed back down several boulders, but then he dragged the wayward torch into view.

He gave her a satisfied smile. "I have it."

"And the rest?"

"They spilled at my feet. Go forth, Enid, I yet follow."

For endless minutes she continued to climb, holding

the torch away from the mist caused by the falling water. The flame sputtered several times, and she prayed it would stay lit, for with such precarious footing, how would she find the flint and steel in the pouch at her waist to relight it?

She looked over her shoulder, but didn't see her husband. "Geraint?"

There was no answer. In a panic, she slid back down between two boulders, pinching her finger painfully, and banging the other elbow. Gradually, the light reached Geraint's upturned face. He was sitting, the torches between his feet, panting for every breath.

When she reached his side, he waved her away. "Go," he whispered. "I just need a moment's rest. I will catch up."

"You won't. Geraint, you are wounded, and the injury saps your strength. Even now I fear the poison of an infection."

"I have had much worse than this," he said, his voice a brave scoff.

"And been treated immediately, instead of wandering through the dank caves of a troll. I will carry the torches."

"Enid—"

"I am the one gifted with strength, my husband. Use the girdle at my waist and strap them to my back."

It didn't take much to convince him, which only increased Enid's fear for him. Together, they managed to secure the extra torches against her back. When she rose easily to her feet, only then did his skepticism fade.

"I hope we don't have to return by this route," he said, standing up. He swayed for only a second before controlling himself.

Enid tried not to let her increasing worry show. "The troll will show us a better way."

"How helpful of him."

Free of the torches, with the dagger at his waist instead of hers, Geraint was able to keep up with her, though she knew the strain on him was severe. Wet moss grew between the boulders and sucked at their feet. Several times she reached back to help him over a difficult passage, and he accepted her aid without complaint. How much longer could he go on? Would she yet have to carry him—or leave him?

In her hurry to reach the top, a boulder came loose beneath her grasp, falling away behind her, each crash echoing upon the next. She screamed Geraint's name. She had to drop the torch to keep from falling herself. The flame went out, and she clung to the path in utter blackness.

"I'm here!" he called out immediately.

It was difficult to hear him over the thundering water.

She almost sobbed her relief. "The rock did not strike you?"

"Nay, but the torch almost did. It was good of you to scream a warning."

She tried not to let a hysterical giggle escape her. Scream a warning? She was only hoping her clumsiness had not killed him.

"I caught the torch as the light died," he shouted. "Shall I relight it for you?"

"You caught the torch?" she said in disbelief. "Thank the gods. Do you need my flint and steel?"

"I can reach mine."

She waited in the dark, grateful for the rest. Below

her, she could see the sparks Geraint struck, but not an answering flame.

"I think this torch is spent," he called. "Wait there and I will come up to help you find the next one. I am not far behind."

He wasn't, but his journey was agonizingly slow. If only she could see him. More than once she almost insisted that she would come to him, but she knew that his pride still ruled him. At last, she heard him scrabble for purchase just below her. Finding his hand in the dark, she hauled him up beside her. He knelt at her feet for several minutes, breathing heavily.

"I'm sitting in a stream of water," she said. "We should ease our thirst."

She heard him grunt, and realized he was attempting an exhausted laugh.

"First I need another torch to light," he said.

When she gave him her back, he pulled a torch free. In only minutes, his spark found its home, and a warm flame burst to life. She gratefully saw his tired, pale face, and he looked beautiful to her.

He smiled. "You need not stare so hard, my wife. I am not a ghost."

"You are pale enough for one."

"From hunger, of course. Is that not your stomach I hear rumbling?"

"You can hear that in this loud place?" She leaned into him, resting her head on his shoulder. He was warm and strong and alive—she would keep him that way. "Drink first, my love," she said. "I sense the troll has begun to move."

"He knows we're here?"

She shrugged. "Mayhap he senses that we have not been tricked by his magic. But he must be curious by now. Drink, and let us go."

The water was brackish, but cold and refreshing. She wanted to examine his bandage, but he was impatient to press on. He must be bleeding and wanted to hide it from her. When they were in the next tunnel, she would rebind him.

He had to last that long.

She continued to climb, ignoring the protest of her strained muscles. They would continue to do her bidding on the strength of will and magic. Would she be able to carry Geraint, if it came to that?

Finally, she sensed something different, an openness above her, rather than an endless tumble of rocks. She held her torch high, continuing to climb with one hand, and at last the boulders subsided before her. She crawled onto flat ground. The river ran fast at her side, heading for its fall into the cave below.

"We're at the top!" she called, then fell to her stomach to reach for Geraint.

When he grasped her hand, she was able to pull him the rest of the way. He collapsed onto his back at her side, his chest heaving from the exertion. She held the torch near his wound and saw the wet stain of blood.

"We're not going anywhere until I rebind that," she said sternly.

Without a protest, he murmured, "Aye, my captain."

As she stripped off the sodden bandage, she tried not to think of his life's blood ebbing away, of losing him. She had to concentrate, for she sensed that she might have to save them both.

"Is he near?" Geraint asked, when they'd begun to walk through the next tunnel.

"Not yet. But there's a definite change in the feel of him, a gathering of strength—of magic."

They walked on, the river moving past them almost silently now. Several times they passed small caves that led nowhere, though often heaps of bones were piled inside.

"We've made a wrong turn," he said, as they stopped for a drink of water.

She scooped water to her mouth, then frowned up at him. "We have not veered from this one tunnel."

"But we've been here before."

She rose to her feet and studied him, but he did not seem feverish. "Perhaps the troll's magic is working on you, Geraint," she said. "Trust me—we have not walked this way before. See, the river is ever on our right, and we have not left it."

He stared at her, obviously baffled, then slowly shook his head. "You must be right, of course. But I feel so *certain*."

She looked ahead of them, to where the tunnel dwindled into blackness. "We're nearer now—the troll may be feeling desperate. I do not think he's in the same place anymore."

"Then let us hurry."

But each time they passed a cave, they felt they had to search it, which slowed them down. There might be food or weapons to aid them in their quest.

In the fifth small alcove, Enid led with her torch—and they saw a flash of bloodred eyes and heard the hiss of an animal's scream.

Chapter 22

• • •

AT the sound of the screech, Geraint reacted instinctively—he pulled Enid back toward him and caught the torch from her hand. He thrust the flame forward again, and now that he wasn't blinded, he could see what it was—a bat, impossibly large, the size of a dog. It hissed and fluttered its wings at them, but it didn't want to leave what it had found.

What it was eating.

"Geraint," she cried, gripping his arm from behind, "'tis been bewitched, changed for an evil purpose."

"Or for good. Mayhap to defeat a troll."

But the bat's purpose did not matter in their defense against it. Only the flame of the torch held it back—thank God they had just lit a new one. Geraint thrust it into the cave, and the bat screamed again. This time he noticed that the ceiling was too low for the bat to take flight. It stood over its meal, wings flapping, but with nowhere to go. When it came at them, Enid moved from Geraint's side, the dagger in her hand.

He wanted to protect her, to defeat the monster himself, but he felt his own weakness, knew of her strength. He was fast losing all ability to help her. Soon he would insist she leave him behind. But he wasn't finished yet. He made himself hold the torch high rather than try to stop her.

The bat hissed again, its fangs dripping with what must be blood. Enid, full of endless courage, advanced on it, and soon it had nowhere to retreat and could only attack. He wanted to shout a warning, but his wife was too well trained not to know what to do. She stepped over the legs of the victim, and the outraged bat launched itself at her. With one slash of the dagger, she cut it in two in midair. It fell in a wet heap to the earthen floor.

Geraint sagged back against the rough wall in relief, then peered down the tunnel both ways before advancing into the small alcove. Enid stood looking down at the bat.

Wearing a look of distaste, she said, "I wonder why the troll permitted such a creature to roam his caves."

He kicked the creature's body aside. "Mayhap it helped more than hindered him. He could have used it in his quest for food. It was feeding on something here."

He held the torch high and saw the body of a lone man, still recognizable as such, though the bat had already eaten into one of his legs.

She grimaced. "He has not been dead long."

"And he did find his way here, closer to the troll,

without succumbing to the deceptive magic. I wonder if he had magic of his own?"

She closed her eyes, and he watched the intensity sweep her face. Had a man ever had a better partner, in battle or in bed?

"I know not what it is," she murmured, "but there is something . . ." She studied the body again. "Bring the light closer."

Together they looked down silently at the dead man, clothed in brigandine and tunic, a shield and sword now useless in the dirt at his side. They found no bag of supplies.

"Look at his boots," she suddenly said.

He held the torch directly over them. They were not made of leather—but what were they made of?

"Do you see the way the light plays on the material—see the patterns and shapes?" she said, her voice rising with excitement.

"Shh," he whispered.

She sent him an apologetic look. "Geraint, I had heard that these were lost to man. Now we know why."

"You have heard of his boots?"

"They are the famed Wind Walkers. They make the wearer feel magically light, able to stride great distances in the blink of an eye. They could help us."

"Maybe that's why the bat was gnawing at his leg. Could his master have wanted the boots?"

"If we're lucky. But now we have them to bargain with. I'll take them off his feet."

He bent over to help her, but the cave began to swirl about him, and he straightened quickly. He hated the weakness of his trembling legs, and the way his wound now burned constantly.

"I can do it," she said, giving him another of her worried looks.

But removing the boots from their wearer proved more difficult, as if they didn't want to leave their owner. Enid tugged hard, and finally she had them in her hands.

She looked at them with awe. "They feel like nothing I have ever touched before."

He ran his hand down them, and the material was slick and yet so very smooth. "Let us try them."

"Do you think 'tis safe within the caves?" she asked doubtfully. "Moving impossibly fast might make us run into walls."

"That's not what killed the last owner. And besides, if your worries were true, wouldn't a person run into trees and hills outside? Perhaps the magic of the boots guides the wearer. I'll put them on."

But when he would have taken them from her, she stayed his hand.

"Geraint, nay. What if you use them and travel so far from me that I can no longer help you?"

"I will return," he said stubbornly.

She pointedly looked at his leg. "What if you cannot? I should wear the boots, just in case. I will hold your hand, and the magic should work for us both."

Though he wanted to continue to protest, he knew her logic was sound. Putting his arms around her, he held her to him, feeling the softness of her hair against his cheek.

"I so worry for you," he whispered. "You have had to take on so much. And all because of me."

She squeezed him once, then let him go. "Not just you. And I would do it all again."

Their gazes met and held, and a feeling of peace burrowed into his soul. Together they would survive. She bent over and slid on the boots. When she straightened, he stared into her face.

"How do they feel?" he asked.

"Like they were made to be worn by me."

She spoke with a reverence that made him uneasy. But she seemed herself when she reached for his hand, holding the torch aloft with the other.

"Hold tight, Geraint. I'll take but one step."

He used one hand to grip her, the other to hold her discarded boots. But when she placed one foot forward, she was wrenched powerfully away from him and he was alone in the dark.

"Enid?" He didn't shout for fear of drawing the troll's attention. What if she couldn't get back? Perhaps the boots had taken her out of the hill itself. Or back to their owner.

But suddenly the light of the torch blinded him, and she was there, grinning. His relief was so great that he felt weak with it. Or maybe the weakness just never left him anymore.

"Forgive me, Geraint, but I could not hold on to you. The power that took me from you was too great."

"Then you should remove the boots."

"Nay, they performed just as I thought. With but one step, I was all the way at the end of the river tunnel, and not far from the troll himself. His magic is powerful in its own right."

"But if I cannot hold your hand—"

"You'll ride on my back. After all, my garments came with me, as did the torch. But we must hurry, for surely the troll knows we are close."

She presented her back, and he eyed it skeptically. He still could not shake the feeling that he would harm a woman with his weight. But Enid was no ordinary woman. He took the torches from her back and tied them to his own.

"I cannot hold on to you," she said, "because I need my hands free for defense. You'll have to grip me hard, but it will not hurt me."

Shaking his head, he picked up the dead man's sword, tucked it into his own girdle, then gingerly put his arms around her neck. Though broad for a woman, her shoulders felt suddenly very fragile. "Enid, when I lift my legs, just go."

He braced himself, and with a jump that shot pain through his leg, he gripped her hips with his thighs.

In an instant the world spun, and she was his only anchor. The light of the torch seemed to stream behind them in this sped-up reality. But only a moment later they were still, and he slid his legs to the ground. He found himself holding on to her for too long, and he forced himself to step away.

"Do you see where we are?" she asked, excitement laced through her voice. "Closer to the source of the river." She pointed back the way they'd come. "Who knows how long the tunnel is? The river is narrower, shallower here, too, as if many streams later join it on its way to the waterfall cave."

"Perhaps we should worry about the troll," he said

dryly, though he could not help but be amused at her childish wonder.

"Of course," she said, smiling at him.

"Should we risk another step, or is he nearby?"

"Nearby," said a darker, hoarse voice.

It could only be the troll, still hidden within the shadows of the cave. Geraint wanted to pull Enid back to his side, but couldn't risk her traveling away from him while she wore the boots. But she stiffened and tilted her head, as if she could sense where the troll was.

A slow, shuffling sound echoed strangely beside the soft murmuring of the river.

"Come no closer," Geraint said, coming to stand beside his wife.

She glanced at him and whispered, "If only I'd had time to take these off."

The troll's voice interrupted them. "They are pretty, your boots." He was just on the edge of the torchlight, a squat, shadowy figure with gleaming eyes.

Without removing her boots, Geraint knew that Enid could not fight properly. Even though he brandished the dead man's sword, he was far too weak to protect them both.

"I sense my rope," the troll said ominously.

"I was bound with it," Enid said. "I will gladly give it back—in exchange for you showing us the way to leave your realm. But I will be honest; the magic vanished."

"I could coerce it to return."

"The men who stole it from you wait outside the hole in the ground that leads into your caves," Geraint said.

The troll hissed. "I thank you for the information."

He shuffled a little closer, and by the light Geraint could see his squat, hunchbacked body. His height would barely reach a man's chest, but his hairy arms looked powerful enough. The hair on his head was long, and a straggly beard masked much. But the lively eyes in his wrinkled face kept darting between both of them—and the boots.

"You defeated the magic of my caves," the troll said reprovingly.

"I have magic of my own," Enid answered.

"Is it to be a duel between us?"

Not while she's wearing those boots, Geraint thought.

"It does not have to be," she said.

"What if I keep the boots and let you go free?"

Geraint frowned. "Why would you do that? Surely we are another meal to you."

The troll made a hissing sound, and his shoulders shook. Geraint thought he must be laughing.

"Meals are easy to come by," the troll said. "Humans are so gullible. But those boots are rare. They could help me. A troll bride wants gold, and with those boots . . ."

"So you're luring a mate," Geraint said. He wanted to keep the troll talking, but his mind felt fuzzy.

" 'Tis lonely here. You would not deny me a bride, would you?" he asked plaintively. "I have one in mind, and she is so very lovely."

Geraint wondered just what a troll would consider "lovely." "We are far from our land. If we give you the boots, how will we get home?"

"Is your land southwest of here?"

"Aye."

"Then let the river take you home. It travels under the hills, and will be safe from intruders."

"But not other trolls," Geraint said.

"You will be traveling through my land, and the land of my future bride. No one will harm you. You will be riding my raft, and it is far too clever to sink. But I need the boots."

Enid glanced at Geraint, then back at the troll. "It is a fair trade. I will remove the boots, but will not give them to you until we have seen the raft."

"And we'll need provisions," Geraint added.

"I have nothing suitable for humans but the water on which you'll ride. Although the meat of a particularly fat cleric might be tender enough to tempt you," the troll added slyly. "I've been saving it for a special occasion."

Geraint saw Enid's face blanch before she said, "Nay, but I thank you for the offer. Stand back while I remove the boots."

The troll obediently shuffled away, out of the light, and Geraint felt that not seeing him was worse. But he took the torch from Enid and stood guard over her as she sat to remove the boots. Even the weight of the torch made Geraint's arm ache, and he barely controlled the trembling. They had to get away from the troll quickly, before the creature realized it might only have to worry about battling Enid. Geraint had never felt so desperate, so useless.

He looked down and saw his wife caressing the boots. "Enid?"

"But they're so pretty," she whispered.

The sound of the shuffling troll made Geraint glance up, but the creature remained outside the circle of torchlight.

"Enid, remove the boots," he said.

He leaned down to tilt her head up. She looked dazed, her eyes glimmering in the flame.

The troll gave his wheezing laugh. "Magic things don't like to leave their wearer. It would be a shame to have to kill her for them."

"Enid, remove them," he said in a more forceful voice.

She licked her lips and nodded. She tugged hard for several moments, and finally the first came off. Holding it at her side, she struggled with the second boot. When they were both off, and Geraint had passed her her own boots, he began to feel better.

Enid rose to her feet, giving him an embarrassed look. She carried the boots in one hand, while the other rested on the hilt of the dagger. "Show us to the raft," she said to the troll.

"Strength enough to conquer the lure of magic," the troll said. "I am impressed."

Geraint stepped toward the troll in time to see it bow its head mockingly and retreat a step. The troll surely must want to keep his raft. Would he try something in the end?

They walked for several hundred paces, always following the river. When they reached a merging stream, the troll turned up it, into a deeper cave. Nowhere on this little journey did Geraint see evidence of torches; the troll must be able to see in the dark. If their torch went out, it would give the troll an advantage.

The cave narrowed along with the stream, and the

troll stopped. Enid held out the torch and they both see a raft made of logs roped together.

"This looks sturdy enough," Geraint said, "but it will not survive the waterfall."

The troll nodded. "On the far side of the river, just before the waterfall, the river separates. A small branch moves through a series of caves and rejoins the main river at a later point. I ride this river to visit my future bride. It can be done."

"But we are taking away your raft," Enid said.

"But I'll have the boots now," the troll said, his dark teeth showing in a grin. "I'll prove my faithfulness by telling you that you must continue on this river until the second appearance of the sky. If you go farther, the raft will be capsize on another waterfall. Leave it on the riverbank and continue south on foot, where you will shortly come to a river. Here it is narrow and there is a bridge. Your land must lie somewhere beyond that, because you are not of the hills." He held out a grimy hand. "Now, the boots."

Geraint leaned down and untied the raft. "Not until we're aboard."

"But you'll take them from me," the troll said, with the beginnings of a whine in his voice.

"On our honor, we will not." Enid tossed one boot at his feet. "This is to show our faithfulness. They are useless to us both right now."

She stepped onto the raft, and it swayed beneath her. When she was sitting, holding the guiding pole across her lap, Geraint gingerly tested the raft with his own weight. Though again it rocked, it seemed sound enough.

He said, "Do not attempt to follow us, troll. As you

know, we can sense your magic. And my lady is capable of destroying you—without any magic at all."

The troll bowed to her. "The boot," he repeated, a little more urgently now.

Geraint pushed off from the riverbank and knelt down in the middle of the raft. Enid tossed the second boot to the troll, and as the stream took a curve to join the main river, their last glimpse of the troll showed him petting the boots, holding them to his chest.

"I think he won't risk following us," she said.

He handed her the torch, took the pole from her, and used it to keep them in the center of the river. "I hope not. And I hope he gave us the correct instructions. Now listen for the waterfall and watch for where the river separates."

They traveled for what seemed like hours, and Geraint knew that the boots had saved them considerable time in their journey. He kept waiting to see the troll appear suddenly beside them, but it didn't happen. He was tense and alert, and able to keep his mind off the throbbing pain that seemed to be spreading from his right thigh up into his hip.

At last they could hear the slowly building roar of the waterfall. Because of the small circle of torchlight, the branching stream appeared so suddenly at their side that he was forced to pole hard to push them into its current. Even then, the force of the main river threatened to re-capture them, but at last they slid within a new tunnel and began a slow descent that circled deeper into the hill. He wiped sweat from his eyes and kept the pole ever ready to adjust their position.

"Let me take a turn," Enid insisted.

He didn't refuse her. He gratefully sat down on the rough, flattened logs and wished he could close his eyes to sleep. But he didn't dare, not until they were well away from the troll.

The narrow cave gradually opened up, and the little stream again rejoined the main river. Their raft spun several times from the force of the strong current, but Enid used the pole with an efficiency that soon had them facing forward again. The rumbling waterfall faded away behind them, and as Geraint's mind drifted, he hoped that the rest of the trip could be uneventful. He thought of his own men, wondering how they fared with his absence. Had they gone to his father? Did an army even now gather to meet the Saxons?

"Geraint," Enid suddenly cried, "when we explored this cave, we saw the river flow into the next tunnel right beneath the wall. I think we'll be capsized!"

Chapter 23

. . .

ENID stared into the face of her husband, pale and dirty by torchlight. His eyes looked red-rimmed. His skin shone with perspiration even though the air within the mountain was cool. He turned his head to look down river, as if he could see the treacherous end of the cave beyond the torchlight.

"The troll lied," he said flatly.

"Perhaps the raft can slide beneath, if we lie down."

"And what about the torch? If only we had thought to ask him for oilskin to wrap them in."

"My jerkin is leather. It will have to do. Hold on to the pole."

She quickly pulled the garment over her head, leaving her in just a long shirt, now ragged at her thighs from where she'd torn it for bandages. Between them, they exchanged the pole and the jerkin.

As he kept glancing forward, he propped the lit torch between his thighs and, leaning sideways, wrapped the unused torches in her garment.

"Enid, throw yourself flat at the last moment. Hold on to the pole and the raft. I'll keep the torches."

"Perhaps I should—"

"I am still capable enough," he said gruffly.

With no food or proper medicine, how much longer would his strength last? And then she'd have to hold the torch *and* pole the raft.

And he might die.

Her chest constricted, and her eyes flooded with tears. Turning her back, she angrily dashed them away. She had to be strong enough for them both.

The cave wall suddenly loomed above them. With a last push at the riverbank to keep the raft centered, she flung herself flat beside Geraint. The raft bumped up against the wall, then one corner slid under and they were wedged.

They stared at each other.

"Should we swim for shore?" she asked.

"And walk all the way home? It would take weeks, and you would have to leave me behind. We should trust our bargain with the troll. But if your breath begins to fail you, leave the raft and save yourself."

"It will not come to that. I sensed no true malice within the troll. Let us go."

She put the pole beneath her body, and he did the same with the wrapped torches. They both put a hand on the wall and shoved upward, forcing the raft down. Water surged over the logs, soaking them. As they slid beneath the tunnel, the water rose higher, and at last she was forced to hold her breath as the river engulfed them and the torch went out.

With her fingers she clung to the raft, and her back scraped repeatedly against the ceiling of the tunnel as they rocked in the strong current. Her lungs strained, her mind panicked, and she wondered how much longer she could last. Then she felt Geraint slide away from her. She frantically reached for him and held on, the pole still secure beneath her.

Then suddenly the water drained from her ears, and she lifted her head. As air rushed into her nose, she breathed it gratefully.

"Enid?"

She met Geraint's fumbling hand with her own. "Aye, I'm here, my love. We survived."

But they were in total darkness. She squirmed to roll onto her back, then lifted her hand high, but did not touch the ceiling.

"We must reach the bank and try to light a torch," he said. "Do you still have the pole?"

"Aye. I'm going to try to kneel."

As she got her knees beneath her and slowly straightened, she felt terribly vulnerable in the absolute blackness. She kept flinching as if the ceiling would slam into her. But she was able to push with the pole, and soon the riverbed scraped beneath them. She gave one last hard push, and they stuck fast against the bank.

Geraint rolled into her, and she caught him. He was shivering.

"You could warn me next time before you use your amazing strength," he said.

She clasped his head and kissed his wet hair. "Forgive me."

"You brought us to land—I guess I can grant you my forgiveness. I am going to attempt to light a torch. You hold on to the raft."

On her knees she followed him to the muddy riverbank and knelt there, her splintered fingers digging into the raft. She could hear his heavy breathing as he unwrapped the torches.

"Finally we have luck," he whispered. "One is damp, but the other two seem dry. And my flint and steel are still in their pouch."

Several sparks flashed briefly in the dark and died away. Then there was a whoosh of flame, and the torch lit. She answered his grin with her own.

Both their stomachs growled in unison, and they shared a shaky laugh.

"Perhaps when we see the sky for the first time, we'll be able to stop and hunt for a meal," Geraint said, offering her the jerkin.

"You keep it for the torches. We can't risk losing them."

"But you'll catch a chill."

"I am never ill, Geraint. You'll see. When our children's noses run and they awaken at night with coughs, I will be able to see them through it without succumbing myself."

His laughter faded to a brief, warm smile. "You'll make a wonderful mother."

"And you a father."

"Are you saying—"

"Nay, I am not with child. But the future yet awaits us, Geraint, and we will reach it."

She held his hand in time to feel a shiver sweep through him.

Standing up, she said, "We have to get you out into the open, where we can build a fire for warmth. Are you ready to go?"

He looked around him. "I never wish to see a cave again. I'll follow you onto the raft."

Once they were aboard and moving, the current grew ever swifter as it was joined by more streams. Enid watched Geraint sleep, the torch propped between his arm and his body. She was glad that he could find rest. When he woke hours later, she thought he looked feverish, but he wouldn't let her touch his skin. He merely insisted that he would man the pole while she rested. To her surprise, she fell instantly asleep, and in her dreams their children laughingly ran about her skirts.

She was startled awake when the raft ran aground. Opening her eyes, she expected to find Geraint slumped in an exhausted heap, the raft lodged against the cave wall. But instead starlight twinkled overhead, and the half moon shined down on her. The pull of its power sizzled inside her, but she ignored it. Though her husband still held the pole wearily, the last effort must have taken its toll, for he was slowly collapsing sideways.

Still holding the torch, she caught him with one arm. "You have succeeded, my husband. Take your well-earned rest."

He nodded, his head lolling against her shoulder, and he slipped into unconsciousness. She gasped at the heat radiating from his skin, burning through his damp, filthy garments.

She whispered his name, shook him, but he didn't answer. She dragged him from the raft, sank the torch shaft in the mud, then quickly pulled the raft ashore before it could float away.

For just a moment, she put her hands on her hips and stared around her. By moonlight she could see the ground stretching away. Hills ringed them on all sides, dark patterns against the sky. The quiet of the night was broken only by the hooting of an owl, and the sound of a rustling animal somewhere off in the distance. Surely there could be no human inhabitants to worry about. She was going to risk a fire regardless. She had to warm Geraint and look to his injury.

After the fire was high and strong, she laid out her own jerkin to dry. When Geraint's ragged hose were removed, she was able to see that the wound in his thigh, left several days untreated, now oozed a smelly pus that made the injury ominous. She had seen more than one man lose a limb from such a deteriorating condition. Using another scrap of her shirt, she cleaned the wound deeply, pulling out shreds of his garments that had lodged inside. Geraint thrashed through it all. Though it made her work more difficult, she was glad to hold him down, if only to prove to herself that he yet fought to live.

But the worst of it was using the heated dagger to burn shut the wound. Geraint woke enough to scream before he passed out again. She was left shivering in despair. Was it too late to save him? While the moon crawled across the night sky, endlessly calling to her, she watched over her husband, spooning water between his lips and bathing him with her river-soaked shirt. She worked on him until his skin finally seemed cool to the touch, and his sleep had eased into restfulness. He even began to lightly snore, and she giggled as the tears ran down her face.

Glancing up once more at the moon, she saw it low on the horizon, weaker now, but still available to her. She had to renew her powers now, or risk losing them.

For the first time, she questioned what she truly wanted.

As she looked at Geraint's beloved face, she knew she loved him beyond all reason. She wanted to be his wife in every way, to remain at his side, to bear his children. And though he seemed to accept all that she had brought on herself in this quest to aid her people, she knew that his father—*his* people—would never understand or accept. If she remained as she was, a disciple of the Lady of the Lake, she would forever be the outsider.

She wanted his love—she wanted his trust. It was time to give up the magic that made her different. She no longer needed it. Through her own intelligence and wit, she would make sure that her tribe and the people of Cornwall never faced each other on opposite sides of a battlefield. And she trusted her husband to commit to the same.

As the moon slid below the horizon, she watched it go, felt its hold on her shiver, then fade away at last. Relieved, confident, she curled up against her husband's side and fell asleep.

• • •

WHEN Geraint awoke, he felt like he'd done battle—and lost. His muscles ached as if with a hundred bruises, but no longer did his thigh throb and burn. When he moved it, a shot of pain made him wince, but it was bearable after what he'd endured poling the raft down river for hours while he let Enid sleep.

Had they rode the river just the past night? He had lost sense of time. The sun was high overhead, and it seemed like an alien thing after their time in the caves. Hills loomed above him on all sides, giving him the feeling of being cut off from the world.

He came up on his elbows and looked around. Though he did not see Enid, evidence of her was everywhere. Their garments were stretched across bushes to dry. A huge fire burned, and the carcass of a rabbit dripped sizzling fat that hissed when it hit the embers. With his eyes closed, he inhaled the delicious odor, and his mouth watered. He realized that he was naked, but the heat of the sun and the fire made him feel warm and comfortable. He could see the blackened scar across his thigh, but there was no blood, no pus. He was healing.

And then he saw Enid, and his very breathing seemed to stop. She was naked but for the braies about her hips. She moved silently through the tall grass, her every step silent and purposeful, watchful and listening. She carried the raft pole, which she slowly hefted like lance. He saw the wicked point she'd carved into it only a moment before she flung it hard. Her body arched with triumph, her fists in the air, her breasts bobbing in time to the movement of her muscles.

She had become his whole world—how could he not have seen that? He had foolishly worried over her loyalty, as if such a woman ever falsely claimed her emotions. A disloyal woman would have left him long ago. She didn't need him to survive, as she had so amply proven on this journey. She had found the troll, gotten them out of the caves. She had nursed him, and was about to feed him—what did she even need him for, if not as her husband?

She hadn't left, because she loved him, because she was loyal to him. His own doubts made him feel like a very small man, unworthy of her. But she must have found something good in him, because she loved him. He would never doubt her again.

He must have made a choked sound, because she stilled and looked at him, panic and worry washing over her face. He sat up, turned his grimace into a grin and gave a little wave. Her smile was surely brighter than the sun, and she ran toward him. His mouth fell open at the grace and beauty she displayed. He would have to keep her naked more often.

"Geraint!" She fell to her knees at his side and cupped his face in both hands. "Your fever is still gone. How do you feel?"

"Tired, but well. You have healed me, my beloved wife."

She grinned, pushing behind her ear a strand of golden hair that had come loose from the leather strap holding it back. "Aye, I might have helped, but time and rest and water did most of the work. This is already our second day here."

"No wonder I'm starving." He sent a longing glance at the rabbit.

"Of course! I managed to get you to swallow small

pieces early this morning, and I just killed another rabbit. Between the two of us, we will be hungry enough to
eat at least a dozen. But start on this one, while I prepare
the next."

He caught her hand when she would have risen. She
gave him a questioning look.

"You have eaten?" he asked softly, caressing her
arm, which had showed its strength in her care of him.

She grinned. "Aye. And I promise I will eat more.
But the rabbit I just killed is a plump one. There will be
plenty. If 'tis all right with you, I think we should remain here another night, to eat and rest and heal. I know
our people must believe us dead . . ." she added with
worry, her gaze darting to the south.

Our people. He loved the sound of that. "Aye, but
they'll understand that we had to keep ourselves alive
to return to them. I am sure that my father will soon
join them, since I'd already sent word about the Saxon
incursion."

"He will be mourning you," she whispered.

"Not for long. We will be back by tomorrow night.
The horses could only have carried us so far." He patted
the ground beside him. "Come back to me soon, Enid,
and rest."

She gave him a quick kiss, then glanced at his lap.
Arching a brow, she said, "If a single kiss does that—"

"And your lovely nakedness."

"Then I'd best hurry."

Though he was tired, he could not sleep for watching
Enid work. There would be time later for slumber—and
other things.

Chapter 24

· · ·

WHEN the sun began to set, and their garments were dry, Geraint watched with regret as Enid clothed herself in her shirt. He had enjoyed every moment of his day with her, even watching her eat. But when the night sky came to life one star at a time, he finally gave his mind permission to reflect on baser needs. And he wanted her to know that he accepted *everything* she was.

She sat near him, warming her hands over the fire, licking her fingers clean of the remains of their meal.

He hesitated, wondering how she would take his questions, but decided to ask them just the same. "Enid, do not fear I mean to censure you, but I am curious."

She froze, her fingertip still in her mouth.

"Tell me how you trained the men."

Her finger popped free of her lips with a soft, wet sound that made his blood begin to heat and pool.

She took a breath. "Trained in . . . battle skills?"

He shook his head.

She leaned away from the fire and clasped her hands in her lap with a nervousness that he regretted. He brought both her hands to his lips, then turned them and kissed the palms. She sucked in her breath.

In a low voice, he said, "I want to know all of you, even this part of your past. I want to take that experience and make it something we share, too, to make it only between us from now on."

She looked at him solemnly. "You know I will never share myself with another man."

"I trust you completely. But show me . . . teach me. Pretend that I am a man who does not yet know how to please a woman."

He sat back and waited. For a moment, he thought she would refuse.

Not meeting his eyes, she said, "No man has ever pleasured me as you do."

"I know."

She finally looked at him in surprise, and they shared a grin. Hers slowly faded as she studied him. Then she reached behind her head and released her hair. She'd washed it in the river, and it was clean and fresh.

"There are more important things to a woman than what is between her legs," she began slowly.

"Aye." He put a hand on her breast and squeezed.

She pushed him away, trying not to smile. "Nay, you betray your youth, lad. A woman wants to be valued for more than your need to have her. Think of her as a pet cat, to be petted and praised. I hope you will woo her with the same gentleness even before the night play."

"I must?"

"Aye, you must. Talk to her, listen to her, care about what she says. You need not agree with it all, but you should be willing to compromise. Respect means everything to a woman. When you have her respect, you have the beginnings of true intimacy."

He had made so many mistakes with her—he thought he'd respected her, but in the end he hadn't shown his trust. He would spend a lifetime making it up to her. But for now he would continue to play his part. "Now can I touch you?"

"Nay. We will begin with a woman's hair."

"The hair between her—"

She covered his mouth with her hand and tried to look stern. "As all men do, you go too quickly. Patience is the key, lad. Just listen and do not speak. Run your hands through her hair, enjoy its softness, while you give your mate the gift of your gentleness."

She bent toward him, and he buried both hands deep in her hair, moving his fingertips along her scalp. He swept his thumbs over her brow, then back over her head.

She purred her response. "Ah, you learn quickly, lad."

"Teach me more," he whispered, not trusting his voice.

"A kiss should not be an assault, or a sudden unwanted mating of the tongues."

"I cannot kiss her?" he said, letting his despair show.

"I did not say that. Just begin gently, reverently, for a woman's skin is softer, more delicate than yours, and it should be treated as such. Later, if you are successful, she will meet your efforts with more enthusiasm. You can respond in kind."

They were still close, facing one another, and all she did was tip her face up to meet him. He pressed his lips to hers gently, over and over again, exploring each moist curve.

His breathing came harder, faster. "Might I kiss more of her face?"

"Of course. But remain gentle."

But she gripped his tunic at the arms with a tightness that betrayed her own needs.

He kissed each part of her face, from her nose to her forehead to her eyelids. He nibbled on her chin, gently bit her earlobe, then hovered over her lips once more.

Her mouth was parted with her breathing, and they stared into each other's eyes.

"I have heard," he began slowly, "that a man may use his tongue."

She licked her lips. "Aye, but not in a wet, intrusive way. Gentle licks, slow strokes that lead into more patient exploration. This works the best to ease the worries of an innocent maiden."

"And later? May I kiss her with a fierceness later?"

She moaned. "Oh, aye, of course."

He licked his way across her lips, then dipped slowly inside. "Is she supposed to answer me in kind?"

"Give her a chance," she whispered, a hint of the frantic about her now.

He entered her mouth more fully, and she met his tongue with her own, stroking and tasting.

"Am I supposed to like this so much?" he said against her mouth.

Her voice was only a whisper of breath. "Aye."

They kissed for several more minutes, until he broke contact. "Now can I grab her womanly parts?"

"Nay, you still hurry too much!"

"Those kisses were not hurried!"

"Your caresses should not be either. Every part of a woman's skin is sensitive, from the curve of her shoulder to the tip of her toes."

"But are not her garments already removed?"

"Nay, you should do that yourself. It helps to increase a woman's arousal."

"Then next she'll strip me?"

She bit her lip, and he loved the smile that teased him.

"Perhaps not the first few times," she admitted. "As a virgin, she will not know what to do until you teach her. If you have succeeded in relaxing her, she will want to remove your clothing to please you—and to please herself."

He fingered the gathered neckline of her shirt, letting his fingers slide beneath to tease her skin. The tension in her muscles pleased him, as if she could barely hold herself back.

"Where should I begin?" he asked. "I do not wish to disturb her sensitive womanly parts too soon."

Her laughter was low, husky. "Later, when you know each other better, she might like that. But for now, caress her gently through her garments, starting with her limbs and then moving to her breasts."

He slid one finger down the slope of her taut breast and was rewarded with a gasp. "I cannot start here right away?"

She clasped his hand before he could do more and placed it on her shoulder. "Feel a woman's skin, notice how different she is than you are. Begin to loosen her clothing as you caress her."

"You are not wearing much."

"Your mate might not be either."

He explored her collarbones like they were the fine bones of a bird's wings. He caressed the lean muscles of her arms, circled her wrists, and explored her long fingers. When she arched toward him, freely offering her chest, he restrained himself and slid his hands down her hips and onto her legs. Her thighs were bare beneath her shirt, so supple and strong. He felt the ripple of scrapes and wounds across her knees, and he bent low over them, full of reverent respect for all she'd gone through.

"I might kiss a woman's wounds?" he asked tentatively.

"Aye, please," she said.

"I can kiss her limbs, not just caress them?"

Her answer was a groan. She fell back against the ground arching up as if needing her lover to rise over her. But not yet. They weren't done with the lessons.

He kissed her bruises and hurts, licked a path behind her knees and down her calves to her ankles. He kissed his way back up again and stopped at her hemline.

"Might I kiss higher?"

Her thighs sagged open in surrender, then suddenly she closed them tight and sat up. "Nay, nay, not the first time. You will scare an innocent maiden, who won't understand the pleasures of such lovemaking."

"Then there is pleasure using one's mouth? I had heard rumors . . ."

She closed her eyes and pressed a hand to her chest. After a moment, she was able to frown at him. "But you have forgotten what comes next, after you caress a woman's limbs."

He let his gaze slide leisurely down her body. "Her breasts?"

With sincerity, she said, "They are so sensitive. Do not maul or grope them. You know how sensitive a man's loins are; so are a woman's breasts."

"Will you demonstrate how sensitive a man's loins are?"

"Later."

She leaned back on her hands, and her proud breasts thrust against the thin, worn cloth of her shirt. He could see the dusky outline of her nipples. He traced the shape of her with a gentle fingertip; she shivered and moaned and pressed against him. He circled the nipple, then delicately squeezed it between his fingers.

"Ah, lad, you learn quickly," she gasped.

He knelt before her, no longer even noticing his own wounds. He cupped both her breasts in his hands and caressed them. Each gasp he wrung from her was pleasure in and of itself.

He tugged on the string at her neckline, and the knot gave way. She dipped her head back, and her long hair slid slowly about her shoulders. The shirt loosened with each tug, baring her shoulders, which gleamed by firelight. Another tug and the upper curves of her breasts

were revealed. Another, and the garment slid to her
waist and wrists.

As he looked at her, her eyelids lowered partway, and
again she licked her lips. Softly, she murmured, "When
a woman bares herself to you, she is giving you all of
her trust. You must never abuse her or betray her."

He stared at her, feeling the sadness of his own actions and how they must have hurt her.

Her eyes widened. "I did not mean that you—I am
just telling you what I say to my students—"

"Hush, I know."

He kissed her then, with gentleness and love. Then
he once again took her breasts in his hands and raised
them both toward his mouth. At the last moment, he
gave her a questioning look.

"I can kiss them now?"

She moaned. "And even use your tongue—gently at
first, of course."

"Without permission?"

She pulled his head to her, and he took the sweetness
of her nipple into his mouth. He suckled her and teased
her, easing her back so that he could reach every part of
her. He treated her like she was unexplored territory,
now his.

"Oh, that's good," she whispered. "Your mate will be
appreciative."

"I can take the rest of her clothes off now?"

"She should let you, as long as you have performed
this well with her."

She removed her sleeves and lifted her hips, and he
slid the last of her garments away. He hesitated, admiring her nudity.

"Should I remove my clothing now?" he asked.

Enid rested her head on her bent arm. "Sometimes a woman will be so shy the first time, that she will not want to see too much of you. After all, men are very different from women."

He stared at the curling hair above her thighs. "I can see that."

"Eventually she will want to see all of you, to touch and kiss you as you have done to her, perhaps even undress you. You will be teaching her that as you please her. But judge her mood the first time, and give her what she needs to feel at ease with you."

"Can I pretend that you are a woman who will not mind seeing my body?"

"Of course." Her voice was strained, and she watched without blinking as he pulled off his tunic and shirt.

Enid could barely think, so consumed was she with the need to feel Geraint on top of her, inside her. Their playacting was enjoyable. But the most important thing was that she would never again worry that he might compare himself to the three men who had lain with her for one night each. He had to know that those acts, between teacher and student, contained none of the glorious feelings that she shared only with him.

But still, the teasing light in Geraint's eyes pleased her, and she was glad to play her part. He rose up on his knees above her, and his erection showed that he was more than ready.

She reached for him, and he pulled back.

"She might touch me, even the first time?" he asked with disbelief.

She settled back onto her elbows and grinned. "Probably not the first time, but eventually she will understand that such things give you pleasure."

He put his hands on her knees. "But I cannot wait much longer. How do I—how will she—" He stopped as if he didn't know what to do next. "Will it not hurt her?"

"Perhaps the first time. When a man caresses her, a woman's body prepares itself for mating. Yet still the maidenhead must be broken. After that, if a woman understands that the pain will be brief, she will relax once again in your arms. Lay with a woman first. Let her feel your skin against hers. You should keep kissing her, caressing her, while she becomes used to the weight of you on top of her."

"Will I not crush her?"

"Not if you hold yourself above her by your elbows or hands. You can even caress her deepest parts, though being shy, the woman might not wish it too much the first time."

He parted her legs and stared between her thighs. "How will I know what to do?"

"Just be gentle." Her voice shook. "You will know by her movements and her breathing and her moans what she likes."

He came down in the grass just to the side of her, letting their legs entwine. She could hardly think, let alone teach, but she would see the game out and be finished with her past. He slid his hand between her thighs, cupping her at first, then sliding his fingers in deeper to explore.

She closed her eyes and tried to speak. "A-a woman deserves to reach her own pleasure, just like a man, though you might have to teach each other what works best for her. She could experience it beforehand, or even while you are inside her."

She felt his arousal hard and insistent against her thigh, but still his fingers worked their magic, circling the sensitive bud of her desire until she was urging him on with soft cries. When he stopped, she could not withhold a groan of dismay.

"Too soon?" he whispered against her lips.

She gasped out her agreement.

This time he slid his fingers inside of her. "Here it is," he said, as if he were proud of his accomplishments.

She turned her face into his shoulder and tried not to giggle. He began to kiss her again, and her arms wrapped around him. His fingers teased and tormented, his mouth found her breasts, and soon she convulsed against him, swept away by the passion she'd only ever shared with him. When he slid on top of her, she opened her thighs to him, and he settled himself in between, the hard length of him teasing her already sensitive flesh.

"Remind the woman to bend her knees," she said raggedly. "It helps the first time. Then you should gently press into her until—"

With a single thrust he was inside her, and she was almost overwhelmed by pleasure again.

"Aye, yes, that's right," she cried.

"I told you I had found it. Now what should I do?" His voice was hoarse with strain.

"Oh, Geraint—"

She moved against him desperately, but he didn't respond, although his muscles trembled, and his breathing was loud.

"I wish not to pound into her and hurt her," he said between gritted teeth.

"Nay, not the first time, although later she will enjoy more enthusiasm." The details were starting to elude her. "But she might be sore the first time, so you should move slowly in and out, and teach her the rhythm of lovemaking."

Against her mouth, he murmured, "Teach me the rhythm."

She moved against him, her hips rising and falling, taking the length of him and then releasing him. She thrust up harder and harder, and he met her ever more boldly. When he shuddered and found his own release, she held him close, her legs wrapped around him, wishing she need never let him go. There could still be so much danger ahead.

Geraint lifted himself up by the arms, their hips still mated, and stared down at her. "I forgot myself, teacher. Did I hurt you?"

She shook her head, trying not to cry with the emotions he inspired in her. She'd turned into a fountain of tears since her marriage, she who had once had the fierce impassivity of a warrior.

He leaned down and nipped her lips with his. "Will I be allowed to do it again?"

"Probably not the first time," she said, laughing. "And you should never immediately leave your mate either. Hold her, talk to her, even as you fall asleep. Show her that she means more to you than a sexual release."

He rolled her to her side and came down behind her, pulling her back against him. He dragged his shirt over the two of them as a blanket.

Caressing her hair gently, he asked, "Did I pass?"

"You met my every expectation." She rolled onto her back and stared up at him. "Geraint, know that when I did this in truth, I never exchanged such banter with my students. They did not talk but for the occasional serious question. They listened and did as I bid. And never— never did I allow them to bring me true pleasure. I instructed them in it, but did not demonstrate."

"Surely such mating could not have been comfortable."

"There are certain oils," she whispered, smiling. Then she stared at him, hoping the love showed in her eyes. "Only with you do I give myself over to the feelings we share."

He kissed her gently, then lay his head down on his arm. "Thank you."

Chapter 25

• • •

B Y the next evening, they'd ridden the raft through the next hill—luckily smaller than the last—and beached it before the waterfall, as the troll had instructed them. It was a short journey down a final hillside to the water's edge, where they found the stone bridge, several hundred years old, that spanned it. Geraint limped to favor his right leg and kept assuring Enid that he was fine. But inside he felt relieved and anxious and worried all at the same time. Had the Saxons already invaded? Was his father even now in battle?

He pointed to the southwest. "Cornwall lies there, only a few leagues' distance."

She stared up at him. "And you know that the Donella tribe lies between us and Cornwall."

"Are you ready to introduce me to your father?"

Her eyes widened. "We have time? Should we not go to your father? The Saxons—"

"But I have need of one of my most important allies. He will surely want to supply us with horses to finish our journey."

"Of course."

Her excitement was contagious, and he told himself to put aside his cares. His father was well prepared, and their reunion could wait another day. Enid had been a long time without her family.

For the rest of the morning she walked and he limped, heading away from the river and deeper into the forest. If there were paths other than animal tracks, he could see none, but his wife moved with purpose. At last she paused and cocked her head. Glancing back, she gave him a grin just as two men jumped out of the trees and landed before her. They were clothed in leather tunics, and both carried bows in their hands as if they were about to use them.

Geraint and both men froze, uncertain and tense. But Enid only laughed.

"Quin and Teague," she said, "you don't look as if you remember who I am."

They both bowed to her, and she smiled and clapped them on their shoulders.

Quin looked at Geraint again. "Enid, you come with a stranger. We worried you were his prisoner."

Geraint rolled his eyes. "As if she would ever allow me to do that."

Enid took his arm. "Allow me to present my husband, Prince Geraint of Cornwall."

Teague looked skeptical. "Druce told us all that you had taken a mate not of our tribe. Your father found it difficult to believe."

"That is only because he does not know my husband," she said primly. "Lead on and we shall follow you into the village."

Geraint's optimism faded as he followed his wife through the forest. Would her father not give his approval of their marriage? Could it be the final reason that the Donella tribe turned against Cornwall?

But Enid seemed confident and fearless. As the forest expanded into small meadows where thatched houses were scattered, she called greetings to all. Children ran to hug her, women left their kitchen gardens to smile at her and stare at him.

When they were walking again, she said, "This is one of the many small villages that make up our tribe. We farm as needed, but mostly we hunt our food. My father's home is just beyond the next ridge of land." She smiled. "It is not so impressive as a castle, but it serves us."

When they crested the ridge and looked down, Geraint saw Enid's pride as he took in her chieftain's home. Built of wood, it sprawled through the trees, making the forest part of the house itself. Lined before it were dozens of warriors, outfitted with swords, yet wearing bows on their backs. And in the center was a gathering of people dressed in draping tunics.

Though several women started to come forward, one man lifted a hand to stop them, then strode toward them himself, followed by a boy nearly grown into his height.

The chieftain was tall and blond and beardless, though his hair was beginning to fade to white. But he had Enid's proud bearing, and even her nose.

Enid ran to hug him. "Father, it is so good to see you!"

"You have been gone many months, daughter. We have missed you."

The man's voice was soft with love, but his gaze was for his new son by marriage. Those eyes assessed Geraint thoroughly, and he waited for judgment, not at all certain what it would be. Even the boy—Enid's brother?—watched him with suspicion.

Enid turned back to Geraint, and wearing a nervous smile, drew him forward. "Father, this is my husband, Prince Geraint of Cornwall. Geraint, meet my father, Chieftain Calder of the Donella tribe."

The boy shot her a scowl.

"And my brother, Dermot," she added quickly.

Geraint bowed. "My father, King Erbin of Cornwall, sends his greetings."

"And he sends you as his ambassador?" the chieftain asked, one eyebrow raised. "On foot and alone but for my daughter? And you look as if you walked through the deepest swamp to get here."

"My father did send me, my lord, although the reason we are without retainers and horses and dressed as poorly as we are is a long story. In fact, my father might believe us dead, so we cannot delay our journey long. Even now the Saxons might be moving ashore in Cornwall."

"So Druce informed me," the chieftain said. "Come into my home and explain yourself, while Enid reassures her mother and sisters."

Geraint turned to his wife. She quickly kissed his cheek, then went running to fling herself into the arms of three women, who laughed and cried and held her.

• • •

ON one side of the great hall, Enid peered between the trees, which towered up through the thatched roof. Her husband and her father were talking, facing one another across a table. Their faces remained so serious, and she could not tell whether they spoke easily—or whether they might like each other. Her brother, Dermot, slumped in a chair near the men. It was obvious that although Dermot listened with interest, sometimes his mind wandered off, as usual.

Her sister Olwen tugged on her arm. "Leave them be, Enid. To them, there are dangers in the world more important than your marriage. But not to us!"

Enid laughed and turned back to her family, seating herself on a cushion in the circle they formed. Her mother, Moira, still could not stop the occasional tear from falling down her cheek. She knew her mother was happy with Enid's happiness. But from now on their separations would be for months, not hours or days, and the reality was sobering.

Olwen seemed much the same, soft and plump again with child. In her eyes, as well as their mother's, was the wisdom of women, of healing and understanding. Cinnia, the beauty of the family, seemed more mature, as if she bore a new knowledge, now that she was truly a woman grown.

And all of them watched Enid with caution, not bothering to hide their concern.

She took her mother's hands. "Do not worry so, Mama. Geraint is a wonderful man, who loves me as I love him. We married quickly, that is true, but we understand and trust each other now."

"And he knows everything?" Cinnia asked sharply.

"Aye, he does."

Olwen sighed. "Then he is the reason you have given up the gifts bestowed by the Lady of the Lake."

Enid shot her a startled look. "Their absence is so evident, then?"

"Of course, especially to us, your sisters."

Their mother sighed. "Why would you risk such a thing, when your mission is not yet complete?"

"But it is, Mama," Enid said. "My mission was to learn the fighting techniques of the British knights. I have done so. After the Saxons are defeated, I will return to teach our warriors. Geraint understands this, and although at first it stood between us, he trusts me now."

Her mother touched her cheek. "But why deny the powers that made you strong, that kept you safe?"

"Because I had no need of them anymore. I want to be one with Geraint and our people, and I cannot do that when I'm forever different. The Lady gave me the gifts as a temporary thing, did she not?"

Olwen looked at her with understanding. "He is part of your family now."

Enid clutched her hand. "Aye, he is, and I no longer wanted to be a worry to him, someone whose behavior he would constantly have to explain to his father. Please worry not. I am so happy."

While Cinnia consoled their mother, Olwen spoke

softly for Enid's ears alone. "You have not told your husband of your decision to relinquish the powers."

Enid stiffened. "It only happened recently. But he will be relieved."

"Then why do you not tell him immediately?" Olwen asked, eyes narrowed.

It had not occurred to Enid that she was again holding something back from her husband. But surely when she told him he would agree that this news was good. "I will find the right moment, I promise you."

Dermot came running to bring them back into the great hall, and Enid saw Geraint and her father holding tankards of ale, more relaxed as they spoke to one another.

Geraint grinned when he saw her.

Cinnia tugged at her arm and whispered, "My, how did you find such a handsome man!"

Enid smiled. "It was all because of my skill with a sword."

"But I want the real story!" Cinnia called.

In the great hall, Chieftain Calder spoke solemnly, but Enid could tell that he was pleased.

"We have renewed the bonds of friendship between us and the people of Cornwall," he said to the courtiers and family members who gathered around him. "Misunderstandings are relics of the past. But we must support each other, if there is to be a future. Even now an enemy approaches."

Enid slid her arm into Geraint's and whispered, "It is true? The Saxons have arrived?"

Geraint nodded. "Your father has had word from his scurriers. The Saxons have disembarked from their ships in Cornwall itself. King Arthur is leading an army, but it may not arrive in time. But my father will stand strong, and your father is sending soldiers."

"We will go, too, of course," she said.

He smiled. "Of course. In the morning, we will depart."

Her mother came to the chieftain's side. "Calder, should our daughter, Enid, not remain with us, away from such danger?"

Enid stared in surprise.

Then her father took her mother's hand. "Enid is a warrior woman, dearling. She is the match of any man on that field."

Olwen stared hard at Enid, and she knew that the time was now.

"Father," Enid said, "Mama only worries because she knows that I have given up the Lady's powers."

Geraint turned her to him, and Enid stared up at him, part hopeful, part afraid.

"We were in the caves," he said, his face drawn with worry. "You were not able to find the moon. I am so sorry, Enid."

She sighed. "Nay, it was afterward, when you were recovering from your wounds."

"Afterward?" he said with a frown. "You gave them up willingly?"

"I have no need of them anymore, Geraint. I only had them to complete my mission, and that is now guaranteed by Cornwall's alliance with the Donella."

He searched her face, and what she saw in the softening of his eyes told her of his understanding.

He spoke softly into her ear. "You would have remained my wife no matter what. My father would have accepted that."

"Perhaps. But I *am* your wife, Geraint, a princess of Cornwall. That is my present and my future. Those magical gifts were my past, and only temporary." She hesitated. "I am still a warrior woman. I can accompany you and give you my sword, my arm."

He met her eyes. "And I value them. I could not be parted from you, not now."

She smiled and came into his arms, and saw Olwen nodding her approval.

• • •

GERAINT and Enid left the next morning with fresh horses, thirty mounted archers, and the promise of more to follow. Geraint knew that the Donella did not yet have the skills to fight armored, mounted warriors, but if Enid was any indication, they would learn quickly.

He thought again of her skill and could not help worrying for her. Now that he knew she was as vulnerable as any other soldier, he found himself dreading the battle ahead. He could not forbid her from it; it would damage their marriage all over again.

But she'd given up everything she'd trained for out of love for him. Though she dismissed it as no sacrifice at all, he knew otherwise.

The Donella had been keeping watch over the brewing confrontation on the moors of Cornwall, and the chieftain had been able to tell Geraint that his small troop had already joined with King Erbin's army. They

were not far from where Geraint had left them. He knew
his father's scurriers would observe the arrival of
mounted warriors, and he made sure to put himself and
Enid visibly in the lead.

They were hailed with great joy some leagues' distant from the encampment, and Geraint was told about
the despondent gloom that had settled over King Erbin
and his army at the thought of his heir's death. As they
rode the final approach, a thousand men greeted their
arrival with a cheer.

He saw the disbelief and joy in his father's face, and
when he dismounted, was greeted with a hug so furious
he couldn't breathe.

"Father," he gasped.

The king released him from the embrace, only to hold
his arms and stare at his face in wonder. "When the scurriers told me about your miraculous reappearance—
Geraint, you cannot know how it made me feel."

The king cleared his throat and glanced at Enid, and
although he seemed embarrassed at his emotional display, there was also something that he kept hidden.
Geraint's happiness dimmed.

Enid was swept into a hug by her squire, Lovell, and
Geraint's men-at-arms each took their turn celebrating
with her. When they finally remembered to congratulate
him on his escape, they seemed apologetic about their
exuberance for Enid. Geraint just shook his head.

"Come have supper at my fire and tell me everything
that has happened," the king said, leading Geraint and
Enid between brightly colored pavilions scattered
across the moor. As he saw his son's limp, he frowned,
but Geraint reassured him that he was on the mend.

After several hours of good food, explanations, and gratitude at the renewal of old alliances, Geraint watched Enid retire to their pavilion, and he turned to find his father watching her as well, wearing an inscrutable expression.

"You said little to my wife, Father," Geraint said as they stood beside the fire, tankards of mulled wine warming them. "When we last met, you seemed willing to accept her."

"I was—for you." King Erbin frowned. "But I have heard things since then, revelations that perhaps you should have known before your marriage."

"I admit to haste," Geraint said evenly, "but it has all turned out for the best. I will not be parted from her."

His father opened his mouth to answer, when suddenly a young soldier ran toward them.

The young man gasped and attempted to speak.

"Slow down, boy," the king said.

"Forgive me . . . sire," the soldier said, breathing heavily. "I-I have come to report that we can see the fires of our enemy in the distance. They are massed in a long line not many leagues south of here."

The king nodded. "Go back to your post, boy. I doubt they will be on the move tonight. I will inform the captain. By dawn we shall be at war, holding Cornwall in the battle for Britain."

"Will King Arthur arrive in time?" Geraint asked, staring off south into the darkness, feeling the Saxon threat like a cold chill.

"His army is still some days' distant. I hope when he arrives we will be able to give him news of victory."

Chapter 26

· · ·

DROWSILY, Enid rolled over on her pallet when Geraint entered the pavilion. She smiled up at him as he began to undress. Sometimes, she still could not believe that every night he would return to her, and they could share simple conversations.

"I looked for my maidservant, Fryda," she told him, "but she returned to Castle Cornwall with Wilton. It seems in her brief time with me, she was quite bereft at the thought of my death."

"I heard Lovell shed tears."

"Do not tease my squire," she said, playfully tossing a cushion at him.

He smiled in a distracted fashion, and when he sat down beside her, she put her hand on his knee and said simply, "The Saxons are near?"

"Aye. Our scurriers could see their camp, although

not well enough to estimate their numbers. I imagine they will at least match our own."

"I have great confidence in your father. He will lead us to victory."

He glanced at her, then away.

Enid cocked her head. "Since you cannot possibly doubt your father's ability at battle, it must be something else."

In a low voice, he said, "He was not as warm to you today as a father by marriage should be."

She bit her lip, tense, but not surprised. "He has had time to hear the stories of our journey. He must fear for your happiness with me. We shall prove his fears groundless, I promise you."

He gave her a slow smile. "You are fearless, even in the face of a king's anger."

She leaned up to kiss him. "Just wait until you see me against the Saxons."

It was not the wisest thing to say, for his smile fled. He looked at her with such a fierce expression of worry that she wondered if he would yet try to forbid her participation in the battle. Instead he kissed her, and made love to her with a hungry intensity that left her sated, exhausted, and grateful that she'd found her true mate.

* * *

WELL before dawn, Enid was dressed for battle. She had agreed to wear a brigandine, but she was too unfamiliar with armor to fight properly while wearing more than that. And so Geraint did not want to leave her side.

Amid torches holding back the night, she put her hands on her hips and scowled at him. "Your place is at your father's side. I will be with Toland and Tyler right behind you."

He glared at the twins, who faced him solemnly. "You will not allow any harm to come to her."

"It will be as if she attended mass, milord," Toland said.

She rolled her eyes, but said nothing. She didn't want Geraint to worry about her instead of himself.

He turned his ferocious frown on her. "And you will remain with them at all times."

"Aye, my prince." She kept her face expressionless, knowing how important this was to him, but how hard it would be once the battle had begun.

She couldn't understand her own confidence, especially now that her unearthly strength was gone. But she'd always been the best fighter, and that ability would see her through the fight.

And besides, the shock of facing a woman across a sword on a field of battle always caused an enemy to hesitate a second too long.

As she moved into position behind Geraint, she stared down both lines of the Cornish army, most of them foot soldiers. She had never seen so many men in one place. Banners flew and trumpeters sounded a glorious march. Behind the lines were the Donella archers, ready to take out as many oncoming Saxons as possible before the two armies met.

Geraint and his fellow knights were a vision in blinding silver armor. Their horses were equally protected, and she couldn't imagine anything more deadly to face on a battlefield.

At last, across the open moor, the Saxon army rode

up from below the plain. They were well over a thousand strong, and their voices were raised in deafening cries of victory and the promise of bloodshed.

King Erbin gave the signal, and the horses, reined and furious, were set free by their riders. Thousands of men rode straight at each other, and over their heads the archers sent their deadly arrows. Dozens of the enemy fell dead in the rush forward. It didn't seem as if it would help in the face of the ferocity of the long-haired, bearded Saxons, who wore padded leather armor rather than the shining suits of the British knights.

The last Enid saw of Geraint was that he was in the lead with King Erbin. Then the two armies broke upon each other with a crash of weapons and the shriek of men dying. Toland and Tyler's good intentions to guard her quickly turned into a fierce battle for their lives. And Enid faced her first Saxon warrior. He saw her from the side, grinned, and pulled on his horse until the animal reared in a turn and came at her.

And then he was dead, his head hanging to the side from a blow of her sword. She wheeled her horse about and looked for her next opponent.

She'd worried that the strength she'd given up would affect her abilities, but she'd had that so briefly. Her own skills took over, and she moved with the fluidity of long practice.

The sun was high overheard before the two armies retreated to regroup. For several long minutes she rode among the men, the wounded and the merely scratched, as they drank from their skins of ale and assessed the damage.

She saw Geraint from a distance, his helmet beneath

his arm as he searched among his battalions. Her relief made her wave furiously. He grinned and returned the gesture, then composed himself and glanced around coolly. She wanted to laugh. They rode up to meet one another, clasped hands, and regardless of the horses, leaned sideways for a quick kiss. Both horses neighed and shied away.

"You were magnificent," he said, handing her his horn.

She drank deeply. "So were you. How does your father feel the battle is going?"

He shrugged. "They might have lost more than we did, thanks to your archers."

"Ever the diplomat," she said, shaking her head.

He smiled. "We were not forced to fall back. It is a good sign. Already there are Saxons retreating toward their ships. Father has sent a battalion to destroy their vessels, trapping the entire army. To defeat both attacks, they'll have to split their forces."

"And thereby weaken them."

"Which could happen to us as well." He narrowed his eyes as he scrutinized her. "Speaking of weakening—"

"I am not weak, my husband. You of all people know my strength and my talents." She wiggled her eyebrows.

He sighed. "This is not a place for jests, Enid."

"It is when someone needs to stop worrying so much. And I have noticed that you are no longer riding the same horse you began the day with. Do you see me panicking for you?" she asked sweetly. But on the inside she was.

He rolled his eyes.

King Erbin's trumpet sounded, calling them back to

battle. Enid gave her husband a jaunty wave and guided her horse behind him, looking for her bodyguards.

The second battle lasted well until dusk. The Saxon line had weakened and finally folded, and the Cornish army was beginning to surround them. Hundreds of Saxons fled toward the rear, to ships that would no longer be able to take them home.

Enid had become separated from Toland and Tyler hours before, but she continued to roam the field, fighting an ever-dwindling enemy.

In a lull between battles, she let her horse pick its way among the fallen men and horses, toward the southern lines where a few Saxons still fought. All around her men and horses moaned and shouted their agony. An evening breeze swept along the moor, chasing away the heat of battle. But the stench of the dead and dying lingered.

"Enid!"

She heard her husband's voice, and she lifted her head to look for him. His horse came thundering across the battlefield from her left, jumping whatever obstacles lay in its path.

She waited for him, but he started motioning furiously.

"Behind you!" he shouted.

She wheeled her horse about and saw two Saxon warriors, still mounted, charging at her. A deadly calm came over her, and every battle instinct rose to replace her exhaustion and fear. She hefted her shield on her left arm, her sword in her right hand, and prepared to do what was necessary to survive.

But she forgot about Geraint. At the last moment, he came galloping between them, and she was forced to veer aside rather than hit him. She wheeled back to find him furiously battling both men at once. She screamed in terror as he was knocked from his saddle. He went down in a crash of armor, yet rolled to his feet and killed the horse from beneath one soldier. The rider went down, and Enid left him to Geraint, kicking her horse into a gallop to meet the still-mounted Saxon.

Her arm shook as their swords met and held. Their horses continued to gallop past, and they were forced to disengage. They wheeled back to face each other, and at the last moment of the charge, Enid saw Geraint rush in to take out her opponent's horse, too. The Saxon tumbled forward, but before he hit the ground, he thrust his sword at Geraint, piercing him at his weakest point, beneath his armpit where only leather protected him.

Enid cried out, and she barely remembered striking the killing blow against the Saxon who would dare wound Geraint. She vaulted from her horse and fell to her knees beside her husband, who lay still. The sun completed its final descent in that moment, and its beam, which had washed orange and red across Geraint's face, went out like a premonition.

How deep had the sword penetrated? Was he even breathing? She frantically pulled his helmet off. His precious eyes were closed, his face pale and haggard. Even when she lifted his arm to assess the bleeding wound, he did not stir.

Oh gods, she had once feared that he might have to choose between her and his kingdom—and he'd chosen. He'd saved her at peril to himself.

Frantically she began to tug at the straps that held the front and back plates of his armor together, but they were sticky with blood. Was it all his? She was kneeling in a morass of mud and blood, surrounded by the dead and the dying—and she vowed that her husband would not be one of those.

"My lady!"

It was Lovell, galloping over the battlefield. A cut streamed blood from above one eyebrow, but he looked whole and well. At his rear rode several mounted knights, and for a moment, she didn't recognize the king.

"Help me, Lovell!" She frantically pulled at the armor straps. As dusk began to settle, it made everything seem grayer. "Gods, please help me," she whispered.

Lovell knelt beside her, and he had to use his dagger to start releasing the straps. Then suddenly they were surrounded by men.

"Take her from my son!" King Erbin thundered.

She was pulled away from Geraint, and she screamed a denial. No one listened. Two knights, strangers to her, held her back. Lovell was pushed aside.

"Sire, let me go to him!" she cried, tugging to no avail. "I know exactly where he is wounded."

"As do I!" the king said, rounding on her in such fury that she shrank back. "I saw everything. He took a blow meant for you!"

She opened her mouth, but she could not refute it.

"A woman does not belong on the battlefield, and the fact that my son allowed it proves that you have bewitched him!"

How could she explain that she had been prepared to defend herself against the Saxons? Then Geraint had rushed in, disrupting everything, taking on the fury of two warriors because of her.

She sagged in the grip of her captors, watching help-lessly as King Erbin ripped apart the last buckles that held his son's armor together. The plates came apart, and he used his dagger against the padded tunic beneath.

"By the saints, there is so much blood!" he cried.

The despising look he cast at her made her shrink away.

Tears ran unchecked down her face. "He's not dead! He cannot be dead!"

"Bring him to the pavilion and send for the healers," the king ordered.

Four men lifted his son.

"Gently, gently," he urged. Then he turned back to Enid. "Keep her restrained. I want no sorcery near my son."

When she tried to follow the procession, the two knights held her back. She struggled violently.

"He said to restrain me, not to take me away. I must be with my husband." She raised her voice in a shout. "I could be carrying Cornwall's heir!" Though it was a lie, she knew such a proclamation would receive atten-tion.

The king came to a halt and slowly turned about. Facing the Saxon fury was easier than staring down this man's hatred. What had he heard that would so turn him against her? She'd done nothing but protect his men.

"She may come, but do not release her," the king said in a low voice laced with fury and contempt.

Back at the encampment, torches were lit and fires were built high against the coming night. There would have been shouts and the celebration of victory, but all the soldiers held an uneasy silence in the face of their prince's grave injuries.

Enid saw sympathetic glances as she passed, but no one would dare to gainsay their king. Lovell walked near her, his shoulders slumped, and his face blotched white and red.

"Lovell, go to my husband," she ordered. "Tell me what they do to him, how he is."

The boy nodded and sprinted away, toward the cluster of people surrounding Geraint's still form. He lay on the ground by the fire. They stripped him of his armor and padded tunic and leggings. She could not see whether his chest rose and fell with breathing. Men were gathered over him, perhaps stanching the blood beneath his shoulder, or looking for signs of life. She didn't know, and it was killing her.

Lovell returned at last, and beneath his wide eyes, dark shadows of despair had appeared. "They say he is not breathing, my lady. They say he's—"

"Nay!"

She drove an elbow into one knight's side behind his armor, then used her knee in the lower back of the other. Breaking free, she flung herself into the horde of men all around Geraint. Many fell back in astonishment, and she was able to put her hands on his chest. She closed her eyes and concentrated. In that frozen moment, she heard the slow beating of his heart.

She was ripped away again.

"Bind her!" the king ordered.

"But he lives!" she cried, eluding first one man, then another. "His heart yet beats."

"You made sure my son is gone from me forever—now you make a mockery of my grief!"

"Sire, there is no need yet for grief. Why will you not listen to me?"

Still gathered around Geraint, men in long robes sadly shook their heads. They put away their bandages, their potions, and backed away from their prince. Geraint looked still and pale, and if she did not hurry, their statements would be fact.

"You witch!" King Erbin cried. "I have heard tales of your dark magic from my loyal knights: your granting of blessings as if you yourself were God, your powers to cheat death itself."

"I have never cheated death. But Geraint might yet! He is alive!" She sobbed the last words, standing alone, surrounded by men who watched her as if she were the devil's handmaiden.

Great tears ran down the king's face. "You bewitched him from the first, forcing a marriage in haste. Was this your plan all along, to take my son from me?"

"I want him to live! Whether he chooses to keep me as wife will be up to him. The power to give a warrior courage runs in my veins. I know I can help him take back the will to live. Would you rather let your only son die than take a chance on my love for him? What could be worse than his death?"

By torchlight, the king's face was stark with grief and indecision.

From the crowd, a young man's voice cried, "She helped me, sire! I lacked the courage for battle, and she shared hers with me."

Bless Severin. All around them a chorus of murmurs

rose. The king turned about like a child's toy, not knowing which way to turn.

Lovell stepped to her side. "She helped me as well, sire. And did you not hear how she healed your son when he was wounded from his fight with the mercenaries?"

Enid pushed past the king and fell to her knees at Geraint's side. She was afraid to call on her abilities as a warrior woman, for fear that without magic, she would deplete her strength just when he needed her most. She needed the magic again, needed the strength of ten men, so that her warrior woman ability might be magnified.

"We can burn the wound, giving him time until I am ready," she said, turning to look up at the king. "Will you let me help him?"

The king stared for only a moment at his son's pale face. And then he nodded.

She sprang to her feet. "Prepare your instruments," she said to the healers. "I hope I can give him the strength to last." She turned to Lovell. "Where is the source of water from which the army drinks?"

"A pond at the base of a spring, my lady. It is on the other side of this pavilion."

"Take me to it."

Chapter 27

. . .

ENID knew she was followed by dozens of men, but she no longer cared. She was of the Donella—with access to magic beyond herself.

But was she too late to ignite her powers? She'd spurned the moon, spurned the Lady's gifts.

As she walked, she stripped off the brigandine, her jerkin and shirt, her boots and braies. She was one with nature, with the night sky and stars.

"Give me your dagger," she said to Lovell, as he jogged at her side and gaped at her. She had somehow lost hers in battle.

Without a word, he did as she commanded. When she reached the pond, she stared in dismay. It had been almost totally drained to slake an army's thirst. In the bottom of the basin, inches of water puddled amidst muddy earth.

It would have to be enough. With the dagger, she cut her finger and dripped blood into the pond. She waited for the moon's reply, but there was none. It was only a distant white face, slumbering. No energy came to life inside her, no buzz like insects along her skin. The moon did not beg her to respond. Where did the wind hide?

"I call on the powers of the Lady!" she cried, lifting her arms to the moon. "I am of the Donella! I forsook you out of my pride, and I offer my apology. Do not abandon me, I beg of you." She said the last in almost a whisper.

She stepped into the pond, and sank only to her ankles. Was the water not enough? Was she being punished?

Then suddenly, the moorland came alive with the rush of a cool wind, and Enid gladly swayed with it, her joy growing. Behind her, men shouted their concern, but she ignored it. The Lady's power rose up inside her, and Enid greeted the awakened moon as an old friend. Her body took on its glow, and at last the energy within her arced with lightning to the moon. As it faded, she was already giving a silent thanks as she strode out of the pond and back to Geraint. She barely felt the cloak that Lovell threw around her.

All along her path men fell back in awe and fear. But the king did not. He was the last to stand between her and Geraint.

He did not look afraid, only grief-stricken and resigned to despair. "It is too late," he whispered.

But he didn't try to stop her. She pushed past him and fell to her knees. Geraint was still there, deeply asleep, his life's force fading. Someone had already burned his wound closed, and he was no longer losing blood. She put her hands on his chest, closed her eyes, and called to the power of a warrior woman. To these she added a call to the Lady of the Lake.

All around her men gasped, and she knew it was because Geraint's skin glowed where it touched hers. She gave him her courage, her strength, willed him to fight the pull of darkness and death, willed him to live.

She fell back, overcome with the deepest exhaustion she'd ever borne, as if she'd never given so much of herself. She could not yet know if she'd succeeded, but she saw his chest rise with the deepest breath he'd taken.

His father saw it, too. With a cry he dropped to his knees on the other side of Geraint. "He is alive?" he demanded of her.

"I told you so," she said tiredly. She had to force her eyes open. "I did not bring him back from the dead— I know of no such powers. But I gave him the strength for this one last battle. I only pray it will be enough."

When the healers moved him into a warm pavilion, Lovell helped her walk there. Throughout the night, Geraint fought a fever, and reopened his wound with his thrashing. Talking to him in quiet moments, she urged him to fight. The healers watched her, their suspicions and fears in their eyes, but she could not help what she was, what she was raised to be.

In the morning, Geraint opened his eyes with lucidness and smiled at his father. The king turned away to hide his tears. Enid came to her husband, stumbling with her exhaustion, glad to rest her head on the cushion beside his. She watched with approval as he took several sips of broth.

He smiled and spoke with a hoarse voice. "I am proving such a weakling that soon you'll leave me."

"Never," she whispered. "Now sleep. I will be here when you awaken."

He glanced down, and she realized that the cloak revealed a hint of her bare breasts.

His eyes alone spoke questions, and she laughed.

"I walked into a pond," she said, "in front of everyone, even your father."

He smiled again and closed his eyes. "Sounds like a story worth hearing."

She kissed him softly and breathed, "I shall tell you all when you awaken."

• • •

BY the afternoon, Enid had slept enough. She could not bear to be apart from Geraint for one more hour. As she walked across the encampment, she looked into the distance, where soldiers buried the dead. Her husband would not be one of them, she thought with relief, though her sorrow for the dead remained.

As her eyes stung with tears, she ran straight into King Erbin. He caught her arm before she stumbled back.

Staring up at him, she said, "Thank you."

He let her go. "I should be the one thanking you. My wife told me of the goodness of your soul. But I could not believe her, not after I heard such strange tales of you, and saw the way my son could not keep his eyes from you."

"Love is not enough reason to stare at each other?" she asked softly.

"Aye, it can be. But how can you blame my fears, after what I saw last night?"

"There is magic in the world, sire, including the magic of a loving bond between two people that results in the miracle of birth. I never thought of myself as having these abilities—I was the warrior of my family, destined to train men. Men never looked at me and saw a woman—not until the moment I met your son. I fell in love with him. And in learning of each other, we've discovered that our love will not fade and die. I am sorry if I am not the sort of woman you thought he deserved."

The king shook his head. "It should never have been my place to judge his choices—or yours. Can you forgive me for believing that you meant him ill?"

She nodded. "Will you trust his choices now? He is an adult, and your continued doubt will only harm him."

"I never meant that," he said in a quiet voice. "He is my son. I could not believe that he was finished learning from me."

"We are never done learning from our parents' experience," she said, touching his arm.

He nodded. "Geraint is asking for you."

"I shall go to him. Thank you for the gift of your understanding, sire."

He gave a faint smile.

Enid ducked beneath the open flap of the pavilion, and to her relief, she saw Geraint propped up amongst cushions. Bandages were wrapped about his chest and shoulder, and none were stained with blood. Though his beloved face showed lines of fatigue and strain, his smile was healthy when he saw her.

The healers bowed to her and left them alone.

She shook her head. "I would like to think that they do that out of respect, but I am not so certain."

Geraint shrugged. "I care not if they're afraid of you as long as they show you respect. I understand that not much was shown to you last night."

He lifted his good arm and she settled beneath it happily.

"I am different, Geraint. You cannot blame your father for questioning my abilities, not with all the rumors he heard."

"I used to blame him for not trusting me," he said dryly. "Only I cannot even do that anymore, because he apologized for his doubts." He took her hand in his and laced their fingers together. "He apologized to me for his behavior last night."

"And to me as well. Grief and fear had taken over his mind. For a moment, I, too, thought you were dead."

"But you would not give up on me."

She looked into his eyes. "I could never give up on the man who knew everything I was and accepted it all."

He winced. "But not immediately. I was as stubborn as my father."

"But you supported me when it counted. You believe in me, Geraint."

He closed his eyes as his head dropped back. "Believe in you? How can you say that after how I treated you? I thought you disloyal. I thought you had to prove yourself to me."

"We all have to prove ourselves to the ones we love—we just did it after the marriage instead of before. How *could* you trust me, Geraint? I was lying to you, over and over again. We shared the same fault, because I could not bestow my trust either."

"Was it the sin of pride then, that we were more

concerned about our families than our marriage, this new family we created?"

"I know not." She sighed and huddled closer to his warmth. "I think we were caught up in our duties, and we had to get through that to see what was most important—each other. I could have succeeded at nothing without you—not my mission, not my transformation from warrior into woman." She caressed his face. "I love you, Geraint. I said it from the beginning, and I was not wrong."

He leaned down to kiss her gently. "I love you, too, Enid. Trust that I have put aside all my doubts and fears for the last time. I love you for the woman you are, warrior and sorceress as well."

She laughed. "I am no longer a sorceress, my husband. The power fled from me so quickly, and left me so exhausted, that I knew it was but one last gift from the Lady. My infamy will have to become only legend, because never again will soldiers see me naked and bathed in moonlight."

Geraint laughed and hugged her. "I reserve that privilege as mine alone."

Epilogue

• • •

GERAINT had found his equal, his partner in life, and a peace he'd never truly known. He no longer had to doubt himself, or his ability to become king.

After the destruction of the Saxon army, and then Geraint's recovery, he and Enid returned to the Donella tribe to complete her mission. Since their people were now close allies, he was able to give them all the training they needed to take their place as Cornwall's equal—no longer would they have to wait behind the battle lines, helping only as archers.

Later that year, King Arthur summoned both Geraint and Enid to Camelot. Together they served as ambassadors for Cornwall and the high king, and once or twice they were known to do battle when necessary. They fought side by side, and their renown spread.

Unless one consulted their children, two boys and two girls, who couldn't understand what all the fuss was about.

Enter the rich world of historical romance with Berkley Books.

Lynn Kurland

Patricia Potter

Betina Krahn

Jodi Thomas

Anne Gracie

Love is timeless.

penguin.com

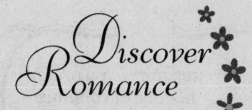